Werewolf Academy Book 4

Taken

By Cheree L. Alsop

TAKEN

Copyright © 2014 by Cheree L. Alsop
All rights reserved. This book or any portion thereof may not be reproduced or used in any manner whatsoever without the express written permission of the author except for the use of brief quotations in a book review.
This is a work of fiction. Names, characters, places, and incidents are a product of the author's imagination. Any resemblance to actual persons, events, or locales is entirely coincidental.
ISBN-13:9781503200371
Cover Design by Robert Emerson and Andy Hair
www.ChereeAlsop.com

ALSO BY CHEREE ALSOP

The Werewolf Academy Series-
Book One: Strays
Book Two: Hunted
Book Three: Instinct
Book Four: Taken
Book Five: Lost
Book Six: Vengeance
Book Seven: Chosen

The Silver Series-
Silver
Black
Crimson
Violet
Azure
Hunter
Silver Moon

Heart of the Wolf Part One
Heart of the Wolf Part Two

The Galdoni Series-
Galdoni
Galdoni 2: Into the Storm
Galdoni 3: Out of Darkness

The Small Town Superheroes Series-
Small Town Superhero
Small Town Superhero II
Small Town Superhero III

TAKEN

Keeper of the Wolves
Stolen
The Million Dollar Gift
Thief Prince

Shadows
Mist- Book Two in the World of Shadows

PRAISE FOR CHEREE ALSOP

The Silver Series

"Cheree Alsop has written *Silver* for the YA reader who enjoys both werewolves and coming-of-age tales. Although I don't fall into this demographic, I still found it an entertaining read on a long plane trip! The author has put a great deal of thought into balancing a tale that could apply to any teen (death of a parent, new school, trying to find one's place in the world) with the added spice of a youngster dealing with being exceptionally different from those around him, and knowing that puts him in danger."
—Robin Hobb, author of the Farseer Trilogy

"I honestly am amazed this isn't absolutely EVERYWHERE! Amazing book. Could NOT put it down! After reading this book, I purchased the entire series!"
—Josephine, Amazon Reviewer

"Great book, Cheree Alsop! The best of this kind I have read in a long time. I just hope there is more like this one."
—Tony Olsen

"I couldn't put the book down. I fell in love with the characters and how wonderfully they were written. Can't wait to read the 2nd!"
—Mary A. F. Hamilton

"A page-turner that kept me wide awake and wanting more. Great characters, well written, tenderly developed, and thrilling. I loved this book, and you will too."
—Valerie McGilvrey

"Super glad that I found this series! I am crushed that it is at its end. I am sure we will see some of the characters in the next series, but it just won't be the same. I am 41 years old, and am only a little embarrassed to say I was crying at 3 a.m. this morning while finishing the last book. Although this is a YA series, all ages will enjoy the Silver Series. Great job by Cheree Alsop. I am excited to see what she comes up with next."

—Jennc, Amazon Reviewer

The Galdoni Series

"This is absolutely one of the best books I have ever read in my life! I loved the characters and their personalities, the storyline and the way it was written. The bravery, courage and sacrifice that Kale showed was amazing and had me scolding myself to get a grip and stop crying! This book had adventure, romance and comedy all rolled into one terrific book I LOVED the lesson in this book, the struggles that the characters had to go through (especially the forbidden love)...I couldn't help wondering what it would be like to live among such strangely beautiful creatures that acted, at times, more caring and compassionate than the humans. Overall, I loved this book...I recommend it to ANYONE who fancies great books."

—iBook Reviewer

"I was pleasantly surprised by this book! The characters were so well written as if the words themselves became life. The sweet romance between hero and heroine made me root

for the underdog more than I usually do! I definitely recommend this book!"
—Sara Phillipp

"Can't wait for the next book!! Original idea and great characters. Could not put the book down; read it in one sitting."
—StanlyDoo- Amazon Reviewer

"5 stars! Amazing read. The story was great- the plot flowed and kept throwing the unexpected at you. Wonderfully established setting in place; great character development, shown very well thru well placed dialogue- which in turn kept the story moving right along! No bog downs or boring parts in this book! Loved the originality that stemmed from ancient mysticism- bringing age old fiction into modern day reality. Recommend for teenage and older- action violence a little intense for preteen years, but overall this is a great action thriller slash mini romance novel."
—That Lisa Girl, Amazon Reviewer

"I was not expecting a free novel to beat anything that I have ever laid eyes upon. This book was touching and made me want more after each sentence."
—Sears1994, iBook Reviewer

"This book was simply heart wrenching. It was an amazing book with a great plot. I almost cried several times. All of the scenes were so real it felt like I was there witnessing everything."
—Jeanine Drake, iBook Reveiwer

"This book was absolutely amazing...It had me tearing at parts, cursing at others, and filled with adrenaline rushing along with the characters at the fights. It is a book for everyone, with themes of love, courage, hardship, good versus evil, humane and inhumane...All around, it is an amazing book!"
—Mkb312, iBook Reviewer

"Galdoni is an amazing book; it is the first to actually make me cry! It is a book that really touches your heart, a romance novel that might change the way you look at someone. It did that to me."
—Coralee2, Reviewer

"Wow. I simply have no words for this. I highly recommend it to anyone who stumbled across this masterpiece. In other words, READ IT!"
—Troublecat101, iBook Reviewer

Keeper of the Wolves

"This is without a doubt the VERY BEST paranormal romance/adventure I have ever read and I've been reading these types of books for over 45 years. Excellent plot, wonderful protagonists—even the evil villains were great. I read this in one sitting on a Saturday morning when there were so many other things I should have been doing. I COULD NOT put it down! I also appreciated the author's research and insights into the behavior of wolf packs. I will CERTAINLY read more by this author and put her on my 'favorites' list."
—N. Darisse

"This is a novel that will emotionally cripple you. Be sure to keep a box of tissues by your side. You will laugh, you will cry, and you will fall in love with Keeper. If you loved *Black Beauty* as a child, then you will truly love *Keeper of the Wolves* as an adult. Put this on your 'must read' list."
—Fortune Ringquist

"Cheree Alsop mastered the mind of a wolf and wrote the most amazing story I've read this year. Once I started, I couldn't stop reading. Personal needs no longer existed. I turned the last page with tears streaming down my face."
—Rachel Andersen, Amazon Reviewer

"I truly enjoyed this book very much. I've spent most of my life reading supernatural books, but this was the first time I've read one written in first person and done so well. I must admit that the last half of this book had me in tears from sorrow and pain for the main character and his dilemma as a man and an animal. . . Suffice it to say that this is one book you REALLY need in your library. I won't ever regret purchasing this book, EVER! It was just that GOOD! I would also recommend you have a big box of tissues handy because you WILL NEED THEM! Get going, get the book..."
—Kathy I, Amazon Reviewer

"I just finished this book. Oh my goodness, did I get emotional in some spots. It was so good. The courage and love portrayed is amazing. I do recommend this book. Thought provoking."
—Candy, Amazon Reviewer

Thief Prince

"I absolutely loved this book! I could not put it down. . . The Thief Prince will whisk you away into a new world that you will not want to leave! I hope that Ms. Alsop has more about this story to write, because I would love more Kit and Andric! This is one of my favorite books so far this year! Five Stars!"
—Crystal, Book Blogger at Books are Sanity

". . . Once I started I couldn't put it down. The story is amazing. The plot is new and the action never stops. The characters are believable and the emotions presented are beautiful and real. If anyone wants a good, clean, fun, romantic read, look no further. I hope there will be more books set in Debria, or better yet, Antor."
—SH Writer, Amazon Reviewer

"This book was a roller coaster of emotions: tears, laughter, anger, and happiness. I absolutely fell in love with all of the characters placed throughout this story. This author knows how to paint a picture with words."
—Kathleen Vales

"Awesome book! It was so action packed, I could not put it down, and it left me wanting more! It was very well written, leaving me feeling like I had a connection with the characters."
—M. A., Amazon Reviewer

"I am a Cheree Alsop junkie and I have to admit, hands down, this is my FAVORITE of anything she has published. In a world separated by race, fear and power are forced to

collide in order to save them all. Who better to free them of the prejudice than the loyal heart of a Duskie? Adventure, incredible amounts of imagination, and description go into this world! It is a 'buy now and don't leave the couch until the last chapter has reached an end' kind of read!"
—Malcay, Amazon Reviewer

"I absolutely loved this book! I could not put it down! Anything with a prince and a princess is usually a winner for me, but this book is even better! It has multiple princes and princesses on scene over the course of the book! I was completely drawn into Kit's world as she was faced with danger and new circumstances…Kit was a strong character, not a weak and simpering girl who couldn't do anything for herself. The Thief Prince (Andric) was a great character as well! I kept seeing glimpses of who he really was and I loved that the author gave us clues as to what he was like under the surface. The Thief Prince will whisk you away into a new world that you will not want to leave!"
—Bookworm, Book Reviewer

Small Town Superhero Series

"A very human superhero- Cheree Alsop has written a great book for youth and adults alike. Kelson, the superhero, is battling his own demons plus bullies in this action packed narrative. Small Town Superhero had me from the first sentence through the end. I felt every sorrow, every pain and the delight of rushing through the dark on a motorcycle. Descriptions in Small Town Superhero are so well written the reader is immersed in the town and lives of its inhabitants."
—Rachel Andersen, Book Reviewer

"Anyone who grew up in a small town or around motorcycles will love this! It has great characters and flows well with martial arts fighting and conflicts involved."
—Karen, Amazon Reviewer

"Fantastic story...and I love motorcycles and heroes who don't like the limelight. Excellent character development. You'll like this series!"
—Michael, Amazon Reviewer

"Another great read; couldn't put it down. Would definitely recommend this book to friends and family. She has put out another great read. Looking forward to reading more!"
—Benton Garrison, Amazon Reviewer

"I enjoyed this book a lot. Good teen reading. Most books I read are adult contemporary; I needed a change and this was a good change. I do recommend reading this book! I will be looking out for more books from this author. Thank you!"
—Cass, Amazon Reviewer

Stolen

"This book will take your heart, make it a little bit bigger, and then fill it with love. I would recommend this book to anyone from 10-100. To put this book in words is like trying to describe love. I had just gotten it and I finished it the next day because I couldn't put it down. If you like action, thrilling fights, and/or romance, then this is the perfect book for you."

—Steven L. Jagerhorn

"Couldn't put this one down! Love Cheree's ability to create totally relatable characters and a story told so fluidly you actually believe it's real."

—Sue McMillin, Amazon Reviewer

"I enjoyed this book it was exciting and kept you interested. The characters were believable. And the teen romance was cute."

—Book Haven- Amazon Reviewer

"This book written by Cheree Alsop was written very well. It is set in the future and what it would be like for government control. The drama was great and the story was very well put together. If you want something different, then this is the book to get and it is a page turner for sure. You will love the main characters as well, and the events that unfold during the story. It will leave you hanging and wanting more."

—Kathy Hallettsville, TX- Amazon Reviewer

"I really liked this book . . . I was pleasantly surprised to discover this well-written book. . .I'm looking forward to reading more from this author."

—Julie M. Peterson- Amazon Reviewer

"Great book! I enjoyed this book very much it keeps you wanting to know more! I couldn't put it down! Great read!"

—Meghan- Amazon Reviewer

"A great read with believable characters that hook you instantly. . . I was left wanting to read more when the book was finished."
—Katie- Goodreads Reviewer

Heart of the Wolf

"Absolutely breathtaking! This book is a roller coaster of emotions that will leave you exhausted!!! A beautiful fantasy filled with action and love. I recommend this book to all fantasy lovers and those who enjoy a heartbreaking love story that rivals that of Romeo and Juliet. I couldn't put this book down!"
—Amy May

"What an awesome book! A continual adventure, with surprises on every page. What a gifted author she is. You just can't put the book down. I read it in two days. Cheree has a way of developing relationships and pulling at your heart. You find yourself identifying with the characters in her book...True life situations make this book come alive for you and gives you increased understanding of your own situation in life. Magnificent story and characters. I've read all of Cheree's books and recommend them all to you...especially if you love adventures."
—Michael, Amazon Reviewer

"You'll like this one and want to start part two as soon as you can! If you are in the mood for an adventure book in a faraway kingdom where there are rival kingdoms plotting and scheming to gain more power, you'll enjoy this novel. The characters are well developed, and of course with Cheree

there is always a unique supernatural twist thrown into the story as well as romantic interests to make the pages fly by."
Karen, Amazon Reviewer

When Death Loved an Angel

"This style of book is quite a change for this author so I wasn't expecting this, but I found an interesting story of two very different souls who stepped outside of their "accepted roles" to find love and forgiveness, and what is truly of value in life and death."
—Karen, Amazon Reviewer

"When Death Loved an Angel by Cheree Alsop is a touching paranormal romance that cranks the readers' thinking mode into high gear."
—Rachel Andersen, Book Reviewer

"Loved this book. I would recommend this book to everyone. And be sure to check out the rest of her books, too!"
—Malcay, Book Reviewer

The Shadows Series

". . . This author has talent. I enjoyed her world, her very well developed characters, and an interesting, entertaining concept and story. Her introduction to her world was well done and concise. . . .Her characters were interesting enough that I became attached to several. I would certainly read a follow-up if only to check on the progress and evolution of the society she created. I recommend this for any age other

than those overly sensitive to some graphic violence. The romance was heartfelt but pg. A good read."
—Mari, Amazon Reviewer

". . . I've fallen for the characters and their world. I've even gone on to share (this book) with my sister. . .So many moments made me smile as well as several which brought tears from the attachment; not sad tears, I might add. When I started Shadows, I didn't expect much because I assumed it was like most of the books I've read lately. But this book was one of the few books to make me happy I was wrong and find myself so far into the books that I lost track of time, ending up reading to the point that my body said I was too tired to continue reading! I can't wait to see what happens in the next book. . . Some of my new favorite quotes will be coming from this lovely novel. Thank you to Cheree Alsop for allowing the budding thoughts to come to life. I am a very hooked reader."
—Stephanie Roberts, Amazon Reviewer

"This was a heart-warming tale of rags to riches. It was also wonderfully described and the characters were vivid and vibrant; a story that teaches of love defying boundaries and of people finding acceptance."
—Sara Phillip, Book Reviewer

"This is the best book I have ever had the pleasure of reading. . . It literally has everything, drama, action, fighting, romance, adventure, & suspense. . . Nexa is one of the most incredible female protagonists ever written. . .It literally had me on pins & needles the ENTIRE time. . . I cannot recommend this book highly enough. Please give yourself a

wonderful treat & read this book… you will NOT be disappointed!!!"
—Jess- Goodreads Reviewer

"Took my breath away; excitement, adventure and suspense. . . This author has extracted a tender subject and created a supernatural fantasy about seeing beyond the surface of an individual. . . Also the romantic scenes would make a girl swoon. . . The fights between allies and foes and blood lust would attract the male readers. . .The conclusion was so powerful and scary this reader was sitting on the edge of her seat."
—Susan Mahoney, Book Blogger

"Adventure, incredible amounts of imagination and description go into this world! It is a buy now, don't leave the couch until the last chapter has reached an end kind of read!"
—Malcay- Amazon Reviewer

"The high action tale with the underlying love story that unfolds makes you want to keep reading and not put it down. I can't wait until the next book in the Shadows Series comes out."
—Karen- Amazon Reviewer

"Really enjoyed this book. A modern fairy tale complete with Kings and Queens, Princesses and Princes, castles and the damsel is not quite in distress. LOVE IT."
—Braine, Talk Supe- Book Blogger

". . . It's refreshing to see a female character portrayed without the girly cliches most writers fall into. She is someone I would like to meet in real life, and it is nice to read the first

person POV of a character who is so well-round that she is brave, but still has the softer feminine side that defines her character. A definite must read."
—S. Teppen- Goodreads Reviewer

"I really enjoyed this book and had a hard time putting it down. . . This premise is interesting and the world building was intriguing. The author infused the tale with the feeling of suspicion and fear . . . The author does a great job with characterization and you grow to really feel for the characters throughout especially as they change and begin to see Nexa's point of view. . . I did enjoy the book and the originality. I would recommend this for young adult fantasy lovers. It's more of a mild dark fantasy, but it would definitely fall more in the traditional fantasy genre. "
—Jill- Goodreads Reviewer

Dawn is the reminder that each day starts with hope.
Chose to hang onto that token of light,
And let it shine with every action.
Impact the lives around you
With the brightness you carry inside.

Thank you to my family,
For the light and joy of
Each and every day.
I love you.

TAKEN

Chapter One

Alex ducked between the buildings. His breath fogged in the crisp winter air as he crouched with his shoulder against the bricks. His ears strained to catch the first whisper of footsteps through the snow.

It had only been two days since the battle against General Jared Carso beneath the mall. The directions Alex had given the General led to the park in Greyton where Alex had learned how to play his first game of soccer. He regretted that it had been the first location to come to his mind, but he couldn't take it back.

Motion caught his gaze. He studied Trent crouched in the alley across the park. His friend's eyes were wide, but Alex knew the werewolf would cover his back no matter what. Cassie and Tennison were across the street to Alex's left. The slight whisper of snow brushing from the roof told of the werewolves waiting above. Jaze's pack, the Black Team, and Pack Jericho, the pack Alex belonged to, hid in strategic positions around the square the park occupied and on top of the building across the street.

Brock's contacts had informed him that the General's men were headed in the direction of the park. Alex's hands clenched and unclenched. He wanted to make the man pay for the fear he had seen in Kalia's eyes. It didn't help that the General was his father. Alex fought back a growl. Sharing blood definitely didn't make the heart any fonder.

A laugh caught his attention.

"Kids are coming this way," Dray said into Alex's earpiece.

"We need to get them clear of the park," Brock answered.

"We can't blow our position," Chet replied.

Five students came into view. Alex's heart skipped a beat

when he recognized Cherish and some of the other students he had played soccer with over the summer. Cherish wore a red bandana instead of a green one over her long black hair, and she was bundled up in a huge coat and a green scarf. Tanner and Sarah walked hand in hand, while Jen ran on ahead and scooped up a snowball to throw at Josh. Jen's red hair was a bright counterbalance to her gray coat.

"I know them," Alex said quietly.

He felt the attention of every werewolf hidden around the park lock on him.

"You know them?" Cassie repeated in shock.

Trent spoke up. "Are they the ones you met on that trip?"

"Yeah," Alex answered. He wasn't sure what to do. The thought of the General's Extremist army and hounds reaching the park while the humans were there sent chills down his spine.

"You need to get them out of there," Jaze replied, his voice commanding. "The General's men have arrived."

At that moment, four black SUVs pulled up to the curb that fronted the park.

"Go, Alex," Trent urged. "You don't have any time."

Alex ran through the snow toward the students. They slowed at the sight of his approach.

"Alex?" Cherish said in surprise.

Sarah grinned. "I didn't think we'd see you again."

"Yeah," her boyfriend Tanner said. "I thought you went to some faraway school or something."

"You guys have got to get out of here," Alex told them. He grabbed Cherish's arm. "You're in danger."

Cherish stared at him. "In danger?" Doubt laced her voice. "Here?" She looked around pointedly, and her gaze locked on the men filing out of the SUVs.

"You mean them?" Josh asked, his curly brown hair visible around the edges of his beanie.

"Yeah." Alex kept his voice steady despite the way his heart thundered in his chest. "They're not here to talk."

The men pulled guns from the vehicles.

Alex heard sharp breaths of surprise from his friends.

"I think we should go," Jen said, clutching Josh's arm, her eyes filled with fright.

"I agree," Sarah echoed, her face pale at the sight of the weapons.

"There's no time," Alex told them as Jaze said the same words into his earpiece. "Follow me."

The students ran across the park in Alex's tracks. He led them to the alley he had left and herded them to the big garbage containers at the end. There was a gap behind them that would work as a temporary hiding place.

"Keep low and stay here," Alex said. He was grateful when they listened.

Tanner pulled Sarah against him, shielding her with his body while Josh did the same for Jen.

Cherish was the closest to the fence that made up the end of the alley. She stared at Alex.

"Just don't move," Alex told her. "I'll keep you safe."

Gunshots erupted in the park. Alex drew his gun and shot two Extremists as they darted across the mouth of the alley. He ran to the opening and fired, taking down two more headed for Trent's hiding place. Other shots rang out, echoing against the buildings as Extremists and werewolves tried to take each other out.

Someone let out a yelp of pain on the rooftop above Alex. More Extremists were massing across the park. Apparently the vehicles on the street hadn't been their only means of transportation. Men in black and gray swarmed from one of the buildings. Alex lost sight of Trent.

Taking careful aim, Alex took out three more men near the vehicles. Another hid behind what remained of a snowman. Alex's breath sounded harsh to his ears. He let it out slowly and squeezed the trigger. The man grabbed his shoulder, then fell to the ground as the tranquilizer took effect.

Bullets hit the wall near Alex's head. He ducked as dust from the bricks peppered his hair.

"Alex, be careful!"

Alex looked back to see Sarah peaking around the corner.

"Are you crazy?" Tanner said, his eyes wide as he pulled her back. "You're going to get yourself shot!"

Alex glanced back at the park in time to see four men taking advantage of his distraction to rush the alley. He fired four times. Three of the men stopped in their tracks while a bullet from the fourth tugged at Alex's sleeve. He shot the man in the chest. The Extremist crashed to the ground and his gun clattered across the sidewalk. Alex turned on his knee and shot three more men crouched near Trent's alley.

There were so many Extremists. They hadn't expected so many. The amount of men Alex had taken down was nothing compared to the Extremists who continued to flood into the park from the streets, the alleys, and the building adjacent to it. Alex didn't know if the men enjoyed being shot by tranquilizers or if the General had them brainwashed like his hounds to do anything he asked. Whenever one was shot, there were two more to take the Extremist's place.

Jen screamed behind him. Alex spun to see three Extremists climbing down the fire escape near the middle of the alley. A fence and the garbage containers blocked off the back; his friends were trapped between the Extremists and any chance of escape.

Alex thought quickly. Two men at the mouth of the alley; two more by Trent. Three by the vehicles and one by the snowman. Four men at the alley, and then another bullet for the one that went wide. Three more by Trent's alley. The Glock held fifteen bullets in the clip and one in the chamber. He was out.

The Extremists pointed their weapons at the students. Alex needed speed and strength. He had no choices left.

Alex tore off his shirt and phased. His paws hit the ground twice before he leaped. He slammed into the back of one man and jumped as the man hit fell. Alex grabbed the second man's gun hand and used his body weight to drag the man to the ground. He released the man's arm and barreled into the third Extremist before the man could bring his gun up. The man hit the wall and collapsed. Alex spun back around in time to see the first man reaching for the gun he had dropped.

A growl rumbled from Alex's chest and he bared his fangs. The man froze with his fingers inches from the weapon. He met Alex's fury-filled gaze and slowly withdrew his hand. Alex moved to the middle of the alley, placing himself between the Extremists and his friends. He met the men's gazes one at a time with his low growl resounding through the alley.

Alex didn't want to tear their throats out. Shooting men using tranquilizers bullets was a lot different than ending their lives with his fangs. He had killed enough to know the consequences. The alarm on the Extremists' faces ate at him, but he would do what was needed in order to protect the humans behind him. The fear that wafted from his friends filled him with resolve. He placed one paw forward.

"I've got them, Alex!"

Three shots rang out. Cries of pain followed and the men

in front of him collapsed. Alex lifted his gaze to Trent who leaned against the alley wall, his eyes wide and chest heaving. A sheen of sweat showed through the small werewolf's buzzed hair.

Alex realized that the sounds of gunfire had stopped. A glance past Trent revealed the park, its snow broken by the bodies of Extremists Jaze's pack and the Black Team gathered up. Chet helped Dray to one of the vehicles. The professor had a bandage around his leg but still had the strength to smile.

"Told you we'd get home before dinner," Dray said.

"It'll be a close thing," Chet replied with his usual frustrated tone. "I hope Cook Jerald didn't feed everything to those vermin."

"And by vermin, you mean the students," Dray replied as they passed from Alex's view.

"Who else would I mean?" Chet growled.

Relief filled Alex. The firefight was over. From what he had seen, the General had kept out of sight, but the werewolves had taken down a significant number of Extremists. It would be up to the Global Protection Agency to take care of them and they would be unable to hunt werewolves any longer.

"A-Alex?"

Alex's relief snuffed out like a match dunked in water. For a brief second, he had forgotten the human students he had protected. They had trusted him and treated him like one of their own. They had given him something invaluable, the feeling of fitting in when the rest of the world regarded his kind with only fear. He had never felt like just another person, but the day he played soccer with them and ate breakfast at the diner, he had forgotten he was different. Now, he had lost that gift.

Alex turned slowly and faced the five students. They stood close to the garbage containers as though debating whether they were truly safe. All eyes traveled from the downed Extremists to Alex. He knew he looked formidable. Werewolves maintained the same weight when phasing since mass couldn't just disappear, and a hundred and sixty-five pound wolf was huge. He wondered how they would look if they saw Vance phase.

"I have your clothes," Trent said quietly. "I'll meet you at the car."

Alex turned away from the scent of fear and the eyes wide with disbelief. He held his head high, though he felt like dragging it on the ground. The Extremists had taken everything from him; it was just one more brick on his shoulders.

Alex phased in the SUV and pulled on his clothes. He sat for a moment contemplating what had happened, reliving the cool metal of his gun in his hand and the way the targets fell as each bullet hit. He pushed his finger through the hole the bullet had torn through his sleeve, grateful it hadn't clipped him. Werewolves healed fast, but bullet holes still hurt.

A tap on the glass jerked him out of his haze of senseless thoughts. He realized that his hands were shaking. He rubbed them together with the understanding that even though he had gone through numerous rescues with Jaze and fired his gun dozens of times, he was still experiencing the effects of shock. Perhaps one never got used to the feeling of shooting another person, no matter their intentions.

He shook his head with a wry smile and pushed the door open.

"What do you—" Alex stared at the five humans waiting beside Jaze.

The dean gave him a smile that said he understood the

werewolf's surprise. "Your *friends* wanted to talk to you." Jaze's emphasis on the word friends made Alex look at them again.

None of the five students looked scared now that the attack had passed. Jen and Sarah were still pale, but Cherish gave him a smile.

"Who would have thought?" she said in her straightforward way.

Tanner pushed his blond hair off his head. "Seriously. I don't think I would have believed it if I hadn't seen it."

"There was that fight with the gang," Josh pointed out. "We should have known." At Jaze's surprised look, Josh took off his beanie and studied the ground.

"Fight with the gang?" Jaze asked.

Alex put on his most innocent expression. "It wasn't a gang, really. There were three thugs who wanted my motorcycle. I talked them out of it." He shrugged. "It was civil, really."

Tanner and Josh both smothered laughs.

Jaze rolled his eyes. "Somehow, I don't believe you." He gave Alex a small smile. "The police are on their way; the GPA can't stall much longer. We'll be leaving in a few minutes."

"Got it," Alex replied.

The humans watched Jaze walk over to several men in black with the letters GPA on their backs.

"That's really him, isn't it?" Cherish asked quietly.

Alex was surprised by the look of awe on their faces. "You know Jaze?"

Josh put his beanie back on. "Everyone knows about Jaze Carso. He's a legend, even with us."

Alex felt the distance the words immediately put between him and the five humans. He was a werewolf; he wasn't one of them. He wondered why it hurt so badly to be reminded of it.

"Have dinner at my house."

Everyone stared at Cherish. Alex couldn't force down his shock when he realized she was talking to him.

"What?" he asked even though he had heard her clearly.

"Have dinner at my house," Cherish repeated. She looked at her friends. "You saved our lives, Alex. If you hadn't done, well, what you did back there, we'd be dead right now. I saw the way those men looked at us."

Sarah cringed as though reliving the memory. "Cherish is right. We owe you."

Alex shook his head without meeting her eyes. "You don't owe me anything."

"We do," Tanner said.

Alex kicked at a clump of dirty snow. "Don't feel like you owe me any favors. I'm a werewolf. You shouldn't associate with me." Saying the words aloud made him feel the distance even more. He shoved his hands in his pockets so he would stop balling them into fists.

Cherish touched his arm. Alex met her gaze unwillingly. "Come over on Sunday," she said, her expression earnest. "My mom always cooks something amazing. I want you to be there."

Alex couldn't deny the sincerity of her tone. He glanced at the others and saw that they were watching him expectantly. Tanner nodded, encouraging him to accept. Alex let out a small breath. "Okay."

"Done," Cherish said with a beaming smile. She handed him a piece of paper with an address she had already written hastily on it. "We'll see you there."

Alex watched them go. When he turned, he met the dean's gaze. Jaze's expression was unreadable. He tipped his head toward the SUV, indicating that they needed to leave. Alex climbed inside and waited for Trent to take them home. The piece of paper sat in his pocket, a barely discernable weight he couldn't ignore.

Chapter Two

"I can't believe you know humans," Cassie said late that night. Pack Jericho's quarters felt empty with the Termers still on their holiday break. Alex could barely believe the term was halfway over.

He glanced at her from where he sat on the floor with his back against the couch. "It's not like every human you meet is out to kill you. Take Nikki or Professor Thorson for example."

Tennison skirted around his argument. "They didn't know you were a werewolf, did they?"

Alex fought back a sigh at Cassie's boyfriend's accurate guess. "No, they didn't."

"At least now that they do, I don't have to worry about you going back there," Cassie said with a satisfied nod. "No one would be that crazy."

"Yeah," Alex replied noncommittally. He hadn't mentioned Cherish's invitation to his sister. Cassie would never understand what it meant to him. He hadn't decided whether to actually accept, but just knowing they didn't fear him had helped chase away the regret that he had phased in front of them.

Trent appeared at the door to Pack Jericho's quarters with Terith close behind. Other pack mates lounged around the room and downstairs, enjoying their break after the long school day.

"I need testers for my new watches," Trent said, holding out the objects. When nobody moved, he directed his most compelling smile at one of the Lifer members of their pack. "Jordan, would you like to help me?"

Jordan rolled her eyes. "Why do you need me?" Her short red hair stood up in spikes; Alex had wondered on more than one occasion whether she kept it like that to show off her fiery temper.

"I always need you," Trent replied.

"What was that?" Jordan snapped.

Trent paled. He swallowed and said, "I, uh, said I need you to help me track their range. I haven't had a chance to test how far they can go."

Jordan let out a loud sigh as if he was asking her to scrub the toilets. She rose from her chair anyway. "Fine," she said. "But you know watches are antiquated, right?"

Trent grinned as if he had won the lottery. "I think they make a good accessory. Look; I even made you a red one."

Jordan shoved open the door with another sigh.

Alex fought back a smile. He would have offered to help Trent, but his friend was no doubt much happier with his crush at his side. Jordan didn't put up much of a fight to join Trent on any of his experiments. She seemed to be all bark and no bite where the scrawny werewolf was concerned.

Terith, Trent's sister, took the chair Jordan had vacated.

"What are you playing?" she asked.

Von looked up from the cards he had spread across the carpet in painfully straight lines. "It's a game I made up. The colors are worth certain points and the shapes are worth others. Together, the goal is to get groups of seventeen without going above or below."

"You mean the suits," Terith said. At Von's blank look, she explained, "The shapes on the cards are called suits."

Von's eyebrows pulled together as he thought about it. He finally nodded. "Suits sound better."

"Will you teach me your game?" Terith asked.

Von's face lit up and he nodded emphatically. Terith scooted down to sit next to him.

Alex's good mood began to fade. He looked around at

the werewolves in his pack. Cassie and Tennison sat at the table working on a math algorithm his mom had given them when they asked for a challenge. Trent was off with his crush, Terith and Von were apparently pairing up, and even little Caitlyn and Marky were coloring at the other end of the table, taking a break from their usual roughhousing and causing general chaos. Everyone had somebody.

Alex fought back the urge to sigh louder than Jordan had. It would have been melodramatic and pathetic, two things he tried to avoid at all costs. The werewolves at the Academy were changing. Everyone was pairing up, becoming couples, and having fun together. Alex felt like he was missing something important, and knew that no matter how hard he tried, he wouldn't be able to change the way things were.

The door to their quarters pushed open. Kalia stormed through with a furious expression.

"Come on, Kalia. It's just a walk. It's not like I'm asking you to hold my hand or anything," Torin said from the hallway.

"I said no, Torin," Kalia called over her shoulder. "I have homework to do."

"Homework can wait," Torin said as she shut the door.

Kalia rolled her eyes and leaned against door frame.

"You okay?" Cassie asked.

Kalia nodded, giving her blonde hair an annoyed push back from her shoulder. "He's just so persistent. It's even worse now that I've phased."

Cassie smiled. "He likes you, and the fact that you're an Alpha definitely doesn't hurt."

Kalia's gaze flicked to Alex. He ducked his head before she could meet his eyes, but felt her watching him anyway.

"He doesn't get the fact that I like someone else instead," Kalia said pointedly.

"Someone else doesn't get it, either," Terith replied without a shred of tactfulness.

"You mean Alex, right?" Von said, giving a nasal laugh. The sound of someone being hit followed. "Ow!"

The door opened and Alex looked up to see the dean standing there. "You needed to meet with me, Alex?" Jaze asked.

Alex rose, grateful for the interruption. "Yes." He crossed quickly to the door and followed Jaze down the stairs. When they were out of earshot, he said, "You just rescued me from an extremely uncomfortable situation."

Jaze looked back up at Pack Jericho's quarters. "I thought it felt a bit tense. Anything I should be worried about?"

Alex shook his head. "Just pack stuff." He glanced at Jaze as they walked into the dean's office. The dean had been like a father to him ever since his parents were killed. Sometimes Jaze's insight made all the difference in the world. "Have you ever felt like you're being left behind? Like everyone's changing and you can't because of who you are?" He felt foolish as soon as the words left his mouth, but it was too late to take them back.

Jaze took a seat behind his desk in thoughtful silence. Alex sat on the other side and waited, wishing he'd kept his mouth shut. When Jaze spoke, his gaze was searching. "What do you mean, because of who you are?"

Alex studied the desk in front of him. The wood was dark and worn with the use of nine years at the Academy. There was a deep scratch near the edge; he ran a finger along it. "Sometimes I'm not sure if I'm really one of them."

The dean was silent, waiting for him to continue. Alex appreciated the time to collect his thoughts. When he spoke again, he said what he had never told anyone. "After everything—my parents' murder, the rescues, finding Siale, the body pit..." He swallowed and had to force his voice to remain strong. "Sometimes I feel like the part of me that fits in here has been washed away." He studied the scratch on the desk intently. "I feel like the things here are a bit meaningless."

He looked up at Jaze. He knew how the words sounded. He didn't want the dean to take it as though he felt the Academy was worthless. That wasn't what he meant at all. He tried again. "I mean not that the Academy is meaningless, just my place in it."

The words hung in the room, thick and obscure like fog caught in early morning branches. He felt as though he floated with the fog, just waiting to be dissipated by the rising sun. Except the sun never came.

"Alex, you have a place here," Jaze said quietly.

Alex opened his mouth to tell the dean he wasn't trying to be obstinate, but Jaze raised his hand, asking for Alex's patience. Alex closed his mouth again and nodded, sinking further into the leather chair that gave off the scents of the werewolves who had sat there before him. Boris and Torin had apparently been called to the dean's office quite often.

"I remember feeling the same way."

The experience in the dean's tone caught Alex's attention. Jaze spoke with the honesty Alex always appreciated. "We were in the middle of saving werewolves and trying to track down my uncle Mason and I told my mom the same thing. I told her that school and a normal life felt insignificant compared to the things I was trying to accomplish, and that I was just wasting my time that I could better spend saving people."

For a second, Alex saw the boy in the dean's eyes, the same boy who had looked up to his mother, confused and torn, trying to do his best but not sure when he would reach his limit.

"Do you know what she told me?" Jaze asked, the shadow of the boy lingering in his smile.

Alex shook his head.

Jaze let out a slow breath. "She said I needed to have a normal life in order to keep doing the things I was doing, that school, friends, and being just a teenager needed to be as important to me as it was to her that I had them." The dean's smile deepened and a hint of sadness showed in his brown eyes. "She told me that I needed to have a normal life to remind myself what I was trying to give others; that if I didn't have dreams and goals for myself, I would never find the happiness I deserved."

Alex's voice was quiet when he asked, "What if you don't feel like you deserve that happiness?"

Jaze set his elbow on the desk and looked at Alex with fatherly sternness. "Don't ever give up on your happiness, Alex. You will find it; I promise. I've been to the very end of my sanity and back. I've seen things and had to do things that broke me inside to the point where I felt no one could ever or should ever care for me." His eyes glittered brightly in the light and he blinked. "But I never forgot my promise to my mom that I would find my happiness."

Alex knew the answer before he asked, "Did you?"

Jaze nodded with a warm smile, tears still in his eyes. "I did. I have Nikki and William, and I have you and Cassie and Meredith. I have hundreds of students to care for and werewolves to free. I have a loyal pack and friends that I have grown to love like brothers and sisters. My life is so full I can only hope that my mom sees it and knows it's because I followed her advice."

The fact that Alex sat under the roof of Vicki Carso's Preparatory Academy, that it had been his home since he lost his parents, and it was where he knew he was safe and protected, wasn't lost on him. He took in a deep, calming breath.

"Then I won't give up on it, either," he said.

Jaze nodded. "I know you won't."

The proud, fatherly light in his eyes warmed Alex.

The dean sat up and cleared his throat. "I don't think that's what you came here to talk about."

Alex shook his head. He steeled himself. "I wanted to ask if I could go to Cherish's house tomorrow for dinner."

Humor touched Jaze's gaze. "I think that's a question for your mother."

The thought of broaching the subject with Meredith was not a pleasant one. After everything his mom had been through, she didn't trust easily. Asking if he could go to a human's house for dinner wouldn't bode well for either Alex's health or the outcome to his question.

Jaze must have read the foreboding on Alex's face because he smiled. "Want me to ask her?"

"Do you mind?" Alex asked with relief.

In answer, Jaze lifted his phone and requested her presence. A few minutes later, Alex heard his mother's familiar footsteps down the hallway.

"You asked for me?" Meredith said, poking her head in the door. Her smile filled her light blue eyes when she saw Alex sitting at the dean's desk. "I don't suppose Alex is in detention."

Jaze chuckled. "Not this time. He has a request and I thought it best that I run it by you, since you're his mother."

The statement made Meredith's smile deepen. Alex had only found out that Meredith was his mom two years ago. She had confessed over the summer that the moments she was referred to as the twins' mother made it truly feel real, and she said she would be happy hearing it for the rest of her life.

Meredith crossed the room to Alex's side. He rose and gestured for her to take his seat.

"You're so thoughtful," she said, sitting on the edge of the chair.

Jaze spoke without preamble. "Alex rescued five young humans during our last battle with the Extremists and they invited him to dinner. He's asking if he can join them."

Meredith's eyes widened. She jerked around to stare at him, her short dark hair brushing past her shoulders. "Absolutely not! That would be absurd!"

"Alex knows the humans from a previous trip he took to the city," Jaze said calmly. "He assures me that they are friends."

"You never told me about them," Meredith said. She rushed on, "Humans are dangerous and unreliable. They would turn you over to the authorities."

"I can handle authorities," Alex pointed out. He realized as soon as he said it that it had been the wrong thing to say.

"I'll not have you putting your life on the line just for a dinner," Meredith argued. She grabbed his hand. "It wouldn't be safe. You can't mean to put yourself in danger like that."

Alex didn't know what to say. "Mom, I..." He shook his head and tried again. "They're my friends. Nobody's going to hurt me."

Meredith shook her head. "It's not worth the risk."

Alex knew the stubborn set of her jaw. It was the exact same look her sister Mindi used to have when she had her mind set. The look gave Alex a pang of regret. Mindi and her husband Will had raised Alex and Cassie as their own children. They had been wonderful parents, kind and caring, filling the twins' lives with love until the day they were killed.

To Alex, they were his mom and dad, they had held his fingers when he learned to walk, had been there for his first lost tooth, and the first time he phased. His mother used to worry when he would go out roaming with his brother Jet. She would put her foot down with the same stern jaw set as Meredith, but Dad had always been the one to remind her that boys needed freedom, and no one would keep Alex safer than Jet.

"Can I talk to your mother alone for a minute?" Jaze asked, breaking Alex from his thoughts.

Alex nodded and left the room, pulling the door shut behind him. He didn't mean to eavesdrop, but as a werewolf, it was impossible not to hear the voices from other room, even with a closed door in between. He wondered if Jaze had counted on that.

"What if they betray him, Jaze? What then?" Meredith asked, her voice heated with worry.

Jaze's reply was calm and sincere. "To me, the opposite is worse. I worry that werewolves won't learn to trust humans, and that our fear will keep us apart forever. Without trust, our lives will never hold peace. These humans trusted him enough to invite him into their home. Alex can protect himself. If he can trust them in return, perhaps they can make waves that will impact these next generations."

The room was silent for a few minutes. Meredith finally said, "You'll know where he is?"

"At all times," Jaze reassured her.

A smile spread across Alex's face.

Chapter Three

Alex was surprised at how hard his heart was pounding when he parked the motorcycle in front of the apartment building that matched the address Cherish had written down.

"I can't believe you're doing this," Trent said into his headset. "And here I thought my job was to keep you from doing something stupid. Now the dean signs off on this? You're unarmed *and* alone? Who's to make sure you come back in one piece?"

"I am," Alex replied. He had argued with Trent during the entire trip to Greyton. Part of him wondered why he hadn't just turned off the headset the werewolf had placed in his helmet; the other part replied that he liked to frazzle Trent, and visiting the humans was doing a fantastic job.

"You're insane, Alex. You have a death wish. Why else would you willingly meet with five people who are probably planning to put a bullet through your heart, and a silver one at that?"

"Because life is getting just a little too boring," Alex replied. He could hear Trent sputtering on the other end. He grinned and said, "I'll talk to you in a few hours. Don't freak out."

"I'm already freaking out," his friend replied. "Don't be an idiot."

"You've already informed me twenty different ways in which I am being an idiot," Alex said. "And I think you said it in a few different languages as well."

"Cursing you out in Latin at least gives me practice," Trent muttered.

"I'd say your Spanish and French are rusty, but I'd probably be wrong, because I don't speak Spanish or French," Alex told him. "Do you know what I speak?"

"What?" Trent replied, clearly past the edge of his patience.

"I speak Hungarian, because I'm hungry. Get it?"

"That was perhaps the worst joke in the history of the world," Trent said dryly.

"But it made you smile," Alex replied, pulling off his helmet.

"I'm not smiling."

Alex put the helmet on his foot peg.

"Alex, I'm not smiling," Trent shouted.

"I'm going to enjoy my dinner," Alex told him.

He could still hear Trent's protests as he made his way up the steps of the apartment complex. He pulled the front door open and walked inside. The scent of more than a hundred humans living in one building stopped him. He glanced around quickly, more nervous than he cared to admit. He had left all weapons at the Academy to make a point; he was starting to regret the decision.

Alex pulled the paper out of his pocket. The directions said third floor apartment B. He put the paper away and jogged up the stairs. When he reached the third floor, he walked quietly down the thin carpet. To a werewolf, the slightest brush of fibers against the bottom of his shoes would give him away no matter how carefully he walked. To a human, he knew such a sound was inaudible, but it made him self-conscious just the same.

Sounds came from the door marked A. He could hear a baby gurgle and the quiet voice of a woman. A child piped up, asking for a cup of milk. The woman's reply was kind.

Alex crossed to the apartment marked B. The sound of people talking and laughing floated from beneath the door. The scent of spaghetti and meatballs wafted with it. Alex's stomach growled, reminding him that he was truly hungry.

He took a steeling breath and lifted his hand.

His knuckles hit the wood of the door like a tree falling. The talking inside the apartment stopped. Someone hurried to the door and pulled it open.

Alex couldn't help but smile at the look of happy surprise on Cherish's face. "I was hoping you'd come!" she exclaimed. She grabbed his arm and pulled him inside. Her black hair was caught back in a thick braid and she wore a blue dress, looking far from the tom boy Alex had met at the park.

"You look beautiful," he said honestly. He could feel the heat rush to his cheeks.

Cherish laughed. "Don't say that too loud. I don't want the boys to start getting ideas."

She pulled him through the small living room and down a short hall to the source of the spaghetti scent. Alex paused when they reached the kitchen.

The four other human students from the park were already sitting around a table.

"Hey, Alex," Tanner said with a nod.

A woman at the stove turned. Her cheekbones and long black hair with gray at the temples gave no doubt that she was Cherish's mother. She smiled, her eyes creasing at the corners.

"Mom, this is Alex the werewolf."

Alex stared at Cherish.

She laughed at his expression. "It's okay. Mom's best friend growing up was a werewolf. You don't have to worry."

Cherish's mother crossed the small tiled floor and held out a hand to Alex. He shook it carefully.

"Pleased to meet you, Alex," she said without a hint of nervousness. "I'm Mrs. Summers. I'm glad you came for dinner."

"Me, too," Alex replied, but it came out sounding like a

question.

"We saved you a seat," Sarah said. She patted the chair between her and Jen on one side of the rectangular table.

Alex sat, aware of Tanner and Josh's attention from across the wooden surface. It didn't feel thick enough by far to be sitting between both humans' girlfriends.

"Thanks for the other day," Josh said.

"Yeah," Tanner seconded. "That was pretty awesome."

"And scary," Jen said. She pulled on a strand of her red hair as though it was a habit. "I thought we were going to die."

Mrs. Summers set a big bowl of spaghetti in the middle of the table. She gave Alex a warm but worried smile. "The kids told me what you did. That was very brave."

Alex shook his head. "Fighting Extremists is part of being a werewolf. It's the only way I can keep those I care about safe."

"It's dangerous," Sarah said.

Alex was touched by their concern. He hadn't known what to expect at the dinner, but the humans' fear for his safety hadn't crossed his mind.

"It gives me something to fight for," he said quietly.

Mrs. Summers sat down at the head of the table. Cherish took a seat between the two boys across from Alex. She handed him a roll, put one on her plate, then passed the bowl to Tanner.

"What ever happened to your friend?" Josh asked, looking at Mrs. Summers.

She shook her head with a sad expression. "I'm not sure. We were close through high school, and then during our senior year, she disappeared. I still look for her, but haven't been able to find her since."

"I could ask Jaze," Alex said.

Mrs. Summers' eyebrows rose. "You know Jaze Carso?"

Alex nodded. "He's sort of been like my father since my sister and I moved to the Academy."

Josh whistled. "Jaze Carso is your father figure? That's amazing."

"What do you know about him?" Alex asked curiously.

Tanner spoke up. "Only that he's a legend. They tried everything they could to kill him, but they failed and he saved his people anyway. He's the deadliest werewolf there is."

"Yeah, only Jet would have him beat on that title," Josh said.

Alex fought back a smile.

Cherish caught the look. "What is it?"

"Jet was my brother," Alex admitted. He felt no sorrow with the statement, only a surge of pride at the amazement on the humans' faces. It was obvious they had heard more about Jet and Jaze than he realized, and the fact that his words weren't met with fear or loathing filled him with a sense of liberation.

"Maybe we'll find Jacey yet," Mrs. Summers said, passing Sarah the bowl of spaghetti.

"I know Jaze won't give up until he's followed every lead," Alex reassured her. "If you want to write down what you remember about her, I'll make sure it gets to him."

"I sure appreciate that," Mrs. Summers replied.

"All that and you don't even know how to play soccer," Josh said, shaking his head dramatically.

"Hey, I learned," Alex replied.

"After nearly taking out that kid on the slide," Jen said with a laugh.

Alex grinned sheepishly. "I was hoping you would've forgotten about that."

"Guess it'd be hard not to be strong all the time," Cherish

said.

Alex's brow furrowed as he twirled spaghetti around his fork. "I usually don't have to think about it. At the Academy, everyone's a werewolf, so we don't have to hide."

"The whole school is werewolves?" Sarah asked in awe.

Alex nodded, worried for a second that he had made a serious mistake. Nobody was supposed to know that Vicki Carso's Preparatory Academy was only for werewolves. If word got out, the Extremists would attack in full force. The General and Drogan didn't know, or else they would have already leveled the school.

"It makes sense," Mrs. Summers noted before taking a bite of her salad. "You need a place to hide out."

"It's more of somewhere to be normal," Alex explained. He realized the truth of the words as soon as he said them. "Jaze has given us the chance to just be ourselves without having to hide what we are. We can phase without worrying about being seen, and we learn about our wolf heritage as well as our human side."

"Wolf heritage," Josh repeated, his eyes wide. "That's awesome!" He took a huge bite of his spaghetti.

Alex shrugged a bit uncomfortably. To him it was normal, but to humans he wondered how sharing DNA with an animal really came across.

Jen set a hand on Josh's arm and he winced.

"What was that?" Cherish asked.

Josh gave a self-conscious smile and pulled back his sleeve. On his forearm was a firefighter helmet with a badge bearing the words Fire and Rescue below it. The tattoo was red around the edges.

"Did you just get that done?" Tanner asked. "It looks amazing."

Josh nodded. He caught Alex's gaze. "My dad was a

firefighter. He died last year. I've been asking my mom ever since to let me get this done and she finally gave in."

"I think that's a good tribute," Alex told him. Josh gave a grateful smile.

"Does it hurt?" Sarah asked.

Josh shrugged. "A bit when they did it, but it feels more like road rash right now. I'm glad I got it."

Mrs. Summers squeezed his shoulder as she walked by with the empty spaghetti bowl. "Your dad would be so proud of you. You take such good care of your mom and brother."

"I'm glad to have them," Josh replied, pulling his sleeve back down. "And to have this girl." He drew Jen close and gave her a kiss on the cheek.

She laughed and hugged him. "You're so cheesy. I love you."

"I love you, too," Josh replied, smiling down at her.

"Gross," Cherish said.

Everyone laughed.

A few minutes later, Sarah nudged Tanner. "We'd better get home. It's getting late."

Alex glanced outside. The sun was just starting to set. Cherish gave him an apologetic smile. "The city's not safe after sundown."

"You mean with bullies like Ruse?" Alex asked.

Cherish shook her head. "Not exactly. They're mild compared to what else is out there."

Sarah nodded with a shiver as she rose and pulled on her puffy purple coat. "The gangs take over after dark. Depending on what block you're on, you might get robbed, beat up, or end up dead on the sidewalk."

"It's not pleasant," Tanner said, helping her with her yellow scarf.

"Want a bodyguard?" Alex asked.

Tanner chuckled, but Sarah nodded quickly. "Yes, please."

"Were you kidding?" Tanner asked.

Alex shook his head. "Not at all. I'd be glad to make sure you get home safe."

"We'll walk with you, too," Jen said.

Josh rose and helped clear bowls from the table while the girls finished getting ready. Alex washed the dishes in the sink while Cherish wiped down the table.

"It's nice to have so much help," Mrs. Summers said when they were done. "It sure gets everything cleaned up much quicker."

"Are you saying I'm slow, Mom?" Cherish asked with a teasing smile.

"No, honey," Mrs. Summer replied, leaning over to kiss the top of her head. "You just take more time to do things."

"So I'm slow," Cherish repeated with a laugh.

Her mother laughed as well. "Okay, if you want to take it like that."

The others were ready to go. Alex waited by the door.

"Do you need a coat?" Mrs. Summers asked.

Alex shook his head. "I don't really get cold, but thank you for the offer."

"Come on back after," Cherish invited. "We usually have hot cocoa before bed. It helps to keep the chill away."

"I will," Alex promised.

The walk down the stairs and then out to the street was quiet. Though cars rushed down the road, no one was in sight on the sidewalks. It felt eerie to walk between the apartment buildings knowing that they were filled with families but seeing no sign of them. Spray-painted graffiti tagged walls and posts with gang signs and names.

"They're getting bolder," Sarah said quietly. "It used to be you only saw the tags in the alleys or in the Saa."

"What's the *saw*?" Alex asked, repeating the word like it sounded.

"It's the part of the city south of Angel Avenue, so S.A.A. We call it the Saa for short," Josh explained. "Angel Avenue is at the end of the business section and the sky scrapers. After that, the city's made up of slums." He pulled his beanie down tighter as if even talking about the Saa made him nervous. "Everyone avoids the Saa."

"Now the Saa's coming to us," Sarah said, her grip on Tanner's arm tightening.

Chapter Four

Their footsteps echoed against the buildings that lined the sides of the road. Alex could hear the nervous breaths of his friends as they hurried past the alleys that branched away. They were almost to the building where Jen and Josh's families lived. The humans were walking so fast Alex was amazed they didn't break into a run.

A shadow detached from the next alley. Alex's wolven eyesight revealed a man wearing a hoodie with the hood pulled up. The man shoved his hands in his pockets and ambled toward them as though not caring that they were there. It didn't fool the humans any more than the scent of iron and determination that touched Alex's nose belied the man's casual demeanor.

"Oh no," Sarah whispered.

Tanner pulled her close, shielding her with his body. Josh did the same. Jen's fast breaths puffed in the icy evening air. They clung to the edge of the curb as they reached the man. It seemed he would let them go, but at the last second, he pulled out a knife and spun around.

"Give me your—"

Alex grabbed his wrist and ducked under it, flipping the man completely over. He hit the ground on his back and gave a yell of pain.

Alex glanced up in time to see another man come out of the same alley.

"Hey, get off him!" the man yelled. He was short and skinny and moved the lethal grace of a hunting cat. The man pulled out a knife as he ran toward them.

Alex met Josh's terrified gaze. "I've got this," he reassured his friends.

Josh pulled Jen back the way they had come. Tanner and

Sarah followed close behind.

The man beneath Alex struggled. Alex stopped him with a straight punch to the jaw just as the shorter man reached them.

Alex jumped back in time to feel the knife catch in the front of his shirt. He punched the man in the ribs, then took a swing at the man's head.

The skinny human ducked to the side, then lunged again with the deadly skill of a seasoned fighter. Alex blocked his arm and landed another punch before he was forced back by the knife. The man was quick, the blade appearing wherever Alex was, forcing him to guard when he wanted to end the fight and see his friends safely home.

The longer they stayed in the streets, the more likely of a target the humans were going to be. The sun had almost set completely, and only a few of the streetlights flickered to life, lighting lonely orbs along the barren sidewalks. Alex's sensitive ears picked up the scuffs of shoes against cement. They were about to be in much bigger trouble.

Alex grabbed the knife by the blade. It was a stupid move, but it caught his attacker by surprise. Alex slammed a side kick into the skinny man's ribs. He let go of the blade and backed up gasping. Alex kicked his left foot, then brought up the right. The ball of his foot connected with the man's jaw with enough momentum to send him flying backwards into a motionless heap.

The silence that followed was broken only by Alex's harsh breaths and the moans of men at his feet.

"Oh my gosh, Alex..." Jen began.

"We've got to go," Alex told them. He searched both sides of the street. "Others are coming."

None of them second-guessed Alex's warning. They followed him across the street and down a block. More footsteps sounded. They would appear at any moment. Instinct warned Alex that if he didn't act, his friends would be in danger again.

"This way," he said, following his gut.

To his relief, the humans didn't question trailing him into the alley and around the back side of the apartment building. He stood at the door studying the street as Josh and Jen hurried inside.

"Thank you so much," Jen said. She threw her arms around his neck and gave him a tight hug. After, she took a surprised step back. "Geesh," she said. "Werewolves are ripped.

"Jen." Josh rolled his eyes.

A blush touched Jen's cheeks. "Thanks again," she said, slipping her hand into Josh's.

They watched the pair climb the stairs until they were out of sight.

"We're only two more blocks down," Tanner told Alex. "Sarah's apartment is before mine."

"Let's hurry," Sarah said, her voice tight. "It's getting darker."

Tanner glanced at Alex's hand. "Alex, you're bleeding."

Alex wiped his palm on his pants. "It's already healing," he said, holding it up. "No big deal."

Tanner looked like he was about to say something, then he closed his mouth.

"Let's get going," Alex said.

Sarah led the way at almost a run. To everyone's relief, they reached her building without being stopped. Alex waited near the outside doors while Tanner walked her up to her apartment. A few minutes later, he appeared again.

"This city's messed up, huh?" Tanner said, drawing the hood of his blue coat over his short blond hair.

"It's definitely not what I expected," Alex replied. He pulled the door open and leading the way through. "Why do your families stay here?"

"Some parts are nice." Tanner shoved his hands in his pockets and leaned against the wall. "And sometimes the scary stuff you know is easier to face than the stuff you don't."

Alex glanced at him in surprise. "Meaning you'd rather live with the thugs and gangs here instead of finding a place that might be better?"

"It might not," Tanner said. He tipped his head back against the bricks. "My dad's the CEO of Datacorp. I could switch to a private school, but I'd have to leave Sarah and the others behind." He looked at Alex. "I won't do that."

Alex nodded in understanding. "So you protect them."

Tanner snorted. "If you call cowering with the girls while you take care of armed robbers protection, then yeah."

Alex chuckled. "I'm sure if I wasn't here, you would have done something."

"I would have given them my wallet and asked them to leave the girls alone."

The honesty in Tanner's voice said he was speaking from experience.

"Does that work?" Alex asked curiously.

Tanner's gaze flitted to the street. "Sarah got hit once." His clenched jaw said how much that affected him. "She was so scared that she was crying, and then he hit her. It left a bruise that took forever to go away."

Alex's voice was quiet when he said, "I can teach you how to defend them."

Tanner looked at him, really looked at him, his green gaze searching as he took in Alex's lack of jacket and his clenched fists. Alex couldn't help the frustration that rose in him at the thought of his friends living lives of fear that could be stopped.

"Let me see your hand," Tanner said.

Alex opened his fist. Dried blood showed where the knife had cut his palm. When he wiped it on his pants, he held out his hand again to reveal only a shallow mark where the wound had been.

"That's amazing." Tanner shook his head, his gaze darkening. "I can't do what you do."

"You don't have to," Alex told him. "And you don't have to be helpless against these guys."

Tanner walked slowly toward his building a block away. Alex followed quietly, checking with all of his senses for any danger by habit. His ears strained for the sound of feet while each breath was colored with scents of rubber and asphalt, the sour-sweet smell of fermenting garbage, and the merest whisper of rain that wafted with the evening breeze.

A candy wrapper swirled on the sidewalk. Tanner stepped on it without noticing. He reached the apartment building, and then hesitated at the steps.

"It would be nice not to be afraid," Tanner finally said in a voice so quiet another human wouldn't have heard it.

"Let me know when you're ready," Alex told him. "I can teach you, and you could teach them."

"I'll let you know," Tanner replied. He jogged up the steps and put his hand on the door.

Alex turned away.

"Hey, Alex?"

When the werewolf glanced back, Tanner said, "Thanks again."

"Anytime," Alex replied with a wave.

Tanner smiled and ducked inside his apartment building.

Nobody bothered Alex on his way back to Cherish's

apartment. Whether they heard of him beating the two men or just had a shred of common sense, Alex didn't know, but the darkness didn't bother him any more than the shadows in the alleys and the voices that grew hushed when he passed by.

"You're okay?" Cherish asked. Before Alex could say a word, she yelled over her shoulder. "He's okay!"

"Of course he's okay," Mrs. Summers replied from the kitchen. "I told you not to worry."

Alex fought back a smile. "You were worried about me?"

Cherish chuckled. "I guess I shouldn't have been. Did everyone make it home safe?"

Alex nodded.

"Cocoa's ready," Mrs. Summers called. "Come get it while it's hot."

Alex followed Cherish into the kitchen. Mrs. Summers sat with them for a few minutes drinking the much smaller portion of hot chocolate she had poured for herself.

"Sounds like things are rough living here," Alex said after a few minutes of silence.

Cherish nodded. She held the cup of cocoa with both hands as though trying to absorb all of the warmth. Both she and Mrs. Summers had blankets around their shoulders. Alex wondered why they didn't just turn up the heat.

"It's what it is," Mrs. Summers replied. She smiled at her daughter. "We make due, and we're comfortable enough for now."

"For now?" Alex asked, picking up on the woman's lingering tone.

"I'm going to be a doctor," Cherish said with a determined expression. "Then I can get us somewhere better and save lives at the same time. That's why I don't have time for boys. I don't need them interfering in my plans."

"What if you interfere with theirs?" Alex asked.

Cherish's eyes widened. "Whoa, now, wolfie boy. Just because you're cute in a rugged you-don't-know-how-attractive-you-are kind-of way, doesn't mean that I—"

Alex almost held up both hands, which would have meant throwing his hot chocolate across the room. He stopped himself just in time. "It's not like that at all!"

Cherish lifted her eyebrows in a pointed look of disbelief.

"My cocoa's gone," Mrs. Summers said, rising from the table and giving them both a warm smile. "Have a good night you two."

Cherish shook her head after her mother set her empty mug in the sink and left the room.

"She's about a subtle as a hammer."

Alex laughed. "She means well."

Cherish rolled her eyes. "She's determined for me to have a boyfriend, and I think she finds you suitable for the job."

"You don't think she cares that I'm a werewolf?" Alex asked in surprise.

"No offense," Cherish replied. "But I think she'd be thrilled if I fell for anything on two legs by this point. I'm just not in that mindset right now."

"You don't have to worry." Alex sat back in his chair. "I have a gir...well, I have someone."

One corner of Cherish's mouth lifted in a half smile. "You just about said girlfriend."

"Yeah." Alex set his half-empty mug on the table. "I guess we haven't exactly had a normal conversation, so I don't know what you'd call it."

"Then why did you say it?" Cherish's voice was soft as if she guessed there was more to the story than Alex let on.

Alex debated whether to tell her. He was used to being closed in when it came to Siale. Tensions at the Academy with Kalia didn't exactly leave room to discuss matters of the heart, and werewolves didn't bring into the open anything that might be used against them as a weakness. Yet instinct bade him to trust Cherish, and his instincts had served him well so far.

He studied a drop of cocoa that was making its way slowly down the outside of his mug to join the small ring on the table.

"I saved her life and fell in love with her." He glanced up at Cherish. "I really haven't been able to think of much else since."

Cherish's mouth opened slightly as though she had expected anything but that. "I think if I found a boy who would say stuff like that to me, my mom could relax."

Alex grinned, feeling foolish. "It's not exactly a normal situation."

Cherish took a sip of her hot chocolate, then said, "Which part? You saving lives or that a girl taking up all of your thoughts?"

"Uh, both, actually," Alex replied. He quickly amended, "I do help Jaze save werewolves, but she was the first one I actually saved myself. I mean, without me, she wouldn't have made it." Thoughts of that night stormed his mind, the body pit, the darkness, feeling Siale's life slip between his fingers with each heartbeat.

"Alex?"

Cherish's voice was hesitant.

He looked up at her, shaken from his thoughts.

"Where did you go?" she asked gently. "You looked so...lost."

Alex took a shuddering breath. "It wasn't easy." He sat up straighter, pushing the memories away. "And in answer to your second question, no, I don't usually have a girl take up all of my thoughts. It's confusing."

Cherish smiled. "Sounds like it. That's why I avoid relationships."

Alex ran his fingers along the rough line on his palm that was all that was left of the knife wound. "It's different for werewolves; at least, that's what I've been told. We form a bond of sorts. It's strong, so strong, and we both feel it. We're pulled together." He blew out a small breath. "I worry about her and can't stop thinking of her, and I know it's not going to go away until I know she's safe beside me."

"Beside you," Cherish said with a smile. "That's fast."

Alex shook his head with an answering smile. "I'm not going to propose to her the next time I see her or anything, but I worry they'll find her." He smile slipped. "I can't let the General hurt her again."

Cherish stared at him. "You rescued her from General Carso?"

Alex nodded. "What do you know about him?"

She sat back in her chair and pulled her knees up under her chin. "They don't let much information through. If you search on the Internet, it's like the stories are being erased as quickly as they're put up." Her eyebrows drew together. "But from what I've seen, he's done some very horrible things." She tipped her head to look at him. "Like kill your brother."

"And his son killed my parents." Alex leaned his elbow on the table. "They're not a very nice family." His heart clenched at the thought that he was a part of that family.

"What is it?" Cherish asked. "You're holding something in."

Alex studied her. "Are you sure you don't want to be a psychiatrist?"

Cherish gave a soft laugh in reply. "Let's just say I'm a pretty good judge of people."

Alex nodded. "I'll give you that."

She crossed her arms around her knees. "So you're not going to tell me?"

Alex hesitated, then shook his head. "I think I've told you more tonight than any of my friends know. I don't know why I did that."

Cherish shrugged. "I'm a good listener?"

Alex smiled. "Yes, you are. Thank you."

"Any time," Cherish replied. She tried to stifle a yawn, but it escaped. "Sorry," she said. "I guess it's late."

Alex rose. "I should get going. We both have school tomorrow."

"Yeah," Cherish said, standing up. "I don't want to keep you from your ninja combat classes."

Alex laughed. "That's not all we learn." He grinned at her. "We have poetry classes as well."

Cherish opened the door with a shake of her head. "I'd love to see werewolves reciting poetry."

Alex grimaced. "It's not always good poetry. Trust me. Torin, one of the Alphas, once wrote a poem about a shoe."

"That doesn't sound so bad."

"He rhymed sole with potato."

It was Cherish's turn to grimace. "That is bad."

Alex stepped out into the hallway. "Thanks again," he told her. "This was nice. Really nice."

"Come back soon," she told him. "Our house is open to everyone for Sunday dinner." She gave a teasing smile. "Maybe you could bring your girlfriend when you finally get to telling her how you feel."

"If it was that simple," Alex replied with a dramatic shake of his head.

Cherish laughed. "Goodnight, Alex."

"Goodnight, Cherish."

Chapter Five

Alex pushed the receiver button near the shield on his helmet as he climbed onto the motorcycle. "Trent?"

"Finally," Trent replied immediately.

"Have you been waiting all day?" Alex asked.

"Well, yeah." Trent's dismay was obvious. "Your mother insisted, and she calls down every five minutes to see if I've heard from you. She's convinced the humans have eaten you for dinner or something." His voice lowered. "It's late enough that I was getting concerned, too."

Alex smiled. "You know I can handle myself."

"I don't know how many there are, if they've contacted the General, if they know about silver, if they—"

"Okay, okay, I get the point," Alex said, his tone gentle despite the sarcasm of his words. "I think my mom's gotten to you."

"I do, too," Trent said with a half-laugh.

Alex cleared the last building. The dark horizon swept away, rolling hills scattered with small towns where lights only showed in a few windows at the late hour. "I'm already clear of Greyton and on my way home. That should give both of you some relief."

"I already knew that," Trent replied, reminding him of the tracking device beneath the motorcycle's gas cap.

Alex had debated removing the device, but he knew the freedom the dean gave him was bought with trust, even if Trent was on the tracking end of that trust. He would leave the chip unless he had a real need to take it out.

"Will you put me through to Siale?"

"Alex, it's two in the morning. I don't think she'll be awake."

"Just humor me," Alex said.

"Fine," Trent replied, but there was long-suffering in his dramatic sigh that told Alex he actually enjoyed doing the werewolf's bidding.

Alex didn't know what he had done to deserve such a friend, but knowing that Trent was always at the other end of the line keeping an eye on him made him feel better rather than trapped. Wolves were meant to be pack animals. It was good to know that his pack always had his back.

"Alex?"

The sound of Siale's voice sent a rush of warmth through him. A smile spread across his face even though she couldn't see it. "Hi, Siale. Sorry to wake you."

"I wasn't asleep," she said.

"Liar," he replied at the grogginess in her voice.

She laughed. "Yeah, well, decent werewolves go to bed at a decent hour."

"Is that a quote from your dad?"

"How'd you guess?" Siale asked wryly.

Alex's smile refused to go away. Just hearing her voice put him in an extremely good mood. "It just seems like something Red would say; although that really doesn't apply on full moons."

"No," she said. "It really doesn't. I'll have to ask him how he feels about that."

Alex laughed. "I'm sure he'll have an answer." He weaved the motorcycle around a patch of snow that had been blown into the road.

"What are you doing out so late?"

"I had dinner with some human friends," Alex replied. While everyone else might only know pieces of his life, he had decided from the moment he met Siale that she would know everything she wanted to. That way, it was up to her to decide whether she truly wanted to be a part of his life.

"That's a new one," Siale said with a hint of surprise. "Do you have dinner with humans often?"

"Tonight was the first time, actually," Alex admitted. "And it was nice."

"No silver daggers?"

Alex laughed. "Now you sound like Trent."

"I don't want that to happen," Siale replied in a tone of mock worry.

"I'll introduce you when you get to the Academy," Alex promised. "He and his sister are great."

"I'm looking forward to it," Siale replied sincerely.

The thought of Siale coming to the Academy filled Alex with hope that things would look up. It was going to be difficult with Kalia, he had no doubt about that, but having Siale close by was more than he had dared to hope when he watched her be lifted out of the body pit. How she had survived the entire night let alone make it through her recovery as well as she had still amazed him.

"Dad's been insisting that he and I need to watch old movies together," Siale said. She sighed. "He has a whole collection. I guess he and Mom used to watch them together all the time, so I really can't say no."

"Have you seen anything good?"

"He showed me 'My Fair Lady.' It made me cry."

The thought of Siale crying made Alex's hands clench. He had to force himself to relax his grip on the gas. "Is that a good thing?" he asked carefully.

"Yes," Siale replied. "It's a beautiful movie."

Alex let out a slow breath.

"Are you okay?" she asked.

"Yeah," Alex told her honestly. "I just don't like to hear about you crying. It makes me want to hit something."

The laugh Siale gave was warm as though his words

touched her. "You don't have to worry about me, Alex. It's okay if I cry once in a while."

"I'm not so sure about that," Alex replied quietly.

"You worry too much. Now who's sounding like Trent?" she asked.

Alex snorted. "I just don't know if you need other things to make you cry after what you've been through."

"We were there together," Siale reminded him, her voice gentle. "You're the one who pulled us both through. If it wasn't for you..."

"I would do it again a million times," Alex told her truthfully.

"I don't think I could."

"I'll make sure you never have to," Alex vowed.

Silence filled the space between them. The hum of the tires on the frozen asphalt filled Alex with peace. "It's beautiful tonight," he told her, glancing up at the stars. "You should see the sky."

"Light pollution out here's kind-of killed that for me," Siale replied. "I don't remember the last time I actually saw more than two or three stars at a time." She paused, then said, "Describe what you see."

Alex smiled at the request. He pushed back the shield on his helmet and looked up as he drove. "The sky's so dark it looks like someone's wrapped the world in black velvet, and the stars shine through bright and clear as though the same person poked a hole in the velvet in a million places and is shining a light through." He paused. "I'm not a poet," he said, embarrassed.

"It sounds beautiful," Siale replied with a hint of longing.

"It is." Alex looked back at the road with just enough time to register the deer standing in his lane, its eyes reflecting the light of his headlight. "Crap."

Even his werewolf skills didn't give him enough time to react. He slammed into the deer so hard he flew over the top of the motorcycle. He managed to pull his arms in before he hit the road on his side. He slid along the asphalt, hearing the scrape of the gravel tear his shirt and the skin of his shoulder.

Alex stopped in the middle of the road. He glanced over his aching shoulder far enough to confirm that he wasn't about to be run over. At the sight of the unbroken expanse of black road trailing like a ribbon into the night, Alex let his head fall back to the pavement.

"Alex, are you okay?" Siale asked in panic.

Alex gave a short, painful chuckle. "Yes, just stupid."

"What happened?" Relief filled her words at the sound of his voice.

"I hit a deer."

"On your motorcycle? Are you sure you're okay?"

Alex took in a testing breath and let it out slowly. "Just a bit road burned, and a few bruised ribs." He sat up gingerly. A glance at the deer showed it motionless near his motorcycle. "But I'm afraid I can't say the same for the deer."

Alex stood. His vision swam for a moment, telling him he should probably have waited longer before moving. He gritted his teeth and limped toward the animal.

The deer was definitely dead. Its neck was bent at an unnatural angle across his fallen motorcycle and its eyes were glazed over.

"At least I don't have to kill it," Alex said quietly. He knelt by the animal's side with a flood of remorse. He set a hand on its neck. The animal's fur was still warm. He could smell the fresh blood spilling out on the ground. At least the animal hadn't suffered.

"What are you going to do?" Siale asked. "Do you need help?"

"Let's see what I have to work with."

Alex limped around the deer to his motorcycle. A quick check of his aching leg showed the skin from his knee to his ankle had been removed by the abrasive road. He knew his shoulder didn't look much better. The gravel and dirt embedded in the wounds would slow the healing process if he didn't get them cleaned out.

He grabbed a bottle of water from the saddlebag on the side of the motorcycle. He didn't realize his hands were shaking until he tried to open the lid.

"Apparently I can fight Extremists and hounds without a problem, but let me hit a deer on my bike and I'm shaking like a leaf," Alex said wryly.

"Alex, you've been through a trauma," Siale told him, her voice thick with concern. "You're probably in shock."

"I'll get over it," Alex replied. He tipped his helmet back enough that he could drink some water but still stay in contact with Siale. The cool liquid calmed his nerves. He shoved his helmet back on and bent over so he could pour water on his leg.

"What was that?" Siale asked.

Alex hadn't realized he'd made a sound. "Oh, just cleaning my leg."

"Sounds like it hurts," she replied quietly.

"Or your boyfriend's just a sissy."

Alex paused. He hadn't meant to call himself her boyfriend. As he had told Cherish, they had only spoken face to face twice. The first time was in the body pit when she was half-unconscious from pain, and the second was when she had removed a bullet from his shoulder before the silver could kill him. Neither had led to the discussion of relationships.

"You're not a sissy," Siale replied without addressing his

poorly timed words.

Gratitude filled him at her discretion. "I hate to admit it, but sometimes I am." He poured the rest of the water bottle over his shoulder. The twisting it took to reach the wound told him that there were a few other injuries he didn't want to take into account.

When the bottle was empty, Alex found a piece of his shirt that hadn't been torn up by the road and scrubbed both wounds.

"Alex, you're really quiet. It worries me," Siale said.

"I'm trying to clean my road rash without further confirming my sissy status," Alex replied tightly as he worked several stubborn rocks from his leg. Thankfully, his shoulder proved a bit less rock-filled. He finished them both and tucked the remains of his shirt into the saddlebag with the empty water bottle.

"Now for the part I've been dreading," Alex said. "Let's see what the damage to the motorcycle is."

"That's the part you've been dreading?" Siale repeated with a little laugh.

Alex clenched his jaw at the pull to his wounds as he righted the motorcycle.

"How's your bike?"

"Better than I thought it would be," Alex replied with relief. While the road had scraped a good amount of paint from the side and broken the left saddlebag, the frame and roll bar had prevented a lot more damage. The deer's body had broken his headlight and dented the front fender, but Alex was able to straighten it with his hands enough that it didn't rub on the tire.

He looked from the still form of the deer to the motorcycle.

"I have an idea," he said.

"Are you doing what I think you're doing?" Siale asked suspiciously.

Alex grinned as he hefted the deer onto his shoulders. "If you think I'm tying the deer to the back of my motorcycle so I can take it back to Rafe's pack, then yeah."

Siale laughed. "That's what I thought you were doing."

Alex set the deer on the back of the seat and used the straps from his saddlebags to tie it down. "I couldn't just leave it. It seems like such a waste. At least if I feed the wolves, its death will have a purpose."

"I like that," Siale replied. "But are you sure you can drive a motorcycle with a deer on the back?"

"We'll see," Alex said. He brought his leg around gingerly and sat on the seat. He rolled his shoulders in an effort to work out their stiffness. "At least I still have over an hour before I get back to the Academy."

"Why is that good?"

"Because I can heal before Trent sees that his worry is for a good reason."

Siale laughed. "Someone needs to take care of you."

Alex thought of Cassie and his mom. "Don't worry. There will be plenty of scolding when I get back."

"Glad to hear it," Siale told him.

"Whose side are you on?" Alex asked good-naturedly as he kicked the motorcycle into gear and eased it up the road.

"Whoever's side will keep you from getting yourself killed," Siale replied.

"It's probably the side of those who will be doing the scolding," Alex admitted with a chuckle. He shifted the motorcycle into a higher gear. The weight of the deer on the back made him steer with more conscious thought, but he had evened it out the best he could and it didn't tip the motorcycle too strongly to either side. He settled into the highest gear and sped down the road, this time searching the forest for deer. He wasn't sure he or the motorcycle could take another hit.

"I guess I should let you go," Alex finally said with reluctance. "You need your sleep. I shouldn't have woken you up."

"I'm glad you did."

"Why?" Alex asked in surprise.

He could hear the smile in Siale's voice when she replied, "You learn a lot about someone when they hit a der on their motorcycle after describing the stars."

Alex laughed outright. "I guess you do."

"Goodnight, Alex," she said, her voice sweet.

"Goodnight, Siale." Her side of the conversation clicked off with a sound Alex felt in his chest. He longed for the day he wouldn't have to say goodnight to her. At least when she came to the Academy, she would only be down the hall.

Chapter Six

The click of the headset told Alex that Trent was back on the line. "What's taking so long?" Trent asked, his voice filled with suspicion. "The motorcycle stopped for a while."

"Uh, I caught a deer for Rafe's pack?" Alex answered in the form of a question. He steered carefully around another patch of snow on the road.

"One question," Trent replied with his usual tone of long-suffering. "How did you kill the deer."

Alex grimaced. "I used the motorcycle as a weapon. It was very effective."

Trent replied flatly, "Alex, you hit a deer with the motorcycle."

"Is that a question?" Alex asked.

He knew Trent was shaking his head in disbelief back at the Wolf Den beneath the Academy. "Does it need to be?"

"No, not really," Alex replied. "So now that you know, can you tell Rafe I'm bringing a kill for his wolves?"

Trent sighed. "I'll let him know. How's the bike?"

The thought of the damage to the motorcycle Trent had made for him made Alex cringe inside. "It's, uh, had better days," Alex said. "But I would like to help repair it."

"You want to help fix the motorcycle?" Trent asked in disbelief.

Alex smiled. "You act like I've never helped you build anything before." As soon as he said the words, he knew they both thought of the time Trent asked for his help to fix a lawn mower. With Alex's assistance, the thing actually blew up. Jaze banned Alex from ever helping Trent on anything after that.

"I think you could help with the paint," Trent said as though he was reaching for anything he thought Alex could handle without putting both of their lives and the Academy in jeopardy.

"Sure," Alex replied. "Do I get to use an airbrush? What if we mixed glow in the dark paint with it. It'd look like it was on fire and—"

"On second thought, maybe I should paint it. Jaze did say you were banned from assisting me," Trent reminded him.

"Okay, fine," Alex let in.

"Thank goodness," Trent whispered in relief

"Hey!" Alex protested. "It would have been fun!"

"It would have been something," Trent replied.

Alex reached the open gates to the Academy and his heart fell. Meredith stood near the courtyard steps with her arms crossed and a very worried look on her usually calm face. Alex pulled the motorcycle to a stop just as her eyes widened.

"What happened to you?" she asked in alarm.

Alex looked down at his bare chest. Blood had dripped from his shoulders and streaked his skin in dark liquid. He quickly pulled off the helmet.

"Don't worry; it's not from me. It's from the deer," he explained.

His mom seemed to suddenly notice the animal tied to the back of his motorcycle. "Do I want to ask why you have a deer?"

Alex shook his head. At her pointed look, he sighed. "I hit it with the motorcycle and thought Rafe's wolves could use it."

He thought she would flip out at the mention of hitting the deer, but instead, Meredith surprised him. She merely shook her head and crossed to his side.

"Are you okay?"

At his nod, she took a calming breath and let it out. "Good. Let me help you with this thing."

Alex stared in awe as his mother untied the deer and dragged it off his motorcycle while he held the bike steady. She then crouched to help him carry it.

"I can do it," he protested.

She shook her head. "I want to help."

Alex helped her carry it around the side of the Academy in the dark. After a few moments of silence, he asked, "Uh, why are you doing this?"

Meredith took a few more quiet steps, then replied, "I realize that my outburst with Jaze was uncalled for. You and Cassie have survived this far without me."

Alex tried to cut her off, but she stopped him with a look over the upside-down deer's stomach.

"We both know it's true. I had no right to argue against Jaze's agreement of your request, and I have no right to second-guess any of your decisions. You are in charge of your life, and I'm just happy to be a part of it." She blinked quickly, then said, "If you still want me to."

Alex set the deer down, giving Meredith no choice but to lower her side as well. He crossed to her without a word and gave her a tight hug. "My mom will always have a place in my life," he said.

"Are you sure?" Meredith asked. She looked up at him, her light blue eyes bright with tears that she wouldn't let fall.

Alex nodded, his throat tight. "Of course I'm sure. I lost you once. I'm not going to lose you again."

"Oh, Alex," his mom said. She gave him another tight hug before stepping back. "You're getting taller."

Alex smiled as he picked up the deer again. "Cassie's mad I've outgrown her. I told her way back when we were little and she was taller than me that I would eventually catch up."

Meredith laughed as she carried her side of the deer. "You were right. I think she'll stay my height."

"That's good," Alex said. At his mother's questioning look, he grinned. "That way I can look down on her."

Meredith laughed. "That was corny."

"I know," Alex replied. "But it made you laugh."

They walked through the gate and set the deer in the snow. It took Alex a minute to realize someone was leaning against one of the nearby trees, a part of the shadows that made up the forest at night. A quick breath told him it was Rafe.

"Call them in," the werewolf said, detaching from the tree.

Rafe was the only werewolf at the Academy who had been raised by wolves. Offspring from that pack made up the wolves that ran through Rafe's forest now. Though Alex had run with the werewolf and his wolves many times, he was always in awe of the half-wild werewolf Professor Colleen had pledged her heart to.

A little nervous about doing the call wrong, Alex put his hands to his mouth and attempted to hit the notes Rafe had taught the students. It was hard to match the full tones of a wolf just with the mouth, so Colleen and Rafe had taught them how to compensate with their hands to round out the sounds.

"Cup your hands a little bit more," Rafe directed.

The werewolf had reached his side soundlessly despite the crunchy snow beneath their feet.

Alex did as the golden-eyed werewolf instructed, giving his hands more space in between which lowered his notes just enough.

Howls answered his call. A shiver ran through Alex. His instincts wanted him to phase. Alex glanced at Rafe. The werewolf's golden eyes glowed in the moonlight.

"They're here," he said, his eyes focusing on the shadows.

Wolves appeared beneath the trees. The scent of blood made them anxious. Alex wondered if winter had been hard on them. They looked gaunt and worn out.

"The deer have been harder to find," Rafe said softly, answering his unspoken question. "They'll be grateful for this."

The Alpha, a big, tawny colored female, approached the deer slowly. She glanced at Rafe questioningly. The werewolf gave a low grunt of approval. The Alpha latched onto the deer's leg. The other wolves quickly followed, helping their Alpha drag it into the trees. Soon, only a trail of blood across the snow and the sounds of the wolves eating in the forest remained.

"Thanks for bringing the deer back," Rafe said, saying more than the werewolf usually did. "You okay?"

"Much better now," Alex said. At Rafe's curious look, he explained, "I couldn't just leave it there. Thinking that I'd killed it for nothing, even by accident, would have been horrible. At least now it didn't die for no reason."

"Life is a circle," Rafe said. He gave Meredith and Alex a smile. "Out here, it's simple. Kill or be killed; eat or be eaten." He tipped his head toward the Academy. "It's more complicated in there."

"Sometimes it feels like the same thing," Alex replied.

To his surprise, Rafe actually laughed. He couldn't recall ever hearing the werewolf do such a thing. "If things get crazy, the forest is waiting," he invited.

The offer touched Alex. "I'll keep that in mind."

"The wolves were sure grateful," Meredith noted.

"I'm glad," Alex said, glancing at his mom. When he looked back, Rafe was gone, vanishing beneath the trees as soundlessly as he had appeared.

Alex and Meredith made their way quietly back to the

front of the Academy. Alex was surprised Meredith didn't question him about his time with the humans. A quick check showed a determined expression on her face. He knew she was trying to give him his space and freedom.

He decided to give her a break. "You can ask me whatever you'd like."

"Are you sure?" she asked, giving him a quick look. "I don't want to pry."

Alex nodded. "Ask away."

She smiled in relief. "How was it?"

"Nice," Alex said.

Meredith laughed. "Now I know why Cassie says you're like talking to a wall."

Alex chuckled. "She said that?" At his mother's nod, he gave in. "I guess I have been a bit preoccupied."

"She said self-centered."

Alex could picture Cassie calling him exactly that. "Well, with Tennison around, there hadn't exactly been as much time to talk."

"She told me that, too," Meredith said. His mom gave him a warm smile. "She just worries about you. She knows she hasn't had as much time to be there for you, and so she asked me if I would make sure you're doing okay."

The thought made Alex smile. "I can't exactly hold it against her. She's happy, and I can't ask for better than that."

Meredith squeezed his shoulder. "You're a good brother, Alex."

Alex thought about the dinner with the humans. "They were really nice, Mom. Cherish, the girl who invited me, acted like I was just another one of her friends, and the rest of them did, too. It was refreshing. I didn't even have to worry about letting werewolf stuff slip, because they already knew. And they weren't afraid of me."

"Not at all?" Meredith asked.

Alex shook his head. "We talked a lot about what it was like being a werewolf, and about their lives. Cherish is planning to be a doctor and her mother is very supportive."

"Is it just the two of them?"

"Yeah," Alex said. "I don't know about her dad. I didn't think it was a good idea to ask."

"Good call," Meredith replied. "She'll probably tell you if she wants to."

Alex stared at her. "So you don't mind if I go over there?"

Meredith shook her head. "I did. I was so worried." She let out a small sigh. "Sometimes it's hard to remember that we need the humans if you guys are ever going to have the chance to live a normal life. Maybe Jaze is right. Perhaps your connection with these students can help things in the long run. I just have to be patient."

"Me, too," Alex admitted. Meredith watched him quietly, waiting for him to decide whether he wanted to explain. They had reached the side of the Academy and he could see Trent surveying the motorcycle. Alex wasn't ready to go over there yet. He wandered to Jet's statue and set a hand on the silver seven emblazoned on the wolf's shoulder.

"The humans have problems too," Alex said softly. He glanced over his shoulder at Meredith. "Their city is a mess. There's a place called the Saa where gangs and thugs live who pretty much run the city after sundown. Cherish's friends don't even dare go outside at night, and for a good reason." He thought of the thugs with knives. "It's like two packs trying to live in one territory, only one is living in peace, and the other is determined to tear everything apart."

"You worry about them," Meredith surmised.

Alex turned around to face her. "I do, a lot. They

shouldn't have to live in fear."

Meredith's gaze moved from Alex's face to the Academy. "That's why Jaze built this place, so you wouldn't have to live in fear, either."

Alex's brow furrowed. "Maybe we have a lot more in common with the humans than we think."

"Maybe," Meredith conceded softly.

"There's a leak from the gas line," Trent called from beside the motorcycle. "You're lucky you didn't blow yourself up. I'm going to have to check the engine casings, cables, and forks. I wouldn't be surprised if you bent the steering stem bearing. Your shifting lever's also messed up. How did you get home?"

Alex and Meredith exchanged a glance.

"Good luck," Meredith whispered.

"Thanks" Alex said. "I'm going to need it."

"I'll catch you inside," his mother said.

Alex jogged across the grass to Trent. The scrawny werewolf looked at his bloodstained chest and merely shook his head. "You should get cleaned up."

"I could drive it inside," Alex offered.

Trent put up a hand. "No need," he said. "We don't want to start it up again until I've had a chance to take it apart. There are a few upgrades I've been wanting to make to the engine anyway."

"You have to take it apart?" The thought of the beautiful motorcycle lying in pieces made Alex cringe.

Trent nodded, rubbing his hands together as if he relished the thought. "It's the only way to ensure you haven't damaged more of the engine that I can see here. Give me a week."

"Fine," Alex finally let in. "How about putting a deer guard on the front of it when you're done."

Trent laughed. "That would look amazing. Like a train. You could catch more deer for Rafe's pack."

"On second thought, let's not do that."

Trent chuckled as Alex pushed the bike toward the Academy.

Exhausted but happy at the day's events, Alex stepped into what he thought would be the sleeping Pack Jericho's quarters. He froze when a set of icy blue eyes locked on his.

"What on earth happened?" Kalia demanded. She rose from the couch, her gaze on his chest.

"Nothing," Alex said. "This is deer blood."

"We need to get you cleaned up," she said hurrying over to him. "What if some of this blood is really yours and you don't know—"

"Kalia, I'm fine," Alex protested. He backed away.

"Alex, you're not fine. You look like death right now."

"Thanks," Alex said wryly.

Kalia steered him toward the shower rooms. He wanted to tell her that her hands were getting dirty, but knew she would just ignore him. She reached in and turned on one of the showers.

"Kalia, this is getting out of hand," Alex argued.

"Don't take that tone with me, Alex. You could be hurt and not even know it. Now change out of those clothes."

Alex's mouth dropped open. "Kalia, seriously. I can take care of myself."

She put her hands on her hips and tapped one toe on the floor. "I'm not so sure about that. Now that I'm an Alpha, next term, things are going to be different."

Alex rolled his eyes. "I'm going to shower, and I need you to leave while I do."

"What clothes are you going to change into when you're done?"

Alex hadn't thought that far ahead. He shrugged. "I'll figure it out."

Kalia sighed. "Fine, but I'm going to wait on the couch so you can call me if you need me."

Alex's frustration finally got the better of him. "I don't need you. When are you going to figure that out?"

The look of hurt that swept across Kalia's face made Alex immediately regret his words.

"Kalia, I—"

She stormed out of the shower room without looking back. A few seconds later, the unmistakable bang of her door slamming shut let Alex know she didn't care about waking up the entire pack, and the other packs sleeping down the main hall as well.

Later, Alex padded to his room in his soggy wolf form. He pushed the door open with his nose and collapsed on the bed without bothering to phase. If the room smelled like a wet dog the next morning, maybe it would be enough to keep Kalia from tormenting him.

Chapter Seven

Alex ran through the woods in wolf form. The snow was long gone and the fresh smell of loam beneath his paws filled him with joy. The Termers had left a few days ago, and Alex was relieved he didn't have to worry about Kalia for a few months. The furry tail Professor Colleen had doused in orange oil coated his mouth with bitterness. He wondered if Professor Chet had given input to the scent. He enjoyed tormenting the students in his own small ways.

The shushing sound of footprints warned him a second before a cream-colored wolf would have slammed into his side. Alex jumped out of the way and Cassie skittered to a stop in the meadow, her tongue out and dark blue eyes dancing with laughter. Tennison appeared a second later, his lanky wolf stride effortlessly eating up the forest floor. Alex darted past them both, keeping his prize away from them as he loped deeper into the forest.

The sound of other paws reached Alex's ears as additional Lifers fought to claim the prize for themselves. A reward of Cook Jerald's famous blackberry cream cheese pie awaited whichever Lifer returned the fox tail Colleen had hidden deep in the forest. Alex loved blackberry cream cheese pie and was determined to be the one to claim it. Whether he shared it with his twin sister and her boyfriend teetered on how much they interfered with him winning the reward.

Tennison beat him at the next turn and made a grab for the tail. Alex spun to the right. The tall werewolf's fangs snapped shut millimeters from the prize. Cassie had anticipated the move and was already there. Only Alex's quick reflexes saved him. He jerked his head up, flinging the tail into the air. Both werewolves stopped short in surprise, giving Alex the chance to leap over Cassie and catch it in his mouth before it hit the ground. He took off again in a cloud of dirt and pine needles his sister would no doubt scold him for later.

Two gray forms blocked the path to the next clearing. Alex could either take the long way around and risk running into Torin and Sid, or take his chances with Trent and Terith. Alex loped toward the siblings, sizing them up. Terith's stance was firm, and she had a mock snarl on her face. Trent's eyes widened at Alex's approach. Alex galloped through the sunflower meadow without slowing. Just before he bowled the siblings over, Alex gathered his legs and leaped.

The wind rustled through Alex's dark gray fur, tormenting him with the thought of actually flying. The sunflowers parted beneath him in the wake of his jump. Landing between the trees at the edge of the clearing would be perfect. Alex looked down at the siblings, expecting to see them both staring up at him wide-eyed as he jumped over them. Instead, Terith had bowled her brother over and was using him as leverage, her paws on his shoulders as she reached for the fox tail that dangled from Alex's jaws.

The werewolf managed to grab the tip of the tail as Alex passed overhead. The sudden halt to his momentum flung Alex so hard into the dirt that he lay there stunned for a moment. His head shook back and forth, and it took him a few seconds to realize that it was Terith attempting to yank the tail from his jaws.

Alex gave his head one hard shake and then rolled over, pinning the tail beneath his shoulder as he did so. The movement threw a surprise Terith to the ground, driving her snout into the dirt. She was forced to let go of the tail and dodge out of the way before Alex rolled over her as well. Faster than they were prepared to react, Alex had his legs back underneath him and was running again.

By this time, Cassie and Tennison were on his heels. Terith and Trent quickly fell in behind. Alex could hear the thunder of paws in the forest on either side. He had to do something to lose them all, or it was going to be an all-out fight for possession of the tail.

A thought occurred to him. He altered his course slightly and felt the ground begin to rise beneath his paws. He would have grinned except for the risk of losing the orange-oil coated tail. Cassie pushed to catch up, no doubt guessing his intentions. Alex ducked his head and ran faster, driving his legs to even greater speeds. He reached the boulders and began to jump, scrambling up one and leaping for the next as soon as he could get his paws beneath him. The werewolves kept close behind.

Alex broke through the top of the steep rise into the bright noonday sunlight. The rays reflected off the lake far below, illuminating the jump he had only made one other time. Barks sounded behind him. He recognized Cassie's voice without looking back. The others would be below her, gaining on Alex's position. There was only one way to shake them completely.

Alex clenched his teeth and leaped off the cliff.

The water rushed to meet him. As soon as he hit the mirror surface, the air he had sucked in burst out of his lungs. His paws began to paddle on instinct while his brain screamed at him for taking stupid risks with his life all for a fox tail and a piece of pie. The other irrational side of him replied that it was totally worth it just to annoy Cassie.

Alex's head broke the surface. He took in huge gulping breaths, then realized gulping breaths shouldn't have been so easy with his mouth closed. He looked around quickly for the fox tail and found it drifting near the shore. Alex quickly swam over to it. The thought wasn't lost on him that he had also doggy paddled the last time he had jumped off the cliff, and he hadn't been in wolf form. At least swimming that way was much less tease-able as an actual animal because it was his only option.

As soon as Alex's paws touched the sandy bottom of the small lake, a growl met his ears. The fur stood up on the back of Alex's neck. The sound was a challenge, and an Alpha challenge at that.

With his ears back, Alex looked up into Torin's dark face. The werewolf's green eyes bored into his, daring him to accept the challenge or give up the fox tail. Alex knew he wouldn't be permitted on shore without choosing one or the other.

A glance to the left showed Cassie and the others bunched near the shore. Apparently it was a lot easier to climb down the cliff than it had to climb up. They looked agitated at Torin's challenge, but none of them could do anything against the Alpha.

Torin's ears flattened back and he growled again.

Alex thought quickly through his options. He could choose to fight the Alpha, but Torin had Sid at his back. Alex still had the painful memory of being beaten by Torin's pack over rescuing a kitten. Sid had proved he wouldn't hesitate to jump in despite rank duel protocol. If Sid dove into the fight, Alex knew the rest of the Lifers would race to defend him. He didn't want any of his friends hurt over a fox tail and a pie.

Alex jerked his head sideways, flinging the tail at Torin. The one satisfaction he received was when Torin missed the grab and the tail smacked Sid wetly in the face before falling to the ground. Torin picked it up and trotted back into the woods. Sid snarled at Alex, then followed the Alpha back toward the Academy.

Alex stepped slowly from the lake and shook himself on the beach. Cassie snorted, and he turned to find his friends covered in the water he had rid from his coat. Alex smothered a grin at Cassie's bared teeth. His sister shook her head and started back along the path. The others followed her, and Alex fell in behind.

Gone was the lightness of their steps and the laughter in their eyes. Torin had singlehandedly stolen the thrill of the chase. Alex bit back the urge to give the Alpha a piece of his mind. It would only get him into another fight and perhaps risk his pack mates as well. Alex snorted softly, his eyes on the forest around them.

A pine branch had fallen next to the trail. With its brown needles and layered twigs, it looked a lot like the fox tail. On a whim, Alex grabbed it in his mouth. He fought back the urge to spit it out again. Pine sap tasted almost as bad as the orange oil had. The combination of both of them in his mouth left a taste nobody would enjoy.

Ignoring the unpleasantness, Alex trotted to the front of the group. He spun without warning, forcing the others to stop or run into him. At Cassie's questioning gaze, Alex turned his head from side to side, flourishing the pine branch.

Tennison gave a wolfish grin and tried to bite the branch. Alex backed up just fast enough to keep it out of the werewolf's reach. Cassie snorted a laugh and joined in. Soon, the four Lifers were chasing Alex through the forest again. He led them down every path he knew, jumping over fallen trees and darting under windrows carved into tunnels by the water that overflowed the river in the spring. By the time they piled through the Academy gates, everyone's good humor had been restored.

Alex trotted into the Academy with his head held high.

Pack Torin lounged in human form on the steps below their Alpha. Torin held up the pie he ate by himself as Alex's pack trotted up the stairs.

"Looks like you made it home with a pathetic branch," the Alpha noted. "Perhaps Cook Jerald will turn it into sap soup for you."

Sid and the other Lifers snickered. Alex rolled his eyes at them. As he climbed past Torin, he allowed his back paws to slip on the wooden stairs. The loss of balance made him fall into Torin's back, which in turn sent the Alpha's face directly into the blackberry cream cheese pie.

"You did that on purpose!" Torin yelled.

Alex widened his eyes dramatically, but he couldn't help a snort of laughter at the look of Torin's cream cheese covered face. Even the other Lifers on the stairs were having a hard time controlling their expressions. Sid actually chuckled before covering his mouth at Torin's enraged glare.

"You think you can get away with anything," Torin said, his eyes narrowed in anger. "I'll get you back. Just you wait."

Alex hurried to the top of the steps filled with wry gratitude that the Alpha was so bad at trash talking. Instead of quaking in fear of retaliation, he couldn't stop picturing Torin's face covered in frosting. Giving him the fox tail had been well worth it.

Chapter Eight

Summer passed quickly at the Academy. Soon, it was time for the Termers to arrive again. The Lifers had been asked to gather before the buses came. Jaze actually looked nervous as he stood on the raised stage at the end of the Great Hall. The professors behind him looked almost as concerned. Alex wondered what was going on. A glance back at Cassie showed the same trepidation on her face.

"I've asked you all here before the term students arrive for a very important reason. Things are going to change this school year, and I ask each of you to be patient and to go along with the changes. It will be different, it may be difficult, but I'm asking you to trust me."

A howl cut through the air. Anticipation surged through Alex. His muscles tensed as he waited for the dean to release them.

Jaze smiled, his brown eyes bright. "They've arrived. Let's go welcome the Termers to our new year at the Academy."

Students rushed out the doors to the Academy courtyard. As much as Alex wanted to be the first one to the buses and cars, he held back for the other Lifers to hurry by.

"Alex."

He turned to see Jaze approaching. The dean gave him a warm smile. "You ready for this?"

Alex nodded, though his chest tightened at the thought of Siale and Kalia being under the same roof.

"Just promise me one thing," Jaze said. "Trust me."

The request surprised Alex. Jaze was the only father figure in his life, and had done everything in his power to help Alex and Cassie through their trials. "Of course I trust you."

The dean let out a breath. "I just have a feeling that if you go along with what's going to happen this term, the rest of the werewolves will follow."

Alex gave a wry smile. "You might be overestimating my impact here."

"I don't think so," Jaze said with an answering smile. He looked out the wide glass doors, watching the students file from the vehicles in the courtyard. Lifers rushed to welcome their friends back.

Alex searched for wavy brown hair and soft gray eyes.

"You'd better go," Jaze said with understanding in his voice. "She's bound to be looking for you, and I wouldn't want her to get overwhelmed."

At that moment, Boris grabbed Parker, his usual Second, and got into a mock wrestling match with the werewolf in the middle of the courtyard. Soon, all of Pack Boris was involved in an all-out battle.

"What's overwhelming?" Alex asked dryly.

He heard Jaze chuckle as he hurried out the door.

Alex's heart slowed the moment his eyes locked on Siale. She stepped slowly from the bus, her gray eyes wide as she looked around at the student-filled courtyard. Her hand hesitated on the door frame as though she debated whether to step down or return inside. The expression of uncertainty that crossed her face gripped Alex's heart. He rushed through the crowd.

"Siale!"

At his voice, the uncertainty swept from her face as though it had never existed. She quickly searched the crowd, and when her eyes met his, Alex stopped in his tracks so quickly he was almost ran over by Shannon and Shaylee.

"Out of the way, Alex," Shannon snapped.

"Seriously, dude. Watch where you're going," her twin echoed.

"Sorry," Alex said reflexively, his attention completely on Siale.

The way her mouth pulled into a smile made his heart stutter. He put a hand to it, willing it to calm. He had forgotten the way her gaze made him feel. It was as if she saw every corner of his soul, the dark along with the light. He felt bare and exposed, but safe at the same time as if whatever she found was exactly what she was looking for.

Her smile soothed the ragged edges of his mind, the places where memories still tormented him, tearing out throats of werewolves possessed as the General's hounds, watching his parents die without the ability to save them, holding Siale as her lifeblood slipped between his fingers. He had failed in so many ways, yet she stood in front of him, watching him from the door of a bus the exact color of the sunflowers that waved in the breeze near the edge of the gate.

Her hair got caught in the same wisp of air and tangled around her shoulders. Alex drew in a breath as it brushed past him. Siale's lavender and sage scent filled his nose. He held the air in his chest as long as he could before letting it out again. The action freed his feet. He walked to her without noticing the dozen werewolves he passed. Several might have yelled at him, but he didn't pay attention.

"I'm so glad you're here," he said. The words felt inadequate to describe the emotions rising in his chest at seeing her again.

"I'm happy to be here, now," she replied, the look on her face indicating that 'now' meant 'now that he was here.'

Unable to contain himself any longer, Alex grabbed her around the waist and spun her around. Happiness that she was finally there threatened to make his heart burst. She laughed and grinned down at him with her hands on his shoulders.

"What was that about?" she asked when he set her on the ground.

He shrugged. "Just helping you down from the bus."

She laughed. "Is that right? Are you going to carry my luggage, too?" she asked, her tone teasing.

"Of course," Alex replied. "What kind of a boyfriend would I be if I didn't?"

Siale stared at him, but the humor failed to leave her face. "So you're using the boyfriend label right off the bat?"

Alex had known it was a risk to push things so far, but he had already done it, so he figured he might as well own up to it. "Yes," he said simply.

His lack of explanation made her laugh. The sound was music to his ears, like a mixture of the river when it was low enough to run over the rocks near the green houses, and the call of the meadow lark as it welcomed the light of day. He knew he was infatuated, and wanted to stay that way every moment of his life if it made him feel how he did right then.

"Fine, boyfriend, get my suitcase."

Alex grinned. "I have a name, you know."

She shrugged. "It's up to me if I decide to use it."

Alex picked up the lone black suitcase that remained of the pile the bus driver had left at the side of his vehicle. He held out his arm and Siale slipped her hand though, holding his elbow as if she was indeed a fine lady being escorted from a carriage.

"Everyone's going to think you're mad," she said quietly into his ear.

A shiver ran down Alex's spine at the brush of her breath against his skin. "That's nothing new."

They were almost to the steps when another voice called out, "Alex!"

His heart fell. He wanted to keep going, but Siale turned,

curiosity on her face.

Kalia stormed through the werewolves still milling around the courtyard. Those who didn't have the brains or speed to get out of her way were pushed to the sides without hesitation. Kalia's icy blue gaze flashed in anger as she took in Siale's fingers on Alex's arm. Her expression had enough venom that Siale let her hand fall to her side.

"I was calling you," Kalia said, her tone strained as if she was trying to keep her voice calm.

"Sorry," Alex replied, plastering a smile on his face. "I didn't hear you." He gestured to the courtyard. "It's pretty noisy out here."

Kalia nodded. "Will you, uh, will you help me with my luggage?"

"Kalia, you're perfectly capable of carrying it yourself," Alex pointed out.

"Let's help," Siale said.

"That's kind of you," Kalia replied, her voice cold enough to freeze the sun.

She turned away and Siale fell in at her side. Alex trailed behind the pair, his thoughts so bewildered he was doing good just to put one foot in front of the other. Kalia kept looking back at him and smiling warmly. Siale talked to her, but Alex couldn't focus enough to hear what she said.

He picked up Kalia's two suitcases, two smaller pieces of luggage, and a small bag the driver had placed at the side of the limousine. They weren't heavy, just awkward as Alex juggled them on his way to the doors. Kalia and Siale spoke like they were old friends, but the few phrases of conversation Alex was able to catch revealed the same icy tone Kalia had used earlier when speaking to Siale. He wanted to stop her, but wasn't sure if Siale would appreciate it.

Alex dropped Kalia's luggage in a heap inside the door

where the rest of the students had piled their stuff in anticipation of the Choosing Ceremony. He carefully set Siale's only suitcase near the window where it wouldn't get trampled by the students.

"She's nice in an ice queen sort of way." Siale said from his elbow.

Kalia was nowhere in sight. Alex breathed a sigh of relief. "I thought she was going to kill you."

"It sounds like she'd rather kill you," Siale said. At his worried look, she laughed. "Don't worry. She said things will be better this term. I'm not sure why that is, but she seemed happy about it."

"Calling all students to the Great Hall," Nikki's voice said over the speakers. "Please assemble for the Choosing Ceremony."

Surprised conversations filled the entryway. Jaze usually gave the specifics of the Choosing Ceremony while they were still in the courtyard for the benefit of any new students who had arrived for the term. He then gave them time to converse so that the Alphas could get to know those they might want in their packs. Heading straight to the Ceremony threw everyone off.

"What's the Choosing Ceremony?" Siale whispered as they followed the flow of students into the Great Hall.

"It's where we get divided into packs," Alex explained. "The Alphas choose and if you want to go in their pack, you accept the choosing. It's as easy as that." He gave Siale a warm smile. "Don't worry. I'll make sure you're in good hands."

She smiled back at him, but he could feel her fingers tremble slightly on his arm as she followed him to the seats by Pack Jericho.

"Is this Siale?" Jericho asked as soon as they sat down.

The tall, dark-eyed Alpha gave Siale a warm smile.

"I am," she replied.

He shook her hand. "It's a pleasure to make your acquaintance. Alex has kept us all very intrigued about, well, everything regarding you. But it's clear his obsession was well founded."

Siale laughed. "I sure hope so."

The members of Pack Jericho smiled in return. Alex realized the way he felt about her laugh wasn't due to his infatuation. Everyone couldn't help but join her. Even Trent was smiling despite his concern about the coming Ceremony.

"I wish I knew what's going on," he said.

"I think things are going to get cleared up," Jericho replied.

Jaze crossed to the front of the stage. Instead of nervous, he appeared self-assured and confident. He looked around at the students with the smile that made everyone feel important and welcome. Kids sat up straighter and smiled back in return.

Chapter Nine

"Welcome to Vicki Carso's Preparatory Academy," Jaze said. "This is the ninth term our school has been open, and I am proud to say that our students have excelled in every area of study. Those of you finishing college courses will be well ahead of human students when you go out into the world. Our goal is to provide you with the keys you need to live happy, full, safe lives." He met Alex's gaze. "And so it is with that in mind that we change our areas of focus for this term."

The dean lifted his eyes to take in the entire student body. "We have spent the last few terms honing your skills as a wolf. You can hunt, track, fight, and live as wolves; however, in doing so, we have hindered you as well. You are each so quick to call yourself a wolf and embrace your wolf side. This term, we are going to help you accept the fact that you also have a human side. You have talents and abilities that need polishing for that side as well if you are to integrate into society and eventually lead normal lives."

The dean looked back at his wife who sat behind him with the other professors. Nikki smiled and gave an encouraging nod. Little William sat on her lap and waved at his dad. Jaze smiled and turned back to the students. "Human life involves learning how to work in populations with diverse personalities. You don't always get to choose who you work with and associate with on a daily basis. Learning how to get along with others no matter what the circumstances may be is very important to survival in real life. With that in mind, at this Choosing Ceremony, no Alpha will be allowed to choose a werewolf who has previously been in his or her pack."

Alex's chest tightened. He felt like he could barely breathe.

Jaze continued despite the rush of conversation that rose

up in the room. "Also, due to funding needs and other circumstances, Professor Vance has also been approved to begin his football team for competition against other schools in the district. Those of you chosen for the team must learn to use restraint in order to hide the fact that you are werewolves. This is going to be a new practice for most." Alex followed Jaze's gaze to where Pack Boris and Pack Torin argued about the Choosing change. "But I know you will be able to handle it," Jaze concluded.

Alex doubted many werewolves heard the part about Vance's football team. Everyone, including himself, was stuck on the fact that no one would be able to stay on the same pack they had grown comfortable with over the terms.

All eyes were on Torin when the dean opened the floor for the Choosing Ceremony. The Alpha Lifer looked over the crowd of anxious students. No one knew what would happen now that things had been shaken so dramatically. Whispers of, "Who would pick me?" and "I hope I get a good pack," filled the air.

Torin looked at Sid, his normal Second, but it was impossible for him to choose the Lifer again. His head tipped slightly to the side and in the next instant, his gaze locked on Alex. Alex felt the bottom drop out of his stomach.

"I choose Alex Davies."

The Alpha's words rang through the suddenly silent auditorium. Everyone turned from staring at Torin to stare at Alex.

"Alex?" Cassie whispered from behind him.

Tennison squeezed his shoulder. "You don't have to go," his sister's boyfriend said.

Alex looked around quickly, calculating his position. He had been Jericho's second for the past four years. The Termers despised him because he was a Lifer, and the only other Lifer Alphas had options they would no doubt rather take.

His gaze settled on Kalia. The new Alpha gave him a smile and mouthed, "I'll pick you."

Alex took a steeling breath. Life as Torin's Second would be miserable, but unless he wanted to go with Kalia, he was going to have a serious demotion in rank.

Alex grabbed Jericho's shoulder. "Promise me you'll take care of Siale."

"I promise," the surprised Alpha said. "What are you going to do?"

"Something probably really stupid," Alex replied quietly. He tipped his head close to Siale. "Stick with Jericho. We'll talk after this."

At Siale's nod, Alex stood up. "I accept the Choosing," he said.

The whispers that had circulated through the crowd were nothing compared to the exclamations and shocked chatter that buzzed around him as he walked to the stage.

"Seriously?" Torin said when Alex stopped in front of him and turned to face the crowd. "This is going to be a fun term."

Alex just gritted his teeth and kept silent. He looked at Kalia, and instantly regretted it. The hurt he saw on her face tore at his heart. She blinked quickly, fighting back tears, and the moment their eyes met, she looked away and glared at the ground.

Alex hated hurting her, but didn't regret his decision. Being Torin's Second might make for a miserable term, but if Kalia had chosen him, dissuading her of her feelings for him would be even more difficult. He kept his eyes on the ground and listened to the other Alphas choose different werewolves for their packs.

Boris chose Daniel, Drake's usual Second. Drake went with Parker, an obvious decision. The rest of the Alphas pretty much switched Seconds until the Choosing reached Jericho.

The Alpha was quiet for a moment, then said, "I choose Siale Andrews."

Alex's head jerked up. Jericho stood behind him, already watching him with a calm expression.

"When I asked you to watch over her, I didn't mean you had to choose her as your Second," Alex whispered.

The Alpha smiled. "I figured having you as a Second was interesting enough. Your girlfriend was bound to add to the adventure."

Alex couldn't help but smile back. "Thank you."

"Anytime," Jericho said seriously.

As the last phasing Alpha, it was Kalia's turn to choose. She took her place on the dais and looked out over the crowd. Alex turned away when he felt her eyes on him.

"I choose Cassie Davies."

Alex let out a breath of relief. At least his sister was with a friend. Kalia wouldn't take out her frustrations regarding him on his twin. She and Cassie got along too well for that. It would be Cassie's first term as Second. His sister smiled the entire way to the stage and gave Kalia a grateful hug before taking her place in front of the Alpha.

The rest of the Choosing Ceremony rushed by in a blur. Pack Jericho was divided up by the other Alphas as were the other set packs. Students stood next to each other as stranger who had never shared quarters or eaten at the same table. Jaze's strategy to shake things up had definitely done just that.

Trent and Terith went with Kalia, as did Pip and Amos. Jericho chose both Lifers and Termers as was his usual policy, though he looked as unhappy about the changes as the rest of the assembly. Siale waited a few places away from Alex. She threw him several uncertain glances, and he forced himself to smile in return. They wouldn't be in the same quarters, probably would have one class together if any, and couldn't sit at the same table to eat. The light that had been shining on Alex's new term had suddenly become dim and watered down. His only relief was that Jericho would make sure she was alright.

By the end of the Ceremony, students were talking and acclimating themselves to their new packs. Torin leaned down and grabbed Alex's shoulder hard.

"You have toilet duty when we reach our quarters," the Alpha growled in his ear.

"Nobody's even had the chance to use the toilet," Alex pointed out.

"My face better shine in that bowl when you're through," Torin said.

"Your face would look better inside the bowl," Alex muttered.

"What was that?" the Alpha snapped.

"Nothing," Alex replied.

Torin stepped closer so that his nose was inches from Alex's. "I don't know why you accepted me as your Alpha, but know this. I will make you regret the day you didn't die beside your parents."

Alex let the jab slide by. "Is this about Kalia?" he asked.

Torin's eyes narrowed. "What do you think?"

He stormed away, leaving Alex with the feeling that a whole lot of the term was about to revolve around Kalia Dickson.

"Why, Alex?"

Alex gritted his teeth and turned. Kalia's eyes were red and faint stains from the tears she had unsuccessfully wiped away marked her cheeks. "You know this term could have been great."

"I couldn't do it," Alex said.

"What does that mean?"

Alex winced at Kalia's demanding tone. "It means that distance right now might keep us from killing each other."

"It also might keep you from realizing that I'm your girl," Kalia pointed out. Her eyes flitted past Alex's shoulder, then narrowed. "You think you love her, but you're wrong."

"I know what my heart tells me."

"You're heart's wrong, Alex. You told the General that I was your girl and you loved me.

Alex's eyes widened. "I was trying to save your life! He would have killed you right then if I didn't say those things. Kalia, I'm sorry I hurt you—"

"Hurt?" Kalia spat. "I'm not hurt, Alex. I'm lost, frustrated, and heartbroken. I don't know why I'm not good enough for you."

The last words were spoken quietly as though she hadn't meant to say them at all. Alex took a step forward. "Kalia, I—"

"Leave me alone, Alex. I need some time to think." Kalia stormed out of the Great Hall without looking back.

Alex leaned against the stage and fought back the urge to bury his face in his hands in frustration.

"Alex?"

His heart turned over. He forced a calm expression on his face and looked at Siale.

"I take it this is the first time the Choosing Ceremony has been so crazy?" she guessed, her gray eyes filled with understanding.

Alex was about to nod, but a memory made him smile. "Four years ago, a crazy new Alpha named Jericho chose me as his Second. I think that really got the ball rolling."

"You're welcome," Jericho said over Siale's shoulder. "And I haven't regretted my decision yet."

"Do you need Siale?" Alex asked, reading the familiar patient expression on the Alpha's face.

Jericho nodded. "I'm just gathering my new pack together so we can find our luggage and our quarters. I thought Siale might like the tour along with the other new students."

She met Alex's gaze. "I would like that."

He nodded. "Have a good time. I'll meet you after dinner."

To his surprise, she stood on her tiptoes and kissed him on the cheek.

"What was that for?" he asked, putting his hand over the suddenly warm place.

"To chase the worry from your eyes," she replied with a smile before joining her new pack mates.

"She's going to have to do that every day if that's the case," Jericho said, watching his pack sort through their luggage.

"I won't complain," Alex said.

Jericho chuckled. "I'm going to miss having you in my pack."

"Just promise me you'll watch over her. I don't trust Torin or Boris' old packs as far as I could throw them."

Jericho nodded. "Will do, but it sounds like Torin will be watching your every move."

Alex sighed. "I'm not sure how much freedom I'm going to have this term. I already got toilet duty."

Jericho shook his head with an answering sigh. "Maybe we can petition to have things back to their old ways next term."

"I hope so."

Alex watched the new Pack Jericho follow their Alpha up the stairs. He wondered who would get the room he had gotten used to thinking of as his over the last four years.

Chapter Ten

Nightfall found Alex lying on the grass beneath Jet's statue. He had scrubbed the toilets until even Torin couldn't complain about the quality, then he had been forced to clean Torin's chosen room until it smelled of four layers of lemon polish. Alex couldn't remember the last time he had worked so hard at scrubbing other peoples' filth.

But he didn't argue. The fact that he was the Alpha's Second wasn't lost on him, and pack protocol dictated that a Second never second-guessed his Alpha's decision unless it was a matter of life and death. Solidarity within a pack depended on unity between the leaders. Alex was determined not to give in to the Alpha's pathetic attempts to cow him.

He turned his head at the sound of familiar footsteps.

"Pack Torin, really? You could have gone with any pack," Jaze said as he settled onto the grass next to Alex.

"I like a challenge," Alex replied. At the dean's skeptical look, he chuckled. "Maybe I didn't think it through, but the toilets in Pack Torin's quarters have never been cleaner."

Jaze sighed as he looked up at the stars. "My goal in diversifying the packs wasn't so the Alphas could torment everyone."

"It's not going to be like that. Torin just has a vendetta and I'm an easy target." He turned his attention to the Orion constellation that hung over their heads. "Maybe it's good for me to remember that not all Alphas are as nice as Jericho."

Jaze gave a noncommittal grunt. "An Alpha is supposed to take care of those beneath him, not abuse his power over them like a dictator."

"Maybe I'm the one who can teach Torin that."

Alex felt the dean studying him. He kept his gaze on the stars and the black form of the statue above him. No matter what Torin did, the Alpha couldn't keep him from his favorite place. As long as he was able to escape and settle his thoughts beneath his brother's statue, he could stay sane.

The sound of other footsteps caught Alex's ear.

"I'll catch you later," Jaze said, excusing himself. Alex watched the dean leave, confused about the werewolf's quick departure until the voice spoke.

"Cassie said I would find you out here."

Warmth flooded through Alex. He sat up and turned on his knees. The sight of Siale standing in the moonlight on the other side of Jet's statue stole Alex's breath. He could only watch her, speechless, motionless, frozen by her beauty and the smile that never failed to fill her face when their eyes met.

"This must be Jet," Siale said. She set a hand softly on the statue's shoulder. There was reverence in her gaze along with sadness. "I wish I'd known him."

"You would have liked him," Alex said, sure of it. He smiled. "And he would have liked you."

"You think so?" she asked as though it was important to her.

Alex nodded. "Definitely. He liked people who weren't afraid to fight for themselves, who wouldn't give up no matter what the odds." His voice dropped as he looked up at the statue. "He understood that."

Siale leaned her forehead against the statue. For a moment, it felt like Alex was intruding on her space, watching something intimate and personal as she closed her eyes and said, "Thank you for saving us, Jet. We'll make your sacrifice worth it."

When Siale stepped back, it was with an expression of peace. "I'm glad he's here for you," she said as she took a seat by Alex's side.

"Sometimes it's hard when he can't answer my

questions," Alex admitted.

"Doesn't he?" Siale asked, searching his gaze.

A shiver ran down Alex's spine. He felt her read his loss and the challenges he fought so hard to overcome.

Her hand lifted to his cheek, heating his skin beneath her palm.

"You're not crazy," she said softly.

"You don't know that," he whispered.

"Yes," she said with a smile that made her soft gray eyes glow. "Yes, I do."

She put her lips to his, kissing him gently. When she sat back, Alex could only stare at her. Her taste lingered on his lips, teasing him, begging him for more. It was only through sheer willpower that he was able to hold still.

"Why did you do that?" he asked.

"To remind you that you're not alone."

He took in a deep breath filled with her lavender and sage scent. "I'm not sure if you want to dive into this," he warned her. "I'm not who you deserve."

Siale sat back against the statue. When the metal base touched her back, she smiled and reached up a hand to touch Jet's paw.

"Alex, you've seen the darkest parts of life. I know that. I've seen the despair in your eyes, and I know there are so many times when you must feel like you are on the verge of losing your humanity altogether, but I've already been there with you."

Her words enveloped and defined him, calling out the emptiest parts of his soul and surrounding them.

She let go of the statue and slipped her hand into Alex's. Her palm was cold from contact with the metal. "If it wasn't for you, I would have lost mine. I couldn't have stayed in that pit alone and survived even if I hadn't been hurt." She blinked, looking deep into his eyes. "Alex, what I see inside you is more strength than I could ever imagine lived in one person. You are stronger than you know, and you are going to carry us and this school further than anyone could even imagine. I believe in you, Alex."

He took a shuddering breath. "But what if I break?" It was the question that toyed in the back of his mind when the memories of his parents' death and the body pit threatened to overwhelm him. The question defined his worst fear.

Siale squeezed his fingers. "I'll be there to pick up the pieces and put you back together."

The words made a smile spread across Alex's face. He pulled her close and she leaned against his shoulder. He loved holding her in his arms, knowing that she was complete and whole, and that she felt safe with him. He would take care of her, and somehow, in some way, she would take care of him as well.

***

"Okay, ladies, let's get some gear on," Vance told them.

"I don't see why we need gear," Matt, a whiny Lifer from Pack Torin, pointed out. "We're werewolves."

Vance rolled his eyes as he towered above them. "How do you expect to play football with humans and not have them guess you're werewolves?" His eyebrows lifted as if he thought the students before him were completely stupid. "You have to dress like them, act like them, and play football like them."

"It's degrading," Torin said.

Alex shook his head at the unfortunate luck of being in Pack Torin for football training. The whining would never stop. Luckily, they had also been paired with Pack Kalia. He would at least get the chance to spend some time with his old pack members, if just for training. He had no idea what would happen when actual football practice started.

Vance grabbed the facemask of the helmet Torin has put on and lifted the Alpha off the bench. "Degrading is watching you sissies attempt to tie your shoelaces. Your mother isn't here to throw the ball. If humans can do it, you can do it. Remember that and you might actually make a good team. Understood?"

"Understood," Torin replied in a grumble.

Vance let him go and stalked across the grass Professor Dray had marked with white lines on the far side of the Academy. He turned near the end and shouted at them, "From this moment on, you will call me Coach Vance, and if anyone asks a question or makes a statement I feel is beneath you, you will do one hundred pushups."

"One hundred?" Nate asked. "I can barely do ten." The words were said in a lisp due to the big gap between Nate's front teeth.

Vance speared the skinny werewolf with a humorless look. "I'll be happy to help you start practicing."

Nate's face washed white.

"While Nate is doing his pushups, I want the rest of you to pick up the footballs and pair up. Each time you catch the ball, take ten steps back. I want you throwing from either side of the field by the time class is over."

Alex felt bad leaving Nate as the kid knelt in the grass. A glance at Trent said that the other werewolf felt the same way. At Vance's fierce look, the Lifer put his hands down and gave a weak attempt at a push up.

"What was that?" Vance asked. The hulking werewolf looked like a bear towering over a muskrat.

"A p-push up," Nate stammered.

"You're a werewolf," the coach pointed out. "You should have more strength than that in your pinky finger."

"Catch."

Alex caught the football thrown hard enough to knock the air from his lungs. He glared at Torin.

"What's wrong? Can't take a throw?" the Alpha asked.

Alex's jaw clenched as he threw the football back. Torin took ten steps and chucked it again. This time, Alex was ready. He caught the ball and used his arms to slow the momentum before the Alpha's strength could drive it into his sternum. He threw it back as though it didn't bother him. Torin took ten more steps back.

"Keep it up, Alex, and you'll be contending for starting quarterback," Vance called.

Normally, Alex would have been thrilled at the werewolf's compliment. It was known throughout the Academy that the professor very seldom said anything kind. This time, however, Torin speared him with a glare before the football sailed through the air. Alex caught it again and sent it back in a tight spiral that made the Alpha's look ugly.

By the end of the class period, Alex's hands ached from catching footballs thrown much harder than any human ever could. His left hand throbbed when he clenched it into a fist. By the swelling, he wouldn't doubt if a few of the bones were broken or at least cracked. He knew he could stop by Meredith's office in the medical wing, but chose to live with the pain. It would heal and sometimes the sharp throbbing reminded him to watch what he did to avoid becoming an even bigger target in Torin's eyes.

"You guys get to play football while we're stuck learning gymnastics?" Cassie complained when they met back in the hallway. "That's sexist."

"Vance, uh, Coach Vance, said no girls play on the human school teams, so we couldn't do it here. We have to do everything right to avoid suspicion," Tennison explained.

"But gymnastics?" Cassie said, leaning against him as he put his arm around her shoulders. "I thought it'd be easy, but Colleen had us swinging on hanging rings and bars until I thought my shoulders would fall off."

"I didn't think Colleen would be a hard on you guys," Tennison said.

Cassie shook her head. "She's not. She's really nice and encouraging, it's just that there're skills we haven't learned yet."

"The muscle memory will take a while to sink in," Trent said, explaining the same thing to his frustrated sister. "As soon as you learn it, I'm sure gymnastics will be easy. Easier than football at least." The small werewolf had a big bruise on the side of his face.

Alex caught a glimpse of Kalia waiting at the end of the hallway. As soon as she spotted him, she turned away. Alex was about to go after her when a voice stopped him.

"Hey, scumbag. Did you forget whose pack you're on?"

The hair on the back of Alex's neck stood up. He turned slowly, willing his body not to phase.

Torin's eyes narrowed. "Have you cleaned those toilets?"

Alex fought back a surge of embarrassment at acknowledging in front of his friends what the Alpha had made him do. "I already cleaned them yesterday," he reminded Torin in a tone he had to force to remain steady.

A light of enjoyment showed in Torin's green eyes when he replied, "They're due for another cleaning today."

Alex glanced at his old pack mates. Pity showed on Tennison's face. Alex clenched his hands into fists. The sharp pain reminded him what was at stake.

"Whatever you say, Torin," he replied.

Torin nodded with satisfied smile and shoved past him. The rest of Pack Torin followed.

"I've got to go," Alex told his friends. "Catch you later."

Chapter Eleven

He walked into his next class just as Gem was addressing everyone. The professor's usually short pink hair had been dyed neon green. She wore a huge smile on her face and was writing quickly on the white board as though there wasn't enough time to get everything done she wanted.

"And so you see, social networking is just a way of learning about your neighbors in order to better associate with them," she explained.

"What if we don't want to associate with them?" Sid asked.

Alex took a seat at the back of Pack Torin's side of the room and stifled a sigh. He had hoped the change up would keep him from having to deal with Torin's usual Second, but they had been paired with Maliki for social networking. Alex knew Gem was no pushover from his rescue missions with Jaze; he could only hope Sid would give her the chance to put him in his place.

Instead, Gem gave a patient smile. "Life in the human world is all about making social acquaintants. School, work, even getting a bite to eat opens one to many different social situations. In this class, we're going to address the protocols for many situations you might face on your own in the world."

"Why don't we just kill them all?" Torin muttered loud enough for everyone to hear.

Gem's blue eyes narrowed. She turned and wrote Torin's question on the white board. As she wrote, the sleeve of her shirt slipped back from her wrist to reveal dark lines running down her arm. Alex knew from Jaze that she had been tortured with a silver whip. Vance also carried the same marks and made no effort to hide them. As soon as Gem saw that her sleeve had moved down, she pushed it up again.

"Why don't we just kill them all," she repeated. The words sounded ugly coming from her kind voice. "Let's address that."

Alex tried to save her from a frustrating explanation. "I don't think Torin meant—"

"Shut up, Alex," Torin growled. "Unless you want to challenge your Alpha?"

Tension hung in the air along with the question. Triumph already filled Torin's gaze as though he knew what Alex's answer would be.

For a moment, Alex debated whether to accept the challenge. Part of him said to go for it and end the torment the Alpha was putting him through. The other part argued that he had survived the body pit; Torin would never be able to do anything worse than that. It was better to cultivate peace rather than fight over something so meaningless.

Alex let out a slow breath and shook his head.

Torin smiled in triumph and motioned for Gem to continue.

She did so in a quieter voice and without the usual bouncing from foot to foot as though she could barely contain her excitement at teaching them.

"Why don't we just kill them all? Why don't we give into our baser instincts and just slay any opposition in our path?"

Torin and several other students nodded at Gem's words.

"Why don't we accept that werewolves are the top dog in this world and get rid of any who stand in our way," Gem concluded.

"That's what I want to know," Torin said. Answering laughter followed.

Gem shook her head, her short green hair bright around her face. "You want to act like animals, yet part of you is human. You want to be like wolves in the wild and deny the fact that you contain any humanity." The disappointment on her face was enough to quiet even Torin's laughter. Gem waved her arm to indicate the world outside the classroom. "You want to prove them right that werewolves can't learn to live in peace with humans, and in doing so, you spit on the sacrifice of every werewolf who died to get you here." Her voice was quiet when she asked, "Why did they die for you?"

Nobody looked at the professor. Students stared at the textbooks in front of them, their laughter gone.

Alex raised his hand.

"Drop it," Torin growled.

"Yes, Alex?" Gem asked when he ignored the Alpha.

Alex didn't look at anyone when he said, "They died so we could live."

"Well said," Gem replied. She lifted her voice. "They died so we could live. Is hiding behind the Academy walls for the rest of your lives a way of living?"

Several students shook their heads.

Gem nodded. "Exactly. Wolves and humans weren't meant to live in cages, and neither were you. The classes Dean Jaze and the professors have selected this term are designed to help integration when we get to a point where that is a possibility."

"What if we never get to that point?" Instead of being obstinate, Maliki's question was colored with true concern.

Gem tipped her head to one side, considering his question. "You can only do so much living away from society. You will get back to the world, whether hiding your wolf side or with the ability to embrace it."

The surety in her words filled Alex with a sense of release. Guilt had remained at the back of his mind when he thought of his dinner at Cherish's, as though having such an enjoyable evening with humans was something against his werewolf nature. The knowledge that his forays into the human life would eventually be joined by the others eased his longing for that world.

"Let's begin our first social lesson, shall we?" Gem said. "Take out your papers and write five things about yourself you think no one else in this class knows. I'm going to shuffle the pages and we'll see if anyone can guess their pack mates correctly."

The sound of pencils scratching across paper followed.

***

"Who can explain the principles of supply and demand?" Professor Thorson asked from the front of their Economics class.

"I demand everyone's cookies at lunch and they supply them to me," Torin replied.

Even Alex could help smiling at Professor Thorson's answering chuckle.

"In a way, you're right," the professor acknowledged. "At least, you are if you take it to the next step. If the cookies are gone, apparently eaten by yourself," Professor Thorson nodded at Torin. "Then we have a shortage of cookies and they become a valuable commodity. If you were to turn around and trade them back to your pack mates for say two pieces of steak..."

"That's way too pricey!" Nate piped up.

The professor nodded. "But if others are willing to trade, you have just profited on the principles of supply and demand."

"Huh," Torin said.

Alex was surprised to see the Alpha's attention to the lesson. Instead of lounging back in his seat shooting spit wads at the other packs, Torin actually looked interested.

"So you're saying that a normal object can become valuable if enough people need it?" the Alpha asked.

Professor Thorson smiled. "Exactly. Let's try an object lesson. I need someone's pencil."

"Alex, give him your pencil," Torin commanded.

Alex held up the object he was going to offer the professor anyway.

"Thank you," Professor Thorson said. "Now, Alex, I need you to write your name on your paper."

"I can't," Alex replied.

Professor Thorson waved the pencil. "So to you, this object has great worth. To the rest of your classmates who already have pencils in their hands, this is just a duplicate of their possession and that decreases its value to them; but since you have the need for it, its worth goes up to you."

He set the pencil on Alex's desk. Before he could pick it up, Torin reached over and snapped the pencil in half. Alex stifled a sigh.

"What if Alex has two smaller pencils instead of one big one?" Torin asked, holding up the object.

"Then he has a duplicate as well," Professor Thorson answered. "It will be of less value to him."

"What if the rest of the class has two smaller pencils?" Torin asked. He threw a glare at the students around him. To Alex's amazement, everyone, including the members of Pack Drake, immediately broke their pencils in half.

Alex shook his head. "Incredible," he muttered under his breath.

"Now everyone has the same two objects," Professor Thorson said. "What is your purpose?"

"Give me the pencils," Torin said.

Students passed their pencil pieces up the rows to Torin's desk. He grinned at Professor Thorson. "Supply and demand, Professor. If anyone wants their pencils back, they will give me a cookie and half their steak at lunch today."

"Torin, I didn't mean for this to be—"

"If they want to go through the rest of the day without a pencil, that's up to them. Otherwise," Torin sat back with the stack of broken pencils in front of him, "I am really going to enjoy lunch."

True to his word, Torin had a towering stack of cookies and extra pieces of steak in front of him at lunch. He sat in his usual seat with his arms folded like a cookie baron, bartering them like coins for whatever he wanted. At least someone had offered to clean the toilets for his pencils back after Torin said he had enough cookies and needed to up the price. Alex was relieved to be spared that duty for at least one night.

"Hoarding cookies? What was that about?" Cassie asked when Alex met them outside after finishing his lunch, minus the cookie and half of his steak as his Alpha had demanded.

Alex shook his head. "Professor Thorson taught Torin how to run the school using economics."

"Great," Trent replied, rolling his eyes. "What's going to happen when he learns about game theory?"

"What's that?" Siale asked as she joined them. She slipped her arm through Alex's and smiled at him.

"It's the study of mathematical models of conflict and cooperation between decision-makers and applies to economics through the belief that one person's gains exactly equal the net losses of the other participants," Trent explained.

Alex and Siale exchanged a confused look. "Does that answer your question?" Alex asked, trying to hide a smile.

"Oh, sure. He should have said that in the first place," Siale replied.

Trent let out a huff of air. "What is means is that if Torin learns game theory, he'll understand how groups of people will react when confronted with certain situations. He could prey on the entire student population for things like food and weapons by understanding what people want and how far they are willing to go for them."

"But you're bound to have deviations," Terith spoke up.

"Oh, deviations, naturally," Alex seconded with a grin.

Trent shook his head at Alex. "You have no idea what we're talking about, do you?"

Alex shrugged. "No clue, but the fact that you know it means we're all safe. Anyone up for a run before lunch is over?"

"I am!" Siale said.

"Me, too," Cassie seconded.

"Why not," Tennison answered with his arm around Cassie's shoulder. He bent down and she gave him a quick kiss. She saw Alex watching and a blush stole across her cheeks.

"Let's hurry, please," Alex said dryly. "As much as I enjoy watching you two make out, I have a tyrant to get back to who will no doubt come up with more demands from his cookie empire."

"Game theory," Trent muttered as he followed them through the gate. "A game theory tyrant with cookies. Does it get worse than that?"

Alex squeezed Trent's shoulder. "I sure hope so; otherwise, all Torin needs to take over the world is one giant bakery."

Trent shook his head, but couldn't keep from laughing. "You are ridiculous."

"Tell me about it," Alex said.

Chapter Twelve

"How's a day in the life of Torin's Second?" Siale asked when she found Alex wandering the grounds after school.

Alex glanced at her. It was impossible not to smile at the sound of her voice. "Well, let's just say that human and werewolf biology is not a class I would choose to take with my Alpha. He's obsessed with pointing out the differences between werewolves and humans. I think Professor Mouse is going to have a conniption by the time the term's over."

"You could maneuver a counter attack by pointing out all the similarities werewolves have with humans," Siale suggested.

Alex's smile deepened. "I knew I liked you for a good reason."

She laughed. "And here I thought I was just a girl you pawned off on your old Alpha."

Alex took her hand. "Come on."

"Where are we going?" she asked in surprise.

"I want to show you something."

He led the way through the gate and into the forest where they had run during the lunch hour. It was different experience walking through the woods in human form. The scents weren't quite as sharp, but the colors held shades and warmth they didn't carry when he was a wolf. In the animal form, grays took over, highlighting shapes and emphasizing details. It was easier to see at night, but dulled the aesthetics of the sun shining through the green leaves overhead or the way the dapple light illuminated the smaller pools of river water in green and blue hues.

"It's so peaceful out here," Siale said, her voice breathless.

"It's home," he replied. At her questioning look, he smiled. "Sometimes all walls become too much, and when that happens, I can come here and just exist. I don't have to be Alex, I'm not a brother, a friend, a student, or a Second. I'm just a part of this forest."

Siale stopped walking. He looked back at her in time to see her sit on the ground.

"What are you doing?" he asked, crossing to her side.

Siale settled onto her back on the pine needle and leaf-strewn forest floor and smiled up at him. "I'm just going to exist."

Alex took a seat near her, not close enough to touch and distract her, but with only a slight gap between them so that when he laid on his back and closed his eyes, he was still completely aware of her.

He listened to her breathing settle into a steady, slow rhythm, the quiet intake and release of breath between lips he so badly wanted to kiss again. He couldn't believe he was in Rafe's forest with the girl who owned his heart, his mind, his soul, his flaws, and anything else that made him who he was.

He could see her again as she had been in his arms in the body pit. She had been motionless, bleeding. The soft breaths of air that made up her words had been so painful to listen to because he knew how much it took from her. Holding his hands over her wounds and feeling her blood slide between his fingers had felt like the very definition of hopelessness. He couldn't let her go, yet no matter what he did, he had felt her slipping away.

Yet here she was, perfect and whole, lying beside him on the forest floor listening to the breeze as it danced between the leaves and showered them in scents of loam and clover, the coming rain and pine needles, and sage and lavender. He smiled at the realization that the last two scents didn't belong to the forest. They were Siale's, and they were his.

"How do you push it all from your mind?"

Siale's soft words broke through his quiet contemplation. He looked over to find Siale watching him. A tear stole slowly from the corner of her eye, drifting down her cheek the way his fingers longed to.

"Why are you crying?" he asked softly. He turned on his side and wiped the tear away with the backs of his fingers. He looked at the moisture on his skin, then again into Siale's soft gray eyes. The blue flecks that hid in the depths were dark with her pain. He cupped her cheek in his hand. "Siale, please talk to me."

She closed her eyes, shutting him out, closing away everything around them. Alex felt helpless to do anything. He wanted to hold her, to tell her everything was alright, but he couldn't fix something if he didn't know how it was broken.

After what felt like an eternity, Siale said, "I can't shut it all the way out. The second I close my eyes, it all comes rushing back, the General, the knives, the experiments." A shudder ran down her body and she curled into a fetal position. "Landing on the bodies of my friends, knowing they were dead and that I was going to join them." Her voice tightened. "Knowing my mother was among them somewhere."

"Oh, Siale."

Tears flowed down her cheeks from her tightly closed eyes as if she couldn't stop them from coming. Alex put his forehead against hers, willing her to feel some form of comfort from being near someone who understood.

She had never spoken of her mother, and he hadn't wanted to pry. Red, her father, had told him that both his daughter and wife had been taken, and that he felt fortunate to have one of them back. Knowing that Siale had lost her mother to whatever horrors the General had created had been enough to keep Alex from asking questions. He knew all too well what it was like to lose family members and be helpless to do anything about it.

"You're so strong," Alex whispered, the skin of his forehead warm against hers. "You carry it all inside so much better than I do."

She let out a breath that brushed his lips. "I feel like I'm going to explode, but that it wouldn't make a difference if I did." Her eyes opened inches from his, staring up at him. "I'm just scars, Alex, horrible memories pieced together in the place where my soul used to be. I don't even know where one ends and the next begins anymore."

Alex sat up and pulled off his shirt. She seemed surprised by the action until her gaze took in his torso and the scars that lined it.

"What happened to you?" she asked, sitting up and staring at his chest.

Alex shrugged and untangled a leaf from her hair. "The General and his son. Like I told you at the warehouse, sometimes I don't know where the scars end and I begin anymore."

He was about to pull his shirt back on when Siale put her hand on his chest. Her touch shocked him like lightning, coursing through his skin with a million electric fingers, awakening every sense and making him feel again, truly feel.

Her fingers traced the scars from the bullet wounds, the knife scar in his stomach, and the stab wound in his shoulder. Her fingers drifted up to his arm, lingering on the scar from the silver bullet.

"I helped make that one," she said quietly.

Alex shook his head. "You helped me survive that one."

He couldn't hold back any longer. He pulled her onto his lap and bent his head, meeting her mouth in a tender kiss. After a moment, he raised his head and looked down at her.

"What are you doing to me, Siale?"

She tipped her head slightly to one side as she looked up at him. Her wavy brown hair brushed his arm, sending shivers through his skin. "I was about to ask you the same thing."

He smiled and kissed her again.

"Were you going to show me something?" she asked a while later as the sunlight began to lessen and the shadows of the trees lengthened along the path like soldiers lined up to protect those who lived within the forest.

Alex pulled another leaf from her hair. He twirled it in his fingers and smiled at her. "Yes, I was. You distracted me."

She smiled at his mocking accusatory tone. "I did, and it was entirely on purpose."

Alex rose to his feet and held out a hand. "I had a feeling you did." He picked up his tee-shirt and slipped it over his head before taking her fingers in his. "No more distractions."

"Not even a little bit?"

He couldn't keep back the smile at her innocent tone. "Maybe a little bit." He leaned down and stole a kiss from her, then danced back when she tried to swat him away.

"Now who's the distracting one?" she asked.

"I just needed to give you a reason to follow me," he called over his shoulder.

"Like I needed one," she replied with a laugh, running to keep up with him.

Alex led her through the trees as fast as he could. She cut corners and tried to beat him, but he dodged her attempts and turned, steering them up the incline. By the time they reached the top of the cliff, Alex was gasping for air as much as she was.

"You don't give up," he breathed, collapsing onto his back on the cliff edge.

"You, neither," she replied, dropping to her knees beside him. "You'd think with all this forest to run in, you'd be in much better condition."

He laughed up at her. "Yeah, you'd think."

She put a hand on his chest as she stared out at the small lake below the cliff. The sun had sunk beneath the distant mountains, lighting the forest in hues of gold and red. Orange and pink hung in the clouds that darkened overhead, promising rain by nightfall.

"It's so beautiful," Siale whispered. "It's like…"

Curious as to why her words had faded away, Alex looked up at Siale. She was studying him hard, concern sharp in her features. "What's wrong?" he asked.

"Your heart. It skipped."

Alex sat up, slipping away from her hand on his chest. "Yeah," he said, feigning nonchalance. "It's nothing."

"That's not nothing, Alex."

He lifted his shoulders. "It happens sometimes. It's no big deal."

"It is a big deal."

Siale watched him the way Cassie did sometimes, as if she was waiting for him to collapse. Alex couldn't stand being looked at that way. He rose to his feet. "Dr. Benjamin wasn't too concerned." His heart skipped another beat.

Siale stood beside him. "If you're going to lie, you should probably get better at it," she said quietly.

Alex stared at the sunset as if trying to bore a hole in it.

After a few minutes had passed, Siale's arm slipped through his. "I'm sorry," she apologized. "I shouldn't pry."

Alex turned. "I just don't want you to worry," he told her. "You've been through enough. You shouldn't have to worry about me, too." His voice dropped. "The last thing you need is a broken boyfriend."

He studied the ground past her shoulder, unable to meet her gaze.

She let out a little breath, tempering it with a smile. "We're a matched set." She put her arms around his waist and leaned her head against his chest. "We're both broken in our own ways."

He wrapped his arms around her. It was the only choice he had when she was so near. Holding her reminded him that at least one of the hard things he had gone through ended up with something good.

"We'll do what we can to fix each other," Siale said.

Alex smiled down at her. "Good luck with that."

"You're unfixable?" she asked with her teasing smile, her gray eyes bright.

He chuckled. "You're just now figuring that out?"

She slapped his shoulder softly. Taking his hand, she turned to watch the last of the sun's rays reflect off of the lake below.

"Jump with me," Alex said.

The wide-eyed look she gave him made him bite back a smile. "Are you serious?"

He nodded. "Trust me."

"I do trust you, Alex. What I don't trust is leaping from this high of a cliff into a lake that may or may not be filled with sharp rocks on the bottom waiting to smash us to pieces."

"I've done it before," Alex told her. "You won't get hurt."

"What if I told you I can't swim?"

Alex stared at her. "You can't swim?"

She shook her head.

"I'll teach you."

"By making me jump off this cliff?"

Alex shrugged, watching her closely. He didn't want to push her into doing something she wasn't comfortable with, but he knew how strong she was.

"Fine." The resolve in her voice held a touch of fear. "As long as you promise not to let go."

"Done." Alex took her hand and stepped to the edge of the cliff.

"Not like that," Siale protested. She loosened his grip, then interlocked her fingers in his. Only the tightness of her jaw let him know the courage she was drawing on.

Alex studied the water below. "You can count if you want," he offered.

Siale shook her head. "Just jump."

Alex bent his knees, then changed his mind and pulled her to him. He kissed her firmly on the lips. "You're going to be fine," he promised.

She stared at him. Before he gave in to his wish to stay on the cliff top beside her forever, Alex jumped, pulling her off the ledge after him. A little yelp of fear escaped her, then they were under water.

Chapter Thirteen

Alex waited until his feet touched the bottom. He pushed off hard, pulling her up after him. He felt her fingers loosen in her panic, but he held on tight until their heads broke the surface.

"Alex, help me!" she gasped, gulping in air and water.

Alex held her as he kicked, keeping her up.

"Stay calm," he directed.

In her panic, she tried to climb on top of him, pushing him under. Alex kicked back to the surface and ducked behind her. He looped one arm across her chest and used the other to paddle and keep them both afloat. Siale's hands latched onto his arm as thought it was a lifeline.

"You're okay," he said quietly into her ear. "I've got you and I'm not going to let you drown."

"I'm...scared," she said.

He could feel her muscles trembling as she forced herself not to struggle. Her breaths became steady as she let him hold her up, putting her complete trust in his abilities.

"That's it," Alex told her. "Just relax. Easy now."

Soon, they were floating in the middle of the lake, her hands on his arm with a grip that wasn't quite as tight as before.

"Ready to try this?"

Siale nodded, but didn't speak.

"Loosen your grip," he instructed. "I'm going to hold you up."

After a minute, she did as he said. Her fingers released their hold and he held her up gently.

"Stretch out on your back. Keep flat like a plank, and fill your chest with air. It helps with the buoyancy."

There was something so amazing in the way she followed

his words without question. Alex felt like he held the most priceless gift in his hands. He had to tell himself over and over that he was worthy of it.

"That's it. Tip your head back. Hear yourself breathe." Alex kept his voice calm and quiet. "You don't have to kick your legs or move your arms. If you keep your lungs full of air and your back arched, you can stay like this for as long as you need."

He felt her body relax as she followed his directions. With her ears under water, he knew she listened to the rise and fall of her breath, that it blocked out all else, even his words.

He lost track of how much time they stayed in the lake. Siale's eyes closed, and only the slight movements of her hands in the water and her breath let him know that she was alright. He kept one hand on the small of her back, not holding her up, but letting her know that he was there if she needed him. He floated beside her, leaning up now and then to make sure she was doing okay.

Eventually, long after the sun had set, Siale let out her breath and lowered her legs. Alex held her again and her hands settled on his arms, not with bruising force this time, but gently, calmly. He swam them both to shore.

"Next time, we'll work on doggy paddling," he said as they settled on the grass at the edge of the lake. "It's not fancy, but it can save your life."

"It was gone."

Siale's soft words caught Alex's attention. He looked at her to find that she wasn't watching him, but the water. The moonlight played upon the gentle waves brought up by the night breeze. The light was shattered, drifting, like silver leaves floating on a vast black ocean.

"What was gone?" he asked quietly.

"The memories, the fear, the General, and the pit." She

looked up at him, her eyes wide with tears. "It was all gone."

Alarm filled him. "Siale, I'm sorry if—"

She shook her head, cutting him off. "You did it, Alex. You found a way for me to escape it all. For the first time since I was kidnapped, I was able to find peace in my own mind instead of being plagued by the things I went through." The tears broke free, drifting down her already wet cheeks.

"Are you sure you're okay?" he asked.

She nodded, taking his hand. "More than okay." She took a deep breath and let it out. "For the first time, I feel like I can breathe." She smiled up at him. "I needed that more than you know. I felt like I was going crazy, like if I didn't find a way to escape, I was going to be buried under those things forever."

Alex watched her closely. "They're not gone."

She shook her head. "They never will be. But being able to just be, just for a moment, reminded me of who I am beneath it."

"You're amazing."

She leaned up to kiss him tenderly on the cheek. She then cupped his cheek in her hand. "You, Alex, are amazing."

A howl sounded. Alex froze, listening. Another voice joined in, then another.

Siale read the look on his face. "What's wrong?"

Alex stood slowly, his attention on the northern forest. "Those tones mean danger."

Two other howls rose into the night.

Alex tore off his shirt.

"What's going on?" Siale asked in alarm.

"That's Rafe and Colleen. They need help," Alex told her.

"I'm coming with you," Siale said.

Alex was about to protest, but the look on her face said that she wouldn't listen. He ran behind a tree and phased.

When he came back out, she was already waiting in the form of a lithe light gray wolf with white marks on her shoulders and chest.

Alex raised his muzzle to the moon and gave an answering howl, combining the tones of his name along with the notes that said they were on their way. Additional howls rose from the Academy. Jaze and the others would be close behind.

Alex led the way through the trees. He dodged a trunk and leaped over a small bush, grateful for the way his wolf eyesight illuminated the obstacles so he could avoid them. Siale kept close to his side, dodging right when he went left, and clearing the river the same time that he did. Her paws hit the ground almost soundlessly as the pair flew through the midnight forest.

Sounds of fighting reached Alex's ears before they entered the clearing. The small cabin nestled in the secluded valley was an all too familiar of a reminder about the first time he had almost killed Drogan, and in turn nearly been slain by his half-brother.

He didn't have time to think about that. Wolves filled the valley, snarling, angry wolves that fought Rafe's pack tooth and claw. The scent of the valley let Alex know that these were werewolves. He had no idea if it was a territory fight, or if the werewolves meant danger to the Academy. All he knew was that Rafe and Colleen had called for help.

Alex dove in with Siale at his side. He sliced and bit, using his fangs to drive werewolves back all the while keeping Siale in his view so he could protect her if they were too strong.

The logical part of his mind counted two dozen werewolves, more by far than he and Siale could take on even with Rafe and Colleen. The werewolves snarled and drooled as they attacked. Their howls reached a pitch that rang in

Alex's memory. When he realized what it was, he nearly froze in his tracks.

Hounds. The werewolves they fought were hounds from the General, brainwashed werewolves sent to attack and destroy anything in their path. He wondered how the General had found so many. They were everywhere, biting, tearing, and destroying anything they could reach. Fear for Siale filled Alex. He fell back, pushing her behind him. If the hounds were after her, he didn't know how he would be able to defend her against so many.

They surrounded the pair. He could see Rafe and Colleen near the edge of the valley fighting for their lives as well. Fallen wolves lay around them, animals from the valley along with others Alex didn't recognize.

A werewolf latched onto Alex's shoulder, tearing it wide open. Alex grabbed the werewolf by the throat and threw it with a jerk of his head. He took down one intent on Siale, then another was on his shoulders, his jaws digging down toward the place where Alex's skull met his spinal cord.

Alex rolled backwards, slamming the wolf to the ground. He spun and tore out the hound's throat before two more latched onto his sides. Another hound grabbed his back paw, its sharp fangs breaking the small bones. A fourth bit Alex's shoulder where it had already been torn open.

Blue burned at the edges of his vision. Alex heard Siale's cry of pain. The thought of her in trouble caused the blue to overcome everything, his thoughts, his pain, and his actions. His muscles expanded and his limbs lengthened. He rose off the ground with a howl of rage.

The werewolves around him stared in amazed horror. Alex grabbed two of them and smashed them together. He backhanded a third across the face and its head snapped around. The fourth took off yelping in the other direction.

Alex spotted Siale pinned against a pine tree with low sweeping branches. Her muzzle was red and blood colored the white marks on her fur. The sight of Siale bleeding turned everything in Alex's sight into slow motion. He reached the werewolves attacking her in two massive strides. He picked up three of them at once and held them against his chest in a grip so tight he felt their ribcages collapse. He dropped them to the ground and grabbed two more. Their yelping cries cut off with a quick jerk of his clawed hands.

Alex met Siale's stare for one brief moment before he turned away. He dropped onto all fours. His claws tore into the earth as he raced to Rafe and Colleen. He hit the pack of hounds around them like a battering ram. Breaking and then throwing the beasts to each side, Alex cleared a path for Rafe and Colleen to escape. One of Rafe's golden eyes was clouded with blood and he limped as he helped his wife to safety.

The hounds seemed to realize that running from Alex wouldn't work. Changing tactics, they attacked in a group. For a second, Alex was buried beneath the snapping, tearing, writhing bodies of the General's werewolves. He could hear howls as Jaze as the others reached the valley. He knew if the hounds finished him, Siale and the professors would be next, with the Academy close behind.

Alex gathered all of his strange strength and stood with a force that threw the werewolves away from him. He slammed heads together, caught the paws of retreating wolves and threw them against trees, and pounded those who remained into the ground. Eventually, the deranged growls and rolling eyes of the imposters stopped.

Alex sucked in deep breaths, staring at the pile of bodies around him. His hands began to shake. The blue faded from his vision. He collapsed onto the pile as his strength left him.

"Alex!" Jaze shouted.

Running footsteps reached him. He felt gentle hands pull him away. A blanket was set on top of him. His body trembled in the aftermath of morphing.

"You're okay." He recognized Professor Dray's voice.

Alex opened his eyes to see the face of the only other werewolf he knew of who had morphed into something that wasn't wolf or human.

"You're going to be alright," Dray said, his gaze filled with understanding. "You saved them."

Alex looked past Dray into Siale's questioning eyes. There was fear on her face, but it wasn't directed at him. "What were they?" she asked.

"H-hounds," Alex forced out. He tried to sit up. Dray helped with a hand under his shoulder. When Alex winced, the werewolf made him lean forward.

"We need to clean that so it'll heal," Dray said. "Siale, can you stay with him?"

At her nod, Dray left them beneath the tree.

Siale scooted closer and glanced behind him. "Your shoulder," she said, her face white.

"It'll heal," Alex told her. "Are you okay?"

She nodded, but when she set her hand on his knee, her fingers trembled. He covered her hand with his own. The sight of blood beneath his fingernails made his stomach turn over. "Are you sure?"

"Wh-what was that? Wh-why did they..." Her voice faded away.

"The hounds are werewolves the General brainwashed." At the mention of the General, Siale's face paled further. Alex kept her eyes locked with his. "I'm not going to let them get you. I promise."

She nodded. Her eyebrows drew together. "Alex, what

happened to you?" she asked softly.

He shrugged, then winced when the movement pulled at his shoulder. "I'm not sure. Professor Dray calls it morphing." He tried to lean against the tree, but couldn't do so without more pain. "He's the only other werewolf I know that it's happened to."

Dray came back with a bottle of water and Colleen at his side.

"Alex, you saved us," Colleen said, dropping to her knees next to Siale. "We couldn't fight them all."

"Glad I could help," Alex said tightly.

Dray put a hand on his good shoulder. "Can you lean forward again?" he asked.

When Alex gingerly obeyed, the professor poured the water over his wound, flushing out any debris left from the fight. Alex gritted his teeth at the sharp pain of anything touching the gaping flesh.

"There's a tooth in it," Dray said. "I need to pull it out."

Alex leaned his head against his hands. He felt like he was about to pass out.

"Look at me, Alex," Siale instructed.

He opened his eyes to find her face close to his. "You're going to be okay," she said. She put her lips to his mouth.

Alex kissed her as pain filled his shoulder, and then eased. Siale sat back with a hand on his arm.

"Got it," Dray said. Alex didn't have to look back to know the professor was smiling. "That was easy."

Colleen wrapped bandages around the wound to hold it shut while it healed.

"Let's get you into the moonlight," Dray said when Colleen was done. He helped Alex stand and the trio walked beside him to a patch of grass that hadn't been tainted by the night's fight. Jaze walked up as Alex eased back to the ground.

"That was amazing," the dean said.

Alex forced a wry smile. "Just keeping our forest safe."

"And doing a good job," Jaze replied. He tipped his head toward the other professors. "They're going to carry the hounds to the canyon. We have a place we can bury them there."

"Bury them?" Kaynan repeated, reaching the group. "They tried to kill Colleen and Rafe, not to mention the kids here," he said, gesturing at Alex and Siale.

"They were werewolves before the General got to them," Jaze said. Sadness touched his voice. "We'll give them the burials they deserve."

Kaynan nodded without pressing further. "I'm just glad you're okay," he said to Colleen, giving her a hug.

"Colleen is Kaynan's sister," Alex whispered to Siale.

"It was a close thing," Collen said, hugging him back. "Thank goodness we have our own secret weapons." She smiled at Alex.

"Yeah, thank goodness," Kaynan seconded. He squeezed Alex's good shoulder. "Get some rest, champ."

Jaze and Dray followed the crimson-eyed werewolf back to the others.

"Did you know what they were?" Colleen asked, her violet gaze on Alex.

He nodded. "I fought them the last time I went up against the General. He had dozens of them at the mall when we rescued Kalia."

Colleen nodded. She set a hand on his knee. "You saved Rafe and me and also most of the wolf pack. Let me know if there's anything I can do to repay you."

Alex smiled. "How about teaching football?"

Colleen laughed. "And put Vance in charge of

gymnastics? Those poor girls would be doing pushups for the rest of the term."

All three of them watched the huge werewolf sling two hounds over each shoulder and trudge across the valley behind Jaze and Chet.

Alex grinned. "I had to try, but I think I'd rather take our chances."

"The girls appreciate your sacrifice," Siale told him.

Colleen rose. "I guess I should help with the cleanup. It should give you some time to heal before we need to start back."

Alex settled onto his side. He could feel the moonlight already taking affect. It seeped into his bare skin, blanketing his shoulder and his other minor wounds in a healing heat. His eyes closed of their own accord.

"You okay?" Siale asked quietly.

Alex nodded. He opened his eyes to see her lay beside him. She smiled when he put his arm around her.

"Sleep, Alex. I'll watch over you."

He smiled drowsily from the effects of the healing. "I think I'm supposed to be the one saying that."

Siale gave him a fond look. "You've already taken care of all of us. Sleep. You deserve it."

He closed his eyes and fell asleep with a smile on his face.

Chapter Fourteen

"Get up, Second," Torin barked. "You have toilet duty."

Cold water poured on Alex's head. He sat up, then winced at the sudden movement.

Torin's eyes widened. "What happened to you?"

Alex looked down at the healing cuts and scrapes along his chest and sides. A glance at the window showed the bare gray of predawn light. He had only slept for perhaps an hour after they returned to the Academy.

"It was a rough night," Alex said. He slipped his feet into his shoes, then bent gingerly to tie them.

"Go back to sleep, Alex."

Alex glanced over to see Torin staring at his back. His shoulder must have looked as painful as it felt.

"I have toilet duty."

"Forget it," the Alpha said gruffly. He left the room and closed the door behind him. Alex heard Torin muttering as he walked back up the hallway to his own room.

Alex's eyes drifted shut the second his head hit the wet pillow.

***

School was well under way by the time Alex opened his eyes again. He basked for a moment in the silence that filled Pack Torin's quarters before forcing himself to rise. Sleep and the moonlight had done wonders for his body. His shoulder barely ached. He carried a change of clothes to the shower room and checked his back in the mirror. Besides a few dark bruises around the edges of the thick scar that would lessen with time, there was no other sign of the battle with the hounds.

Alex showered quickly and pulled open the panel in the common room. He jogged through the tunnels into the depths of the Academy. One last door slid open to reveal the Wolf Den.

"Sounds like you had an adventurous night," Brock said dryly, spinning in his chair at the command center to look down at Alex.

"It was unexpected," Alex replied.

Brock chuckled. "I'll bet. Sounds like I have you to thank for saving my friends."

Alex smiled. "You forget that the professors are my friends, too."

"I didn't forget," Brock said. He took a big bite of the hotdog he was holding and said around the mouthful, "I just wanted to remind you that they were my friends first."

Alex climbed the steps to the huge monitoring station and took a seat beside Brock. A glance at the screens showed maps, camera views, and heat sensor images. "Watching anything in particular?"

Brock sat back to study the monitors as well. "We've tracked the hounds back to a house at the edge of Haroldsburg. Chet and Dray are searching for clues as to how they got there."

"If we can track them back to the General..." Alex began.

"We can send him a thank you for such a wonderful gift," Brock concluded dryly. He took the last bite of his hotdog and licked his ketchup-covered fingers.

"And they say we're the animals," Alex said, rolling his eyes.

"What?" Brock replied. "Who wants to waste perfectly good ketchup?"

"Not you, apparently," Alex muttered good-naturedly as he studied the screens. Something caught his attention. "Hey, what's that?"

Brock followed his gaze and sat up straight. He hit a few buttons on the keyboard and zoomed in on the image. An icy surge of fear rushed through Alex.

"Chet, get to the roof."

They watched the Alpha climb up the side of the house as if it was nothing. The professor's footsteps slowed when he reached the area Alex had indicated.

"What is this?" Chet asked tightly.

He picked up the objects strung on a rope. Alex's stomach rolled. Chet was without a doubt holding up a string of fingers.

"Did those hounds you fought the other day by any chance happen to be missing fingers?" Brock asked hopefully.

Alex shook his head. "Not that I noticed."

They both knew that meant there were other werewolves under the General's control.

Alex gripped the edge of the desk so hard the wood began to splinter.

"Uh, do you mind?" Brock asked.

Alex sat back. "He knew we'd follow the hounds. Why else would he bait the roof?"

"Any sign of explosives?" Brock asked.

"Nothing," Dray told them from inside the house. "The place is empty, though the werewolves have left it filthy." A second later, he said, "Ew. I stepped in something I don't want to identify."

"Let's get out of here," Chet said. "This place is giving me the creeps."

"Scan the fingers for tracking devices," Brock said.

"Seriously?" Chet replied, though it was obvious his frustration was more at the fact of having to scan other peoples' removed appendages for microchips than at anything Brock recommended. "Clear, and just plain wrong," the Alpha replied when he was done.

"Bring them back. I can cross-reference their DNA with the werewolves we have on file. It might give us a lead," Brock told them.

"Aye-aye, Captain," Chet said dryly.

Brock sat back in his seat. "I'm underappreciated."

"I heard that," Chet said.

"I know," Brock told the werewolf. He then clicked off the microphone. "I didn't mean for him to hear that."

"Why fingers?" Alex mused, trying to keep away the nausea that attempted to rise up his throat at the thought.

"Because the General is a messed up psychopath with a twisted sense of humor," Brock replied.

Alex shook his head. "As much as I've tried to tell myself the same thing, every time I'm up against him, I realize it's the exact opposite. He's shrewd, calculating, and vindictive. Everything he does has a purpose."

Brock studied the monitors in a fresh light. "If he wants to give us a clue, why fingers. Couldn't he just be goading us? And if he's trying to find Drogan, why send the hounds to the cabin instead of the Academy. He would have had a bigger impact."

"Maybe he thought Drogan was at the cabin." Alex didn't believe the words as soon as he said them. The General knew the GPA had Drogan. His whole plan in kidnapping Kalia had been to flush out Drogan's position. The fact that Alex had given him the soccer field as a false location had no doubt stung, especially with the amount of Extremists they were able to take down.

"Was the Academy safe while the cabin was under attack?" Alex asked.

Brock rolled his eyes. "Of course it was. I was here the whole time keeping a close watch on things. What are you implying?"

"Nothing," Alex replied quickly. "I just can't understand why he would try to take out Colleen and Rafe."

"Or the wolves." Brock sat up straight. "What if he needed the wolves out of the picture?"

"You have the forest under surveillance. You don't need the wolves."

Brock ran a hand through his spikey brown hair. "Alright then, what if he's checking our response time?"

"We have flying colors there." Alex rubbed his eyes in an attempt to clear his mind. "What if he had a bunch of hounds he didn't know what to do with, so he sent them to the forest to wreak havoc?"

"What if he wanted to see you morph into your crazy beast form?"

"I don't think he knows about that," Alex said even as ice ran through his veins.

"I saw the remains of that Alpha hound that attacked you and Kalia at the mall." Brock's eyes met his. "Trust me. He knows. No one could do that, not even a werewolf."

"So you think he was watching?"

Brock lifted one skinny shoulder in a half shrug. "It

makes sense to me. You want to figure out which werewolf can take down an Alpha hound, you send a pack of them after people he cares about and verify it with your own eyes."

Alex looked at the monitors without seeing them. "Why would he want to know?"

"I'm not sure," Brock replied. "I'll talk to Jaze about it. Maybe he'll have some ideas."

Alex went back up to Pack Torin's quarters feeling more worried than he had before talking to Brock. If the General was after him because he could morph into the beast, the entire Academy might be in danger. He didn't put it past the General to send even more hounds through the front gates if it would get him what he was after. In fact, the General might do it anyway just for the sheer enjoyment of watching werewolves die.

"You okay?"

Alex looked up from the couch in surprise. He had been so deep in thought he hadn't even heard Torin enter. He stood. "I'm fine."

Torin's gaze narrowed. "I don't believe you."

Alex gave a humorless smile. "Does it really matter?"

Torin rolled his eyes. "Look, Alex. I may hate you for standing in my way of dating Kalia, but I'm also an Alpha. It's my job to know when a member of my pack is in danger."

Surprised at his genuine concern, Alex leaned against the couch. "I've been in danger since the Academy opened. It's nothing new."

"If you mean from me..."

Alex held up his hand with a chuckle. "No, not from you." The Alpha glared as though Alex was making fun of him. Alex decided to go with honesty. "Drogan killed my parents, and ever since we reached the Academy, he's been after me and Cassie. Now that Drogan's with the GPA, his dad, the General, is hot on my trail because he thinks I know where to find his son."

Torin looked as though he was trying to believe everything Alex told him, but was finding it hard to swallow. "Do you?"

"Know where to find his son?" Alex shook his head. "Which is probably a good thing, because when he took Kalia last year, he asked me for the location and I would have given it to him if I'd known."

"You were gone saving her life." Torin spoke the words slowly, his gaze searching inward as though things clicked together for him. The Alpha leaned heavily against the mantle, his jaw clenching and unclenching. "You saved Kalia's life." He met Alex's gaze. "No wonder she won't stop pining for you."

"It's not like that," Alex protested. "She's a friend..."

"To you, maybe. But I've seen the way she looks at you." Torin's words were tight as though the statement was hard to admit. "How do I compete against someone who saved her life?"

"That wasn't the first time," Alex said quietly.

Torin glared at him. "You're not helping yourself not get pounded into the floor."

It took Alex a minute to understand what the Alpha had said. He shook his head. "I think I'd better get some more sleep. This conversation is too confusing right now."

He walked past Torin toward the hallway.

"Is that what happened last night?"

Alex paused at the corner. "The General sent a pack of his hounds, uh, brainwashed werewolves, after Colleen and Rafe. I went to help out."

Torin shook his head. "Here I thought you were just another extremely annoying student."

Alex gave a tired smile. "I'm not sure if proving you wrong was a good idea. Apparently I talk too much when I'm exhausted."

Torin just waved him away. "Go to sleep, Alex. I won't tell anyone what you told me."

Alex reached his door and stepped into the room before the Alpha's voice stopped him.

"You've got toilet duty tomorrow."

"Looking forward to it," Alex replied dryly. He climbed onto his bed and fell asleep without bothering to change out of his clothes.

Chapter Fifteen

"Hungry?"

Alex sat up in surprise at the sound of Siale's voice. She smiled at him. "Torin let me in. He said you could probably use some food right now."

"Torin said that?" Alex asked. The thought amazed him. "And he let you into our quarters?"

"Is that against the rules?" Siale looked suddenly worried. "Do I need to go?"

Alex caught her hand before she could turn away. He sat up and took the plate she held in her other hand.

"Please have a seat," he offered.

He moved off the bed and sat on the floor with his back against the wall. Perching the plate on his knees, he took a bite of the fried chicken. He hadn't realized how hungry he was until he swallowed. He scooped up a spoonful of mashed potatoes and put it in his mouth.

"This tastes amazing," he said, remembering to swallow before he spoke with his mouth full.

She smiled. "Healing makes you hungry." Her eyebrows pulled together. "How's your back?"

Alex rolled his shoulders. "Feels fine. It's good to be a werewolf."

Her smile deepened. "Yes, it is."

She studied him as he ate. He could feel her gaze traveling from his face to his hands. He slowed his movements and glanced up at her. She looked so beautiful sitting on the edge of his bed, her wavy brown hair hanging down in front of her shoulders, and her soft gray eyes filled with curiosity.

"What is it?"

She shook her head. "I probably shouldn't ask."

Alex set his plate on the carpet and knelt in front of her,

taking her hands in his. She watched him with a mixture of humor and concern.

It felt so important to him that she understood. "Siale, you can ask me anything and I will tell you. I promise."

She watched him for a minute as though debating what to say. Her eyes left him and looked at the carpet. "I've never seen anyone fight like you do."

Alex caught her chin gently with his fingers and tipped her face up so she would meet his eyes. "How do I fight?" he asked quietly.

"Like you have nothing to lose," she whispered.

The pain in the depths of her gray eyes made Alex's heart skip a beat. He took a breath, trying to steady it. "I fight that way because I have everything to lose," he told her. "When the General attacks, my thoughts are filled with you, Cassie, Mom, Jaze, Kalia, and the others here at the Academy. I know that if I don't give everything, someone I love could get hurt or worse."

"But you get hurt and that doesn't bother you."

"Because I've been through worse," Alex said honestly. "Physical pain doesn't hurt as badly as watching my parents die or holding you in that body pit. Physical pain doesn't make me feel like I'm going crazy because no sane person should go through those things."

"Is that why you turned into what you did back there?" Siale asked softly.

Alex was quiet for a minute, then he nodded. "I think so. I think if I can stop the horrible stuff from happening, I can figure it out in my mind. When I'm not strong enough, the beast comes out and I can save my loved ones."

Siale set her hand on his cheek. He covered it with his own.

"What about Kalia?"

Cold rushed through Alex's body. "What about her?" He searched Siale's gaze. There was no jealousy there, only curiosity and a touch of sadness.

"I can tell she cares a lot about you, and you said her name when you were listing the people you protect here."

Alex kept ahold of her hand. He knew he could be treading deep water broaching the subject, but Siale had asked, and he had promised to always tell her the truth.

He let out a small breath. "I used to really care about Kalia. I thought she was the one, and it confused me because I didn't feel quite the way they described it. She came here as a werewolf who couldn't phase, and for a long time I was her only friend."

"And now?" Siale asked when he grew silent.

Alex studied the checkered blanket on his bed. "Now, I don't feel that way at all. I think of her as a friend, but she still feels like I'm her one. She's convinced that if she can just keep reminding me how she feels, maybe I'll go back to the way I was before."

"Is there a possibility of that happening?" A slight hint of apprehension touched Siale's voice.

Alex met her gaze, his own serious. "There's no way. You own my heart, Siale. It's been yours since I found you in that pit. I knew from the moment I heard you speak that we were supposed to be together." A hint of a smile touched his lips. "That might be forward, but it's the truth, every bit of it. You are my one. Kalia will always be my friend, but just that."

Siale looked at him for a long moment, the depths of her eyes unreadable. She finally gave him a small, warm smile. "Thank you for telling me," she said. She kissed him softly on the forehead.

He closed his eyes at the feeling of her lips on his skin. Warmth rushed from her touch. He couldn't help but smile as he sat back.

"I could get used to that," he said.

The warmth in her eyes as he picked up the plate again to finish his meal was better than any full stomach.

She took his plate with her when she left. Alex was about to return to his room when the door to Pack Torin's quarters flew open.

"I've got it!"

The excitement on Torin's face filled Alex with trepidation.

"Got what?" he asked warily.

"I've figured out how to make Kalia fall in love with me!"

"Okay," Alex replied, wondering why the Alpha was telling him. "How?"

"You are going to help me."

Alex shook his head quickly. "I've already messed up enough things with Kalia. I don't want to be involved."

Before he could move, Torin grabbed the front of his shirt and pinned him against the wall. "You're going to help me."

"You know there are better ways of getting results than bullying someone," Alex protested, the collar of his shirt tight around his throat.

"Jaze takes you on some of his rescue missions, right?"

What Alex didn't respond, Torin shook him like a terrier with a rat. "Right?" the Alpha shouted.

Alex wanted to attack Torin. He wanted to end the bullying right then and there, starting with a fist to the Alpha's thick jaw. His hands clenched.

A hint of desperation came into Torin's angry green eyes. He lowered Alex just a bit. "Look, Alex. I don't know of any other way. I can't think of life without her. She barely even looks at me, and when she does, it's like she's looking at scum from the bottom of Cook Jerald's sink. I can't take it anymore."

Seeing the Alpha's walls lower broke something inside of Alex. He wasn't Kalia's mate. The way he felt was all too certain. If he had somehow stood in the way of Kalia seeing Torin for his true self, maybe he could do something to help.

"Okay," Alex gave in. "What do you want me to do?"

"Let me go on a mission with you."

Alex shook his head quickly. "I don't think Jaze would appreciate me picking my own team members."

"Sure he will. I've seen the way he looks at you. You and Cassie are Jaze and Nikki's golden children. You can't do anything wrong if you tried. How many times have you been suspended?"

"None," Alex admitted, though he was sure there were circumstances that definitely could have used such a punishment.

"Exactly," Torin replied. "Just get me on one of your missions, and if Kalia's in trouble, I'll be the one to save her. It's that easy."

"I'm not sure anything's that easy," Alex mumbled.

"What was that?" Torin demanded, tightening his grip on Alex's shirt.

"I said fine," Alex replied. He tore Torin's hand away. "Would it hurt you to have an actual conversation instead of bullying people into accepting your way? Maybe that would appeal to Kalia."

Torin gave him a skeptical look. "You think?"

"Yeah," Alex said, rubbing his throat. "It couldn't hurt."

"I consider it," the Alpha replied. "But it might be pushing things a bit too far."

***

"We thought we'd find you out here."

Alex smiled when Cassie's face blocked his view of the stars.

"This is the best place at this school," he said.

"Especially since your living space is filled with members of Pack Torin?" Trent asked, sitting down next to the statue.

"It's not that bad," Alex told them. He sat up next to Trent. "It just makes me appreciate you guys that much more."

"All of us?" Kalia's voice made Alex's heart turn over.

"All of you," he said, trying to keep the smile on his face.

His friends took seats around him. Cassie leaned against Tennison's shoulder near the statue while Terith and Kalia sat facing the others.

"What's it like being Torin's Second?" Terith asked.

Alex thought about it for a moment. "Well, I'm getting really good at scrubbing toilets."

"That's not what Seconds are for," Kalia said grumpily. "If you'd waited to be on my pack, I wouldn't make you do that."

Alex saw Cassie's downcast gaze. Knowing Kalia would have chosen him as Second over his sister definitely hurt her feelings. Alex thought quickly for a change of subject. "So, um, everyone ready for football? Sounds like we're getting serious tomorrow."

"No one should want to be the quarterback," Trent pointed out. "He's the target. It's like being the elk that's limping and bleeding. Everyone's going to be after you."

"Yeah, that'd be stupid," Alex said.

Trent's eyes narrowed at his tone. "Wait. You want to be the quarterback, don't you?"

Alex shrugged as if it didn't matter. "I can throw and I'm

quick."

"Tennison's quick," Cassie said. "But he doesn't want to be the quarterback."

"No way," her boyfriend replied. "Not happening. I would rather catch than throw, and I'd worry about wolfing-out if I got tackled."

Alex smiled. "Wolfing-out?"

Tennison nodded seriously. "Think about it. Your instincts are going to kick in with all that adrenaline. Especially if you get rushed and five guys are chasing you down. It's going to take some real self-control to keep calm in that type of a situation."

"If anyone finds out this school is a werewolf academy, the Extremists will be here for sure," Cassie agreed. "Don't do it, Alex."

Alex feigned a surprised look. "Who says I'm going to do it?"

"I've known you since the day you were born," his sister said. "You can't pass up an opportunity to push the limits."

"And we don't want you to get into a bad situation," Kalia said. She set a hand on Alex's knee. "You could get hurt."

Alex shifted uncomfortably, but Kalia refused to drop her hand. He met Tennison's gaze. "You said it's going to take some real self-control, right?"

Tennison nodded.

"Think about it," Alex continued. "What happens to Torin in this situation?" He looked at Kalia. "Or Boris? What happens if one of our extremely explosive, highly instinct-driven Alphas becomes the quarterback? If they phase, not only will they give away our secret, but I have no doubt human students will be injured as well." Alex drew up on his knees and Kalia's hand slid away. "I want to protect this school. I have self-control, and I think I've proven it plenty of times." He met each of their gazes. The werewolves around him nodded one at a time.

Trent let out a slow breath. "Alex is the only one I would trust out there."

"Me, too," Terith agreed.

Cassie finally gave in. "Do what you need to," she said. "Just be careful."

"I will," Alex promised. "First I've got to win the position."

A grin spread across Trent's face. He unzipped the backpack Alex hadn't noticed he had been wearing. To his surprise, the small werewolf pulled out a football. "Well, let's get practicing."

"You knew it was going to come down to this, didn't you?" Alex asked, rising.

Trent shrugged. "I'm not your best friend for nothing."

Alex laughed and caught the ball the werewolf threw to him. "If you're going to be one of my receivers, you'd better work on those hands."

Trent's eyes widened. "You are not getting me onto that field."

Alex smiled. "Tennison's got speed and agility, and you're the smartest werewolf I know. I need you both out there in case something does go wrong."

Trent sighed. "Fine, but if Torin wins the quarterback position, I quit."

Alex grinned and threw him the football.

Chapter Sixteen

"Tight spirals aren't all I'm looking for," Coach Vance said as he walked down the row of students who had shown up for quarterback tryouts. "You need accuracy, the ability to make snap decisions, and reliability. If your team can't count on you, I can't count on you."

Alex threw the ball and nailed Tennison in the middle of his short route.

"Nice," Vance commented. "Just watch your werewolf strength. It looks too easy."

"It needs to look hard?" Boris asked from a few places down the line.

"If you're throwing the football eighty yards and it looks like you put in the effort of tossing it five, we're going to have a problem," the coach explained, his tone dry. "We need realism here. Strength proves nothing. You all have strength. I need someone who can look like a quarterback as well as throw. You might have to pull a few punches once in a while."

"That makes no sense," Torin muttered. "Who pulls punches?"

Vance snorted. "It means act. I need you guys to learn how to act. If you take a hit, act like it hurt. If someone hits you, let it throw you off balance like it would a human."

"Great," Sid complained. "Not only do we have to learn about them, we have to act like them, too."

Vance stopped behind the student. The coach's hulking stature made the huge werewolf look like a tiny kid. "You're done, Sid. Take a hike."

"But—"

Vance shook his head. "You should know by now the value of humans. I don't like your tone and I don't want you on my team."

"Good," Sid snapped. "I didn't want to be on your stupid football team anyway."

Coach Vance's face took on a look of such anger that the students closest to him backed away. Alex didn't know if Vance would attack Sid for being snide. It took a few seconds for the professor to regain visible control of his emotions.

"Leave, now," Vance finally barked.

Sid ran across the huge expanse of lawn along the side of the Academy that made up the practice field. Alex doubted the werewolf would stop running until he reached his bedroom.

"The rest of you, throw," Vance barked.

Tennison completed another route. Alex ran forward a few steps as though he needed it for momentum and threw the ball in a tight spiral. He leaned into the throw even though he could have done it without moving at all.

"You look like a dork," Boris commented while a few of the others laughed.

"Yeah, we'll he's a dork with a job." Vance gave him a rare smile. "Alex, you've got the position until you screw it up and I give it to someone else."

"Uh, thanks?" Alex replied. With the glares he was receiving from the rest of the werewolves, he wasn't sure the position was much of an honor.

"The rest of you will be divided into defensive and offensive teams. I expect you to practice on your off time as well as on this field." Coach Vance gave the group of them a hard look. "We have our first game in a week. Make practice count."

"One week!" Trent squeaked as soon as the professor was out of earshot. "Is he kidding?"

"I don't think Coach Vance has kidded a day in his life,"

Tennison replied.

Alex felt the weight of the team on his shoulders. "Let's get to work."

Boris was in front of him in an instant. Kalia's huge brother had to duck his head to look Alex in the face. He glared. "Just because you're the quarterback doesn't mean you get to start giving orders, Stray."

"Yes, it does."

Everyone stared at Torin in surprise. The Lifer Alpha crossed his arms. "Alex is our quarterback and my Second. What he says on this field goes."

It appeared for a moment as though Boris was about to challenge Torin. His jaw clenched so tight it looked like the vein in the side of his neck was going to pop out of his skin. Finally, the huge Alpha took a calming breath. "Fine," he growled. "But if your Second steps out of line off this field, he gets to answer to me."

"And me," Torin replied calmly. He looked at Alex. "Where should we start?"

***

By the time they were done practicing routes and running defensive and offensive drills, the entire team was exhausted.

"I don't know how we're going to survive this until the end of December," Trent said, trailing behind Alex as they made their way to the Great Hall for dinner. "Coach Vance is going to kill us."

Alex smiled at his friend's dramatic statement. "If it doesn't kill us, it'll make us stronger."

Trent rolled his eyes. "Is that seriously your motto? No wonder you do so many stupid things."

Alex shrugged. "I'm not dead yet."

"Say it much louder and Boris will help you with that," Tennison said.

Warmth filled Alex at the sight of the girls of his pack sitting around the table. Cassie smiled up at him and Tennison while Terith made room for her brother. Even Kalia looked happy to see him. Alex had almost reached them when he realized he was heading toward the wrong pack.

"Uh, take care," Alex told Trent.

"You, too," the Lifer said with a sad smile. "Wish you were joining us."

Alex was about to reply when he realized that Torin had come up behind him.

"How are those toilets?" the Alpha asked.

Alex gritted his teeth and walked silently to Pack Torin's table. He spent the meal moving the alfredo pasta around his plate without much of an appetite. The only improvement to the evening was when he saw Jordan stop Trent near the garbage can.

"Want to go for a walk tonight?" she asked.

Trent grinned as his face turned red. "Yeah, sure. That sounds great. I mean, that sounds more than great. It's a great night for a walk, and I think we'd have a great time."

Jordan looked like she was fighting back a laugh. "Okay. I'll meet you by the gate."

Trent practically ran to Alex. "She asked me to walk with her!" he said breathlessly.

"Yeah, I think the entire Great Hall heard you say the word 'great' a billion times," Alex replied, smiling back.

Trent grinned. "I guess I was a bit nervous, but it worked!"

"Good job. I'm happy for you," Alex said sincerely.

Trent was about to walk away, then paused. "Any idea where I should take her?"

Alex thought about his own walk with Siale. "How about the cliff above the lake? It's a great place to talk."

Trent nodded quickly. "Good thinking. Thanks."

"Anytime," Alex told him.

He watched the werewolf leave with a feeling of happiness.

"Do you always smile like an idiot after talking to that nerd?" Torin asked.

Alex made sure his face was expressionless when he turned to the Alpha. "I'm just glad things are going his way."

Torin shook his head. "I don't know why you associate with them. They're weird."

"If they're weird, than I'm weird," Alex replied.

Torin studied him for a moment, then shook his head. "I don't understand you. Go scrub the toilets."

Alex sighed and rose from the table.

He was emptying his tray in the garbage when he heard Torin speak again. It was easy to pick out the Alpha's deep, grating voice through the crowd of students eating their dinner. Alex paused, listening.

"So, uh, don't you think it's lame we have to compete

against humans?"

"I think it could be interesting."

Alex was surprised to hear Kalia answer. He glanced over his shoulder.

"Interesting?" Torin's expression was one of disgust.

"Yes," Kalia replied. "A true test to see whether werewolf students could pass for human students."

Torin's mouth twisted at the idea. "Why act like something inferior?"

Kalia huffed a breath of frustration. "Look, Torin. I thought I was human for most of my life. It's not that bad."

Torin rolled his eyes, not bothering to hide his contempt. "At least now you're one of us. You don't have to worry about being one of *them* anymore."

Kalia's grip on her empty tray was so tight her knuckles were white. Alex wondered why she bothered talking to the Alpha at all. "Don't you think maybe you're a little biased?"

Torin shrugged, clearly enjoying himself. "What's biased about being glad I'm a member of the dominant species? I just don't appreciate having to hide my heritage in order to raise a few bucks for the school, that's all. Especially when students like you could afford to pay a bit more for tuition."

Kalia shook her head and stormed away from him. She slammed the tray down on the pile near Alex and stalked past him without saying a word.

Torin spotted Alex and rose. Alex regretted not leaving when he had the chance. He couldn't imagine what the Alpha would do after Alex's advice to have a normal conversation with Kalia had imploded so completely.

"Did you see that?" Torin demanded.

"Yeah," Alex replied. "I'm sorry—"

"Me, too," Torin said. "Sorry that I didn't try having a conversation with her sooner. It went wonderfully, don't you think?"

"I, uh..." Alex groped for words.

"I was quite the charmer." Torin gave a huge smile, which was a terrifying, unnatural sight. "I'll give her a break for the rest of the night before we have another conversation." He winked. "I wouldn't want to lay on the Torin Westwood charm too thick. She'd never have a chance."

Alex couldn't help but stare. "Yeah, you wouldn't want to do that."

Torin nodded, satisfied. "You give good advice." He looked back at their table, studying the students still eating around it. "Hey, Matt."

Matt's head jerked up. His eyes widened at the sight of the Alpha talking to him. "Y-yes, Torin?"

"You've got toilet duty tonight."

Matt looked extremely relieved that toilets were the Alpha's only request. "Y-yes, Torin. I'll get them done, Torin."

Torin turned back to Alex. "You're off duty for good advice."

"Glad to hear it," Alex replied. He shook his head as he walked down the hall, wondering where on earth he had gone wrong.

"What was that?"

The sound of Kalia's frustration turned Alex in his tracks. "What was what?"

She closed the distance between them. "You know what, Alex. I saw you listening. What was your Alpha up to?"

Alex stifled a sigh. "He was trying to have a normal conversation with you."

"That was normal?" Kalia replied with an incredulous laugh. "Insulting my parents and all of the other humans I grew up with?"

Alex shrugged. "At least he's trying to make an effort."

"An effort for what?" Kalia asked.

Alex clenched and unclenched his fists, trying to figure out how to break it to her. "Torin's convinced you're his one, and that if you'll give him a chance, you'll realize it, too."

"That's ridiculous," Kalia replied with a small laugh. When she realized Alex was completely serious, she stared at him. "You're not kidding."

Alex shook his head. "Afraid not."

Kalia leaned against the wall. "Torin thinks I'm his one." Saying the words aloud made her eyes widen. "Torin, bully and Alpha of the Lifers, thinks I, the girl he just accused of paying too little for tuition, am the one he's to be with for the rest of his life? Is he insane?"

"Probably."

Kalia glared at him. "Now's not the time for jokes, Alex."

Alex decided it wasn't the time to point out that he wasn't joking. He rubbed the back of his neck. "Well, maybe you should give him a chance," he suggested.

Kalia's eyes tightened the way they did when she was about to fly off the handle.

Alex held up a hand. "Hear me out. You give him a chance, then let him know you just didn't feel it."

Kalia stared at the wall across from him. She was silent for so long, Alex tried to figure out where he had gone wrong in his advice. He didn't know why everyone seemed to be seeking him out for his opinion; it didn't appear to work out well.

"That's what you did."

Kalia's tone as much as her words gripped Alex's heart. He closed his eyes for a moment. When he opened them again and looked at her, he couldn't deny the pain he saw there. "Yes, it is," he admitted. "I had to tell you the truth. I couldn't keep drawing things on. It wouldn't have been fair to you."

Kalia turned away from him without a word.

"Kalia, wait," Alex said. He jogged to catch up to her.

She turned on him with the speed of a striking snake. "Leave me alone, Alex, and stop playing matchmaker with my life. If I'm not for you, then I'd rather not be for anyone."

She left him standing in the hall feeling as though whatever he did in regards to her was destined to be doomed.

Chapter Seventeen

"Just relax and remember that you've got to keep a tight hold on your wolf side here," Coach Vance told them.

Alex looked at his anxious teammates. Even Boris and Torin appeared on edge at the thought of the football game ahead of them. For many of the Lifer werewolves, the game would be the first time they had been around humans since they arrived at the Academy. For the others, though some had family members and friends that were human, the fate of the Academy and the students within it rested on their ability to maintain control.

"Let's go."

The team followed their coach through the doors from the locker room. A short tiled hallway led to the outside doors. Vance put a hand on Alex's shoulder, holding him back while the others passed by.

"They'll be looking to you for cues," the coach told him, his expression serious. "If you stay calm, so will they. You know how to act around humans." The light in Vance's gaze said he knew about Alex's excursion to Cherish's. Alex wondered if that was why the coach had really picked him as quarterback.

"I'll get us through this," Alex promised.

"I know you will," Vance replied with one of his rare smiles.

Alex and Vance jogged across the field to where the team was waiting in a loose huddle. Alex dropped to one knee with his teammates. For the first time, he chanced a look at his surroundings.

It wasn't a huge school. A few bleachers lined either side of the field and a track with a fence on the outside made up the rest of the view. Fans wearing the red and white colors of the high school they cheered for took up the bleachers nearest to the school. The other side was conspicuously empty.

A whistle blew and they took their positions.

"What's the matter? You guys are so bad your own town doesn't even come out to cheer?" the other quarterback asked. His team burst out laughing.

"Maybe that's why we've never played them," another said.

"I'm gonna tear—"

Alex grabbed Boris' shoulder. The Alpha shot him a glare.

"Focus on the game," Alex said loud enough that the rest of his team could hear.

He crouched back down and held his hands ready. "Hike," he called.

Drake passed him the ball. Alex backed up a few steps, checked the field, and spotted Tennison wide open fifteen yards down. He threw the ball, remembering at the last second to step into the throw to make it look real. Tennison caught the ball and took off down the field.

Alex realized at that moment that everyone was staring at their team. A quick check showed every member on the line holding the rushing team back as if they weighed less than a football. No matter how hard the humans strained, they couldn't move the werewolf team an inch. The player covering Tennison was far behind. When Tennison scored, nobody cheered. Alex felt the stares of a hundred confused humans.

"Time out," he called.

Coach Vance motioned to the referee. The man in black and white blew his whistle, though he looked confused as to why they were taking a time out after scoring a touchdown.

"Guys, seriously!" Alex said, his voice quiet enough that only the team huddled around him could hear. "Can you act like you're getting hit? It's like they're running into a wall!"

"They are," Torin scoffed.

Alex grabbed the Alpha by the face mask and pulled him close. "If the Academy needs money through the football program, it's our job to make it look like we can actually play football. There is a lot more on the line than your pride. Think you can act a little bit more human?"

Alex suddenly realized he had an Alpha by the facemask and was giving him direct orders. He stared at Torin, his chest heaving as he wondered what the Alpha would do.

Torin glanced left and right. The rest of their teammates watched in stunned silence. In that moment, the Alpha did something that shocked Alex entirely.

"Sorry, Alex," he said, lowering his eyes.

Alex let go of Torin's facemask and the Alpha took a step back. He looked at the other members of their team. "Listen to Alex," Torin growled. "The Academy needs this."

"Right," Boris answered. The rest of the team echoed him.

The whistle blew. Alex watched the defense take their positions on the line. To his relief, when the quarterback called hike, his team grunted and staggered with the effort of blocking the other players. When Miguel took down the running back, he actually looked winded when he got back up, and the running back wasn't killed. Alex chalked it up as a point for Vicki Carso's Preparatory Academy.

"What did you say to them?" Coach Vance asked in amazement.

Alex shrugged. "I guess threatening an Alpha really gets in their heads."

"Good," Vance said with a nod. He crossed his arms and

studied the team.

When it was their turn to throw, Alex felt the change in his teammates. They weren't just werewolves, defensive, brutal creatures fighting to defend their territories; instead, they felt like a team, working and acting together to bring money to the Academy. Even those who were Termers needed the Academy. It was a sanctuary, a school, and a place they could call home where they fit in no matter what they did.

Alex released the ball and fell when the defenders dove into him. He struggled free in time to see Tennison catch it and run just fast enough to make it look like the other team was close to taking him down.

"Touchdown!" Trent shouted from the sidelines. To Alex's horror, the buzz-haired werewolf then broke into a touchdown dance. His skinny elbows and knobby knees stuck out in all directions. By the end of his painfully long dance, everyone in the stadium was staring at him.

"At least that takes away the notion that we're super-human," Vance muttered.

By halftime, the score was twenty-eight to zero. The team huddled around Coach Vance in the locker room, their faces flushed with excitement.

"We're killing them, Coach!" Trent said.

Vance nodded with a hint of concern on his face. "That's what I'm worried about. This team was undefeated last year, and now we're destroying them."

"It's awesome!" Boris replied.

"We're unstoppable, and we're not even using our full strength. We're going to dominate!" Torin said. The rest of the team cheered.

Alex crossed to Vance's side. "What do you want us to do?" he asked in an undertone.

Vance met his gaze squarely. "I want you to lose."

Alex let out a breath. "They're not going to be thrilled about that."

The coach was silent for a few moments as he watched his team celebrate their impending victory. "We can't risk shaking things up at such an early stage. We just got accepted into the division." He put a hand on Alex's shoulder. "I need you to make sure we lose this game."

Alex trailed out after the rest of the team.

"What's up?" Trent asked at the door.

Alex shook his head. "Nothing the rest of the team is going to like."

"We have to throw the game."

Alex stared at his friend. "How did you know?"

Trent shrugged. "It makes sense from a statistics point of view. If we destroy the champions, somebody's going to investigate the team. That's the last thing we need."

"So you'll help me?" Alex asked.

Trent nodded. "Of course. Just get Coach to let me play. I'd like to tell Jordan I at least set foot on the field."

"Oh, you'll play," Alex promised.

As soon as the whistle blew, Alex backed up a few quick steps. Tennison and Parker were both wide open. Alex checked center field. Daniel had two players covering him. Alex chucked the ball, letting it slip through his fingers at the last minute.

It wobbled through the air end over end and landed directly in one of the other team's arms. The boy looked surprised to have it. He took off running with Daniel close behind. Alex jogged to intercept him, then tripped and took out Daniel instead. The boy reached the end zone to the cheers and shouts of the crowd.

"What was that?" Boris demanded as soon as they

reached the sidelines.

Alex met his glare. "I'm doing what Coach told me to."

"I'm not going to throw the game," Boris growled.

Alex met his angry gaze. "If you won't, I'll get someone who will."

Boris sat on the bench with a stony glare. When the next drive started, Trent was at Alex's side.

"I can't believe I'm out here!" the scrawny werewolf said. "This is amazing!"

"It's a high school football game," Torin told the werewolf dryly. "Try to maintain some composure."

"Fumble it," Alex whispered.

Trent nodded, his eyes wide.

As soon as Alex got the ball, he handed it off to Trent. The werewolf took off running. He made a very convincing show of tripping over his feet, and before his knees hit the ground, the ball flew out of his hands into the arms of the closest player from the other team. The student was tackled, but he held onto the ball.

"Seriously?" Boris growled. "That was pathetic."

"Shut it," Coach Vance snapped.

"Really?" Torin said, stopping at Alex's side. "We have to lose like this?"

Alex hoped he could somehow get the Alpha to understand. Having Torin on his side might be the only way to pull off the loss. "Coach says we have to lose to keep playing in this division. If we wipe out the champions in our first game, we're going to be investigated for sure. We'll lose our funding and the Academy will come under scrutiny."

Torin nodded. "Fine. Whatever." He leaned close to Miguel and Drake. "Throw the game." When the Alphas stared at him, he nodded toward Coach Vance. "Coach's orders."

Miguel nodded, and Drake followed. They began spreading the orders to the rest of the teammates. Those who had problems were sent to join Boris on the bench. Soon, everyone on the Academy's team was involved in a completely different kind of acting.

"Stop dropping the ball," Torin yelled.

"Give an effort," Drake shouted.

Alex hid a grin as he threw the ball at Tennison. The werewolf took off toward the end zone. This time, instead of scoring, he let the other team catch him. The ball slipped from his hands into the grasp of the other team, and the player took off running.

"Catch him!" Miguel yelled, jumping up and down. "I can't believe he just gave it away!" The Alpha threw his helmet to the ground.

"Tone it down a bit," Vance said under his breath. "I don't want to replace equipment."

"Got it, Coach," Miguel replied.

The crowd cheered as the player crossed the end zone.

"I'm going to miss my touchdown dances," Trent said, shaking his head.

"You're the only one," Torin replied. "You looked like an idiot."

"At least I have school spirit," Trent shot back.

Torin grabbed the front of his jersey. "What did you say?"

Alex caught Torin's hand. "Let's remember what's important here, and that means not pounding Trent's face in. We need him."

"For what?" Torin grumbled, but he set the werewolf back down. "He annoys me."

"It's a skill," Trent replied, straightening out his jersey.

By the end of the game, everyone from Vicki Carso's

Preparatory Academy had perfected their frustrated loser expressions. They sulked as they got onto the bus, and sat quietly until they were out of the city limits.

"That was a blast!" Torin shouted.

"Yeah," Parker replied. "I don't care if we lose as long as we get to play."

"Then what's the point?" Boris demanded. Everyone grew quiet. "If we're not playing to win, why do it?"

Coach Vance stood up from the front of the school bus. He turned to face his students with his hands on the back of the seat. "Because your Academy needs you to. If you don't play, we lose our funding. Several other venues of funds have become unavailable to us, and we need this sport to bring in what we're lacking."

"It still seems stupid to lose," Boris muttered, turning to face the window.

As soon as they reached the Academy, Alex climbed off the bus. He was about to join the others on their way up the courtyard steps when a hand grabbed his jersey and slammed him against the side of the vehicle.

"If you ever, and I mean ever, talk to me like that in front of the other werewolves again, I will tear your arms off," Torin growled with his face inches from Alex's.

Alex nodded and pushed down his pride at the stares of the students on their way to the school. "I know I was out of line. I'm sorry."

Torin lifted his lips in a snarl. "Other Alphas aren't going to be as understanding as I am."

"I appreciate it," Alex replied.

Torin let him down. "Go clean the toilets."

Alex stifled a sigh as he made his way to the Academy.

Chapter Eighteen

"There's joy in slamming another person to the ground."

Alex looked up from his potato salad to see Torin leaning against the wall near where Kalia threw the remains of her food in the garbage.

"I can image," she said dryly.

"It's a feeling of complete power," Torin continued. "I know I'm stronger than any werewolf here."

"Any werewolf?" Kalia asked doubtfully.

Torin shifted his feet. "Well, the students at least. I'll bet I could take on more than a few of the professors as well." He glanced around.

"Right," Kalia said. "I've got to get something from upstairs."

"I'll go with you," Torin told her. He fell in beside her without giving her a chance to argue.

"I almost feel sorry for Kalia," Trent said, pausing near Alex's side.

"Me, too," Alex replied honestly.

Trent gave him a sympathetic smile. "Women."

"What about us?"

Trent stared over his shoulder at Jordan. He gave her a quick smile. "You're beautiful."

The fact that the reply came out as more of a question than a statement didn't seem to matter to Jordan. She smiled as she walked past him. "Why thank you."

Trent lifted his eyebrows at Alex before running to catch up to Jordan. "And by beautiful, I mean absolutely stunning," the werewolf said quickly.

Alex ate his last few bites of food with a smile on his face. He set his tray on top of the stack and made his way through the students to the hallway.

"Finally."

The smile on his face grew at the sound of Siale's voice. He met her gaze. "I've missed you."

"Me, too," she replied, slipping her arm through his. "School, football, and training with Jaze take all of your time. When am I supposed to see you? I'm beginning to think my reasons for coming to the Academy have disappeared." She looked at the walls that surrounded them. Alex knew he didn't imagine the shudder that ran across her skin. "Sometimes I feel a little trapped."

Alex led her outside. The brisk air bit his exposed skin, telling of the closing fingers of winter. He took a deep breath and could smell the icy promise of an approaching storm. The thought made him smile.

"You take a breath and smile? What's that about?" Siale asked, watching him curiously.

Alex grinned. "I love winter. There's something about snow covering everything, changing the landscape, altering the way the animals act and people, too. Sometimes change is nice."

Siale nodded, following Alex around the side of the school. "It's nice if you have a chance to get out and enjoy it."

Alex pulled open the secondary entrance to Trent's workshop. "Well, let's get out and enjoy it."

To his surprise, Trent was already there tinkering with something on a table littered with engine parts. He looked up when they came in.

"I thought you'd be itching to go out pretty soon, especially with football and all that," his friend said, gesturing toward the motorcycle near one corner of the room. "It's all fixed."

"Thank you," Alex said sincerely. He set a hand on the

motorcycle, remembering the condition it had been in when he helped push it back after the accident with the deer. "You've worked a miracle."

The answering smile on Trent's face said enough.

"Do you happen to have another helmet?" Alex asked.

Trent's gaze flicked to Siale. He nodded. "I thought you might be needing that, too." He grabbed a red and black helmet from a hook on the wall and tossed it to Alex.

"We're leaving?" Siale asked. Her eyes shifted to the motorcycle. "On that?"

"You'll love it," Alex told her as he fit the helmet over her long brown hair and fastened it under her chin. "Trust me."

"Oh, I trust you," she replied. "But you forget I was the one talking to you when you ran into that deer."

Alex chuckled. "Then you don't need to worry."

"Why not?"

"Because now I won't have your voice in my ear distracting me."

She hit the top of his helmet. He laughed and climbed onto the motorcycle, then held it upright.

"Let's go," he said with an inviting smile.

Siale didn't hesitate. She climbed on behind him and wrapped her arms around his waist.

Alex started the engine. He pulled the motorcycle carefully toward the door. "Thanks again, Trent!"

"We'll see you soon, I hope," Siale called over the sound of the engine.

Trent waved as Alex revved the engine. They sped through the door and out onto the courtyard. The few students who mingled out there after dinner watched them depart through the gate Trent had thoughtfully opened.

"He's a good friend," Siale said, speaking loud enough to

be heard above the wind.

"He really is," Alex replied. He turned his head slightly and said, "He's always got my back."

Siale's arms tightened around his waist. "Just like me."

The smile that spread across Alex's face stayed as he maneuvered the motorcycle down the long winding road from the Academy. The feeling of the wind pushing against his shirt and the hum of the road beneath his tires chased away all other thought. The fact that Siale was behind him filled him with a warmth the coldest night couldn't chase away. He put his left hand over hers as he drove down the road.

Alex pulled over after darkness set in. "This is where I hit the deer," he said. He turned off the motorcycle, careful to park it far enough off the road that nobody would mess with it.

Siale climbed off after him. "I heard a loud bang and some sort of engine sound. I thought you'd gotten shot," she admitted.

Alex took her hand. "I don't always get shot at," he said, hoping to make her smile.

She did, but with a small shake of her head. "It seems like you do quite often."

He hesitated, then nodded in agreement. "I guess more than the average werewolf. Comes with the whole pack search and rescue thing."

"I suppose," she said.

He glanced at her. "What does that mean?"

She lifted her shoulders in a small shrug. "I think you're a little reckless."

Alex laughed as he led her into the trees along the side of the road. "You've been talking to Cassie, haven't you?"

Siale nodded. "She's convinced you have a death wish."

"It's really the opposite of that," Alex explained as he helped her over a fallen log. "It's more like a wish for a life better than what we've been given. I think werewolves deserve more."

"How will that happen?" Siale asked, ducking under a tree branch.

Alex ran his fingers along the smooth bark of an aspen, careful to keep his gaze from Siale's when he said, "We need to come up with a way to reintroduce werewolves to society."

After a moment of silence, Siale replied, "That would be nice."

Alex stared at her. "I thought you were going to laugh."

Siale shook her head. "You're not the only one who wishes we could leave whenever we want and not feel like there's a target on our backs."

"Exactly," Alex said, glad someone understood. "Werewolves used to live with humans and nobody knew the difference. It was only when the Extremists starting attacking that Jaze had to reveal our race to the world." His voice lowered. "That didn't exactly go over well."

"No, it didn't," Siale said.

At her silence, Alex knew she was thinking about her mother. Thoughts of his parents surfaced, memories he had pushed away to keep the pain at a tolerable distance. Through their young lives, Mindi and Will had been the best parents any child could ask for. The truth that they had adopted the twins hadn't surfaced until Alex's fight with Drogan.

Meredith was a loving mother, but her sister Mindi's face was the one that had smiled down at Alex above the crib. Will had held his fingers as he learned how to walk. He remembered roasting s'mores over the fire pit in the backyard, and learning how to tie his shoes with Mindi's patient guidance.

His thoughts flashed forward to the day they died, to Drogan's hate-filled mismatched eyes, and to the feeling of emptiness when Jet rescued the twins and left them at Two before he sacrificed himself to save hundreds of werewolves from the General.

"It doesn't have to be that way again."

Siale's soft voice broke through Alex's memories. The feeling of her hand was gentle on his cheek. He put his hand over it, willing her touch to chase away the ache in his chest. His heart gave an uneven beat. He took a calming breath and met her gaze. The gray depths of her eyes showed the same pain he felt.

"We'll find a better way," he promised her.

"I know we will."

Alex forced a smile. "This is getting way too serious."

"What do you have in mind?" she asked with a small answering smile.

"Let's run. Really run."

Siale nodded quickly. "Yes, please. It's been way too long."

Alex stepped behind a tree and pulled off his clothes. A chill ran down his skin, replaced by the warmth of thick gray fur as it covered his body. He relished the way the chaos of his thoughts receded, leaving instinct in the forefront. Wolves had no need for worries that cluttered the mind, especially things that had no impact on the daily need for survival.

Siale's lavender and sage fragrance filled his nose. He took a deep breath, reading the scents of a deer that had passed not long ago, along with the sharp, brittle smell of the sap within the pines as it froze from the drop in temperature. Alex shook, settling his limbs and enjoying the feeling of his wolf body. He stepped into the moonlight.

Siale pranced in front of him, her light gray form like a

pale shadow beneath the trees. The white marks on her shoulders and chest stood out in the darkness. She yipped and bent down with her haunches in the air, calling him to play like a puppy.

Alex gave a snort of laughter and took a step forward. Siale darted off into the night. Alex ran after her, his wolf stride eating up the ground with ease. He caught up to her, then loped at her side. The smells of the forest filled his nose. His brain categorized and filed them as quickly as they came to him, the scent of a snowshoe hair, its fur no doubt taking on the pale colors of winter, the droppings of an owl fresh from overhead, the padded footprints of a lynx stalking beneath the trees, and the footprints of two other wolves wandering across the frosty loam.

Alex pulled up short. Siale stopped when she realized he was no longer beside her. Alex sniffed the tracks again, though he didn't need to. His sister's scent and Tennison's cedar trail were unmistakable.

The thought of Cassie and Tennison out beyond the walls filled Alex with worry. He gave a bark and jerked his head toward the tracks, pulling his ears flat against his skull. Siale nodded. Alex took off along the trail and she followed close behind.

Alex's paws drummed along the forest floor in a cadence he usually enjoyed, but this time he was too filled with worry for his sister to think about it. He leaped over a fallen pine, ducked branches, and followed the tracks around a huge boulder. Siale ran beside him with the stealth of a ghost, her footsteps nearly inaudible.

Convinced that he was about to find his sister at the mercy of Extremists or worse, Alex galloped headlong into the next meadow. He nearly ran straight into Cassie and Tennison both in wolf form sitting next to a pond.

Cassie jumped at her brother's sudden appearance. Tennison rose and gave Alex a searching look. Alex checked quickly around the meadow, sure he was missing something. His heart thundered in his chest and he fought to catch his breath and sniff for danger at the same time.

Siale bumped his shoulder with her own. Alex glanced at her, wondering if she had seen any danger. Siale pulled her ears back and she snorted, opening her mouth in a wide, toothy grin. Alex realized how foolish he was being. He sat down with an answering snort of laughter.

Cassie ran up to him and, instead of stopping, bowled him over with her shoulder. Alex grinned up at her apologetically. Instead of appearing upset that their evening had been interrupted, Cassie tipped her head toward the forest. Alex nodded. Siale and Cassie took off side by side into the dark trees. Tennison gave Alex a look as if to say girls will be girls and followed them out of the meadow.

Alex was the last to leave. The moonlit grasses swayed in the gentle midnight breeze. The slight ripple of the water in the pond was musical and light. Crickets chirruped within the grass, their songs quiet as though they knew their green world would soon be blanketed in snow. A squirrel, restless in the night, awoke and scolded its creaking tree before it settled back to sleep.

To Alex, it felt as though the scene was frozen in time, the moonlight dancing along the surface of the water, the stars bathing his shoulders in warmth felt more by his soul than his body. He wanted to hold it in his mind forever, because at that moment, the meadow was filled with such peace. It felt as though everything within it had a place and hope.

Alex smiled inside. Jet had once said that the scent of grass reminded him of hope. Alex thought he finally understood.

A shoulder touched his softly. He looked into Siale's soft gray eyes. She didn't have to smile for the joy in the depths of her gaze to fill him with happiness. She tipped her head, her eyes questioning. He let his tongue hang out in a dopey wolfish grin.

Siale snorted a laugh and trotted back into the trees. Alex followed, pausing one last time to look back at the quiet meadow before he left it behind.

"Scold all you want, Alex. If you can leave the walls, we can, too," Cassie said hours later as she and Tennison followed Alex and Siale back to where they had left the motorcycle. His sister was taking full advantage of the fact that Alex was still in wolf form and couldn't reply to her arguments. "I know you don't approve, but sometimes it's nice to remember that there's a world outside the gate. I'm sure Jaze and Nikki wouldn't be thrilled with us, either, but wolves weren't meant for cages."

"I don't think Alex minds too much," Tennison told her as they walked side by side behind Alex and Siale. "He was out here, too."

"Yes, but Alex seems to think he can do whatever he wants as long as everyone else is safe." Alex glanced back in time to see her spear him with a look. "But he can't expect us to go crazy like I would if I didn't get out from time to time." Her eyes narrowed. "Now don't give me that look, Alex. This isn't the first time, and it won't be the last."

Alex glanced at Siale. The light gray wolf looked like she was going to burst out laughing at any moment. He rolled his eyes and she gave a snort of laughter as though she couldn't it keep inside any longer.

"And furthermore..."

"You're going with 'furthermore'?" Tennison asked.

"Yes," Cassie replied shortly. "This requires a furthermore. Furthermore, I have my own life to live and you can't expect me to be sheltered behind your brotherly protectiveness any longer. I can defend myself."

"She can," Tennison verified.

By the time they reached the motorcycle, Siale looked as though she was holding in the laughter only by sheer willpower while Alex was convinced that if he had to listen to his sister scold him any longer, he was going to explode. He quickly changed into his clothes and stepped out ready with a barrage of answers for her one-sided arguments.

"Don't do it," Tennison said before he opened his mouth.

"But I—"

Tennison shook his head with a quick glance in Cassie's direction. Alex's sister was busy looking the motorcycle over with an obvious expression of disapproval. Siale was in her human form again and watched Cassie with the same laughter in her eyes.

"It's easier if you just let it go."

"I can't let it go," Alex replied. "Otherwise Cass'll think she can do anything she wants. She shouldn't be out here."

Tennison's eyebrows lifted. "Now you're saying exactly what she said you would."

Alex sputtered for a moment, searching for words. "Well, uh, she really needs to be safe. The General's looking for Drogan and if he knew Cassie was my sister, and his daughter, he would kill her for sure."

"But he doesn't know," Tennison replied.

Alex paused with his mouth open. He closed it again, then gave in. "No, he doesn't know."

"And he won't."

"Not if I have anything to do with it," Alex replied

quietly.

Tennison nodded. "That's settled then. You know your sister won't stay within the Academy walls, so you might as well save your breath and not argue with her. She'll be safe from the General as long as he doesn't know she's his daughter, and you're not going to tell him. So that's that."

Alex wanted to argue. He began several arguments in his head, but they quickly tapered off. He finally sighed. "Sounds like she's got you trained."

"I'm glad you wear a helmet," Cassie called from the side of the motorcycle. "At least that's one smart thing you're doing."

Tennison gave a quiet chuckle. "I think she has both of us trained."

Alex grinned ruefully and followed the werewolf back to the motorcycle.

Chapter Nineteen

"It's one thing to lose with style. It's another to let them know we are going to be a team to reckon with," Coach Vance said in yet another high school locker room.

"You mean we get to win this time?" Trent asked tentatively.

Vance nodded. "We've lost enough to keep us out of the finals. Let's win our last game and give them the heads up that next year we'll be a team to contend with."

"Let's do it!" Amos said, jumping up. The huge werewolf almost hit his head on the ceiling. "Me pound humans."

"No, not like that," Vance contradicted.

Amos was a stand-in for Raynen who had failed enough tests that Nikki had removed him from the team until he could improve his grades.

The hulking werewolf grinned down at Alex. "I protect you."

"Yes," Alex told him. "But don't hurt the humans."

"How 'bout a little knock?" Amos asked. The werewolf clenched his hand into a fist and brought it down on top of one of the lockers with enough force to dent it and make the door fly open. "Uh, oops."

"Oops is bad," Alex told him. "If we hurt the humans, we can't play anymore." He was nervous about taking the huge werewolf out there. Though the behemoth had done well in practice, that had been against werewolves who could stand his brute strength. Alex knew the humans wouldn't be able to last against those fists.

"No hurt humans?" Amos' voice carried a comical hint of confusion.

Alex fought back the urge to laugh. The entire team, as well as Coach Vance, was watching, and if he couldn't get

Amos to understand, they would all be running back to the Academy with Extremists on their trail.

"Humans are our friends," Alex began.

"Human lover," Torin muttered.

Several other members of the team broke out in laughter. They quieted at Alex's look.

He tried to speak in terms Amos would understand. "Humans break easily. You have to be careful with them. Don't push or hit too hard."

Amos was silent for a few minutes. He finally nodded. "Okay. Me be nice to humans."

Alex plastered a smile on his face. "Okay. Good. Let's go play."

He watched the others file out to the field. The cheering and talking from the other team competed with the sound of the pep band warming up and the calls of the cheerleaders from the home school as they got the crowd ready for the game.

"You think this is going to work?" Vance asked quietly.

Alex took a breath and let it out slowly. "I sure hope so. I mean, what else can we do at this point?"

Vance shrugged. "Say the team came down with Parvo?"

Alex grinned. "Telling Ridgeline High School that our students caught a dog virus would probably raise a few questions."

"Probably answer a few, too," Vance said with a small chuckle. He led the way outside and Alex followed.

The sun pierced his eyes, bathing the small field regardless of the chill that bit through even Alex's jersey with merciless teeth. The fans in the stands wore coats, scarves, hats, gloves, and anything else they could use to keep the cold at bay. Many held cups of hot cocoa and coffee in an attempt to warm themselves from the inside out.

The cheerleaders from Ridgeline High waved yellow and green pom poms and shouted cheers; their breath left little clouds of fog in the air with each phrase. The few members of the crowd that could be persuaded to stomp and clap appeared to do so as a means of getting warm more than to follow the school spirit infused girls and boys.

"We seriously need to get us some of those," Boris said, nodding his head toward the cheerleaders as Alex and Vance reached the huddle.

"No way," Torin replied. "They hurt my ears."

Boris grinned. "Wimp."

"Come on, ladies, let's show them what we've got," Coach Vance said loudly. He then lowered his voice so only those in the football huddle could hear, "But let's do it in a way that doesn't kill the humans and expose our school. Got it?"

"Got it!" the werewolves replied.

Alex could see the excitement in their eyes beneath their face masks. They were being given a chance to actually win. He knew they couldn't blow the Ridgeline muskrats out of the water completely, but just winning at all would feel great.

"Let's take it nice and easy," he said quietly as they made their way across the field.

"I think we should just plow them all over," Torin responded dryly.

Alex didn't reply. He crouched and looked around. Silence filled the small stadium. The few members of Vicki Carso's Preparatory Academy who had been allowed to attend the last few games based on their ability to stay calm and keep up the professional appearance of the school watched their team with abated breaths. Cassie clutched Siale's hand. Kalia sat near them, her eyes wide. Alex grinned. It was time to give them something worth watching.

"Hike," he yelled.

The ball was in his hands. He backpedaled a few steps and scanned the field for an open receiver. Torin darted left while Boris ran past the player who was covering him with just enough speed to make it look natural. Alex's senses told him a sack was closing in. He threw the ball, then went down with the impact from two members of the opposing team. A glance through the bodies around him showed Boris jumping up to catch the ball. The werewolf brought it to the crook of his arm and ran to the end zone.

Alex let out a whoop. So what if Boris ran just a bit faster than the humans. It didn't matter if one of the Alphas who made Alex's school life miserable had just scored. His team was jumping up and down. Finally, they were going to feel what it meant to win.

After shutting down the other team's attempt to score, Alex was back on the line. Coach Vance had changed the lineup and Amos was on his right. He studied the opposing team. They were fueled up, ready to stop the drive. Alex smiled.

"Hike."

Alex scanned the field. Boris and Torin were doing a good job of acting like their opposition could keep up. Tennison cut around Torin, using the hulking werewolf to shave off the student who kept pace with him. Alex let the ball fly. As soon as he let go, a member of the other team slammed into him and he hit the ground.

"No hurt Alex."

Alex's heart skipped a beat at the sound of rage in Amos' voice. He looked up in time to see the huge werewolf shove players aside as though they were made of paper. There was no doubt in his mind that Amos was about to slam the Centerville player who had just tackled him. If that happened, the student would be hurt or worse. At the sight of Amos' flaring nostrils and small flashing eyes, Alex knew it would be much worse.

He shoved the student away from him and charged across the field. Blue touched the edges of his vision. He hit Amos with the force of a battering ram, pummeling the werewolf to the ground. Time slowed around them. Alex's heart thundered in his chest. He willed his breathing to steady. The realization of what he had just done filled him.

He had tackled a member of his own team who outweighed him by more than a hundred pounds. His momentum had stopped the charging werewolf in his tracks and thrown him onto his back. What did that look like to the Ridgeline fans? How could he play it off?

Amos looked up at him with wide eyes.

"Alex tackle Amos."

Alex nodded. "You were going to hurt that boy."

"He hurt Alex." Confusion was bright in the werewolf's eyes.

Alex said quietly, "I'm a werewolf, remember? They can't hurt me."

"Alex no hurt?"

When Alex shook his head, relief was clear on the hulking werewolf's face.

"I need you to do something for me," Alex said, making sure Amos heard the urgency in his tone.

"Anything for Alex."

Alex smiled. "Good. I want you to get up and start laughing."

"Uh, okay."

Amos clambered to his feet and started laughing. Alex slapped him on the shoulder and laughed with him as though they were friends who had just been fooling around. A few members of their team caught on and joined in the laughter. Chuckles rose from the crowd.

Torin grabbed Alex's shoulder. "Good job," the Alpha said quietly.

Alex glanced around. No one appeared concerned about the quarterback tackling the huge werewolf. The other team was lining up again after Tennison's touchdown. It was time to get off the field.

"Good move," Coach Vance told Alex quietly. "I thought Amos was going to kill him for sure."

"I did, too," Alex replied. He smiled at the sight of Amos talking to Cassie near the fence that separated the stands from the field. Alex jogged over to them. "I hope I didn't hurt you."

Amos gave a deep chuckle. "Alex hurt Amos. No way. Amos tough."

Alex grinned. "That's right. You're tough. Too tough for the other team, if you know what I mean."

Amos nodded his big head. "Cassie tell me they break easy. I play careful."

"Good." Alex replied. He threw his sister a grateful look. "Thanks."

Cassie shrugged. "What are sisters for if not to keep her brother's teammates from smashing the other team into a pulp to protect him?"

Alex laughed. "I didn't think I needed a bodyguard."

That made another smile grow on Amos' face. "I bodyguard." He gave a deep laugh and ambled over to Coach Vance. Alex could hear him telling the coach the same thing.

"Better be careful," Kalia warned, leaning over from Cassie's far side. "Amos might start following you around wherever you go."

Alex shrugged. "He's good company." At the girls' looks,

he said, "Not much of a conversationalist, but he has a great sense of humor."

Siale gave him a warm smile from her seat beside Cassie. "You're a good guy."

Alex winked at her. "Don't spread that around. I don't want to ruin my reputation."

"It's already ruined," Kalia said dryly.

"Alex," Coach Vance barked.

Alex looked over his shoulder. "I've got to go."

"Don't get killed out there," Siale told him.

Alex gave her a smile, grateful for her support.

"I'll try not," he said. "But I can't promise anything."

Siale and Cassie laughed as he hurried back to Vance's side.

The ride home after their win felt completely different from the losses they had been forced to take. Alex sat in the back of the bus with Siale. Cassie and Tennison had the seat on their left with Trent and Jordan one seat ahead of them. Kalia had surprised him by taking the seat in front of him and Siale; Torin insisted on sitting with her.

"That was an awesome game," Siale said. "You guys won, but didn't make it look easy."

"Who would have thought football meant acting," Trent put in. "I think I could do well on a stage."

"Maybe we should ask Nikki about setting up a drama class," Cassie suggested.

"Don't you dare."

Everyone fell quiet at Torin's irate words. "The last thing I want to do is get out on a stage rehearsing some girly play."

"I think it might be nice," Kalia said. "You might be good at it."

She glanced at Alex. Her eyes tightened slightly at the corners, but her expression remained carefully even. He realized she was toying with the Alpha.

"Well, uh, maybe," Torin said with doubt in his voice. He hesitated, then nodded. "I suppose so. If I tried it, I would definitely be good at it."

Cassie lifted her eyebrows at Alex. He smothered a laugh.

Coach Vance's voice crackled on the intercom, cutting through their conversation. "I know it's been hard on you to give up so many games, but I'm proud of you guys."

The players exchanged surprised looks, amazed to hear such positive words.

Vance waved a hand as if he knew what they were thinking. "You can all just wipe the confusion off your faces. I know I'm hard to deal with, but life isn't always easy." A hint of sadness showed in his eyes before he shook his head. "But it's worth living. Make sure you do your best in everything, even losing." He held up a football. "This is the game ball. I'm giving it to the werewolf who deserves it the most."

He walked down the aisle between the seats. The bus swayed and he caught his balance with a hand on the ceiling.

"Seriously, Kaynan? Are you trying to kill me?" he called over his shoulder.

"If I knew it was that easy," the red-eyed werewolf replied, grinning into the mirror above the driver seat.

Coach Vance shook his head. Alex though he heard the coach mutter the word, "Clones."

"This ball goes to Alex," Vance said, handing over the football. He gave Alex a smile. It looked rusty on his face as if it had been a long time since his lips had been forced to do such a thing. "You took us through a frustrating losing season, and helped us win the last game with style. And," he held up a hand to stifle the applause. "You took Amos down before he could kill that player."

Everyone looked at the huge werewolf who took up an entire seat by himself. "Alex smash Amos," he said with a deep laugh.

The bus erupted into answering laughter. Werewolves leaned over and patted Alex's shoulders. He sat back with a feeling of accomplishment. Siale kissed him on the cheek. He offered her the football.

She shook her head. "Keep it. You've earned it." She smiled at him. "Maybe you can teach me how to throw it."

"I'd be glad to," he promised.

Siale leaned against him. He wrapped an arm around her shoulder and caught Cassie's eyes from the next seat. She was snuggled against Tennison. They both smiled at him. Alex tipped his head back and closed his eyes, completely content.

Kalia's voice penetrated his wall of calm. "You guys all need to get a room. It's disgusting."

"I think they're cute," Terith replied.

Alex opened his eyes to see Kalia's annoyed look. "They don't have to shove it in our faces."

"If you want to cuddle, I'm available," Torin offered.

She rolled her eyes. "If I wanted to cuddle with a stinky, small-brained dolt, I'd go find a bear."

Torin refused to be cowed. "They're all hibernating right now." He grinned. "That's right. I listened in class. Would a bear know that?"

"Yeah," Kalia replied dryly. "It's the one hibernating."

Kalia was leaning against the window with her arm over the back of the seat. Torin put his hand over hers. "I guarantee I'd make you happy."

"As if," she said. She pulled her hand away and glared sullenly out the window.

Alex held Siale closer, completely aware that if she hadn't come into his life, he would be the one sitting next to Kalia.

Chapter Twenty

"You asked for me?" Alex said, knocking on the open door of Jaze's office.

The dean looked up from the stack of papers he was perusing. "Alex, yes." He rose. "Please come in and shut the door."

As soon as it was closed, Jaze opened the hidden panel in the wall and led the way through. Alex walked quietly behind the dean down to the small monitoring room that was Brock's normal working space when they weren't on missions. As soon as the door slid open, Brock swiveled around.

"We're positive. She can't go back there," the human said.

"Who are we talking about?" Alex asked. One glance at the surveillance cameras showed exactly who they meant. The Dickson's mansion appeared solitary and silent on its vast expanse of grass. He stepped closer, peering at the screens intently.

"Kalia Dickson's home is being watched," Brock said.

"I see that," Alex replied.

Brock shook his head. "Not by us. By them." He pointed at the monitor.

At that moment, a dark shadow broke from the wall and skirted around the perimeter. Moonlight reflected off of the scope of the rifle the form held in his hands.

Alex's heart sped up. "We've got to warn them!"

"They've been warned," Jaze said quietly. At Alex's questioning look, he explained, "I've already spoken to Adam Dickson and he's increased his security, but evidence says they're the General's men."

"Probably waiting for Kalia and Boris to arrive home for the holiday break," Brock concluded.

Alex let out a breath. "They have to stay here."

"Mr. Dickson agrees. I'll tell Kalia." Jaze's tone said the dean knew exactly how Kalia felt about any time she spent at the Academy. Asking her to stay through the break would be like pulling teeth.

"No, I should tell her," Alex replied. "But she'll kill me for sure."

"Better you than me," Brock told them. He took a big bite of a granola bar. The crunch of the grains sounded loud in the small security room.

"I could talk to her," Jaze said. "But she might take it better coming from you."

Alex nodded. "I'll do it, but if you don't see me around tomorrow, you might want to send out a search for my body."

"Will do," Jaze replied with a sympathetic smile.

Alex wandered down the hallway wondering how to break the news to Kalia and her explosive brother. He rounded the corner and ran straight into her so fast they hit foreheads.

"Ow!" Kalia exclaimed, rubbing her head. "Watch where you're walking."

Alex barely kept himself from replying that she could do the same. He gave her a tentative smile. "Actually, I was looking for you."

Kalia crossed her arms, her expression skeptical. "Why were you looking for me?"

Alex didn't know how to put it into words. He stood there for a minute trying to collect his thoughts, but there was something in her icy blue gaze that kept him from speaking. He knew what it was, recognized it from all of the hours they had spent together. He knew Kalia well enough to see hope when he saw it. For that brief moment, she hoped he was looking for her for many different reasons than being forced to spend the break at the Academy.

"Kalia, we need to talk," Alex told her. He took her hand, a gesture that had once sent tingles up his arm but now filled him with a longing to hold Siale's hand instead. He led Kalia outside away from the prying eyes of the few students who wandered the corridors at night. He gestured to the steps and waited until she took a seat, her gaze still distrustful.

Alex glanced around, making sure they were alone. He caught himself clenching and unclenching his hands, and shoved them in his pockets. "Kalia, I know how you feel."

The hope brightened. The faintest hint of a smile showed on Kalia's lips.

Alex shook his head quickly before she grabbed onto something that wasn't there. "You are not the one for me, and I can't be the one for you."

The hope vanished in a heartbeat, replaced by anger. "How do you know?" Kalia demanded. She rose and grabbed his arm. "How can you really know, Alex? You haven't given me a chance since Siale showed up. I'm invisible." Her voice wavered slightly. "I feel like you don't see me anymore."

"Of course I see you," Alex replied. "You're my friend."

"Just a friend?" Kalia shot back.

"Yes," Alex said, shaking free of her grasp. "Just a friend. A very good friend. Someone I care about." Again the flicker. Alex let out a frustrated breath. "As a friend, but no more than that."

Kalia grimaced. "How can you go from mooning after me last term to pretending I don't exist this term?"

Alex held back the urge to point out that he hadn't been mooning after her. Instead, he closed his eyes and squeezed them with one hand in an attempt to clear his mind. "Kalia, Siale is my one."

The small gasp that escaped her lips broke his heart. He had never said the words because he knew how bad it would hurt her. Watching her shake her head, her eyes wide with disbelief, only made the pain of the truth that much harder to bear.

"I don't believe you, Alex," she said. "There has to be a way to show you that you're wrong. There has to be something I can—"

Without warning, Kalia leaned forward and kissed him. She kept a hand on the back of his head, holding him there as she pressed her mouth firmly against his. Alex could feel her passion, her love, and her desperation in the kiss. He tried to fight it, but her Alpha strength came into play. Alex glanced behind Kalia to the doors. Siale stood there; loss filled her soft gray eyes when she met Alex's gaze.

Anger surged through him. The blue rush flooded his vision. "Kalia, no!" he said, shoving her away. A glance back up at the doors showed Siale gone.

"Tell me you didn't feel anything," Kalia demanded.

"I didn't feel anything," Alex replied. He glared at her. "Don't do that again."

"You liked it."

Alex grimaced. "It was like kissing my sister."

Kalia's mouth fell open. She tried to talk, but no words came out.

Angry that she had possibly hurt things between him and Siale, Alex pushed past her up the stairs. "You and I are never going to happen, Kalia. You need to accept that." He looked back down to see tears in her eyes as she watched him. He grabbed a door handle. "Your house is being watched by the General's men. You and Boris have to stay here for the break."

He pulled the door open and stormed inside.

Familiar footsteps hurried up the stairs. Alex ran forward in time to see Siale reach the top. "Siale, wait," he called.

A door slammed before he reached the last step. Alex ran to the end and pulled open the door to Pack Jericho's quarters. He stopped short at the sight of Jericho and the rest of the pack standing around Siale. She turned at the sound of the door opening. Tears ran down her cheeks, but she didn't speak.

Jericho's hand was on her shoulder. He met Alex's gaze with a stony glare. "Get out of here."

"I need to talk to Siale," Alex told his old Alpha.

"Not if she doesn't want to talk to you," Jericho replied. "She's my Second, and I won't let you hurt her."

Rage burned through Alex. For a moment, he wanted to attack Jericho and teach the Alpha what it meant to stand in his way. Reason washed away the anger before he took a step. Jericho was an Alpha protecting his Second. The werewolf would have done the same to defend Alex, and he had. Jericho chose Siale after promising Alex that he would take care of her. Alex was just witnessing the Alpha holding up his end of the promise.

Alex forced his muscles to relax. He looked at Siale, willing her to listen. "Siale, please. We need to talk," he said gently.

It took a moment for her eyes to lift to his. The bare, pain-filled gaze stole his breath. He could only hold out a hand, his expression pleading.

Siale took a step forward. Pack Jericho moved with her in case she needed him. She drew in a steeling breath and stood straighter. "I'm okay," she said, her voice almost steady.

"Are you sure?" Jericho asked.

At Siale's answering nod, he motioned for the rest of his pack to step back. Siale crossed to the door. Alex held it open for her to pass through to the hallway.

"Alex?" Jericho said.

He glanced back.

"I'm doing what you asked," the Alpha told him with a hint of apology in his voice.

"I appreciate it more than I can tell you," Alex replied. Jericho nodded and Alex gave him a small smile. "I'll resolve this."

"You better," Jericho said. "Because you don't want to mess with Siale's Alpha."

"No, I don't," Alex agreed. He stepped outside the door and pulled it shut behind him.

Siale sat on the top step, her head buried in her hands and her hair hiding her expression from view.

"I'm so sorry," Alex said, crossing quickly to her.

"I can't believe it," Siale spoke in a voice just above a whisper.

Alex took a seat next to her. "It's not what it looked like."

Siale turned her head enough to peer at him through her wavy brown hair. "It looked like Kalia still has feelings for you and is trying to prove that you have the same for her."

Alex swallowed the lump in his throat. "Okay, it's exactly what it looks like." He touched Siale's shoulder. "But it didn't mean anything to me."

She bowed her head. "Nothing at all?"

"Nothing," Alex replied.

"How am I supposed to believe that?" Siale asked quietly. "You liked her before you met me. That much is obvious. What if me coming here was a mistake? What if I—"

Alex tipped her chin up and kissed her. She hesitated for a moment, then kissed him back with a fierceness that surprised him. It chased away the feeling of Kalia's kiss and replaced it with completeness. With a kiss like that, there was no doubt in Alex's mind where Siale stood. He could tell by the small sigh that left her that she felt the same way.

"You're my Alex," she said, drawing back to look up at him. "I'm not going to share you with anyone."

Her words filled him with such warmth he could barely speak. "I like that," he replied softly.

"You better."

They both turned at the sound of Jericho's voice. The entire Pack Jericho stood at the end of the hallway watching them.

"You okay, Siale?" Jericho asked.

"Yes," she replied with a small laugh. She leaned against Alex and he held her tight. "I'm just fine."

Jericho met Alex's gaze and nodded. Alex gave a smile in return. The Alpha pushed his pack mates back into their quarters. "Let's give them some space," Alex heard Jericho say.

Alex looped his fingers through Siale's hair as she leaned against his side. "You're my one, Siale."

"You're my one, Alex," she replied.

The smile he heard in her voice made his heart skip a beat. She set a hand on his chest.

"You need to take care of that."

He shrugged. "I can't help it if being so close to you makes my heartbeat uneven. You have that effect on me."

She looked up at him. "You deserve love, Alex."

He smiled down at her. "I want only you." He covered her mouth with his and smiled when she returned the kiss.

"I don't want to leave," Siale said when Alex leaned back.

As much as Alex wanted her to stay, he admitted the truth. "Your dad would kill me if you skip the holiday break to stay here."

She sighed. "I know. Telling him I have a boyfriend is

going to be hard enough." Her eyes danced. "And telling him it's you is going to be even more difficult."

Alex pretended to be offended. "Red likes me."

"Yeah," she replied. "Until I tell him you kissed his daughter."

"If he kills me, you can tell him it was still worth it."

"Don't worry," Siale said with a warm smile. "I will."

Alex held her close, dreading the morning when she would leave on the school bus out of his life for the next two weeks.

"My life won't be worth living until you return," Alex told her.

"Mine, neither. Maybe I can get Dad to send me back early."

The thought cheered Alex immensely. "That would be great."

"I'll see what I can do," Siale promised.

Alex rested his chin on her head as she held him, her hand still over his heart and the fingers of her other hand tracing patterns on his palm.

Chapter Twenty-one

"We've found another of the General's warehouses," Jaze said, addressing the small group of werewolves that made up Alex's pack while the Termers were gone.

"Is it full of dead werewolves?" Trent asked with a shudder.

"We're hoping we found it soon enough to rescue at least a few," Jaze replied. It was clear the dean didn't relish the thought of another warehouse of bodies.

Terith spoke up next. "How soon are we heading out?"

Jaze tipped his head at Brock.

"Five minutes," Brock replied. "Mouse is getting the chopper ready."

"Great," Kalia muttered. "Death by chopper."

"Don't worry," Terith told her with a grin. "Trent won't be flying."

"I didn't do that bad," Trent argued.

"I'm not getting in a helicopter if he's flying," Torin said.

"I'm not flying it!" Trent replied, exasperated.

Terith and Cassie burst into laughter.

"Mouse will be flying," Alex told the Alpha.

Torin wandered past to look at the array of weapons Brock's cousin Caden had set out.

"Alex, why is he here?" Trent asked in an undertone.

Alex pushed down the feeling of trepidation that was rising in his chest. "Jaze said we needed help. The GPA will be at the warehouse, but the Black Team is occupied somewhere else. The more werewolves we have checking for those who might still be alive, the better."

"I think it's a bad idea," Trent replied.

Alex agreed, but didn't say so. He strapped on his bulletproof vest and picked up his gun. The Glock felt comfortable in his hand, cold, simple, and deadly accurate. He checked the cartridge and slid several more into the pouch on his belt.

"They trust you with that?" Torin asked with doubt heavy in his voice.

"He's saved hundreds of lives," Trent replied defensively.

Torin's eyebrows lifted in surprise. "Guess I should stick near you then."

"Hundreds?" Alex whispered as they made their way to the helicopter.

Trent shrugged with a hint of red in his cheeks. "I might have exaggerated a bit."

Alex stared out the window as they lifted into the air. He barely heard Torin's exclamation of surprise when the ceiling of the cavern split. Alex's thoughts were on Siale, what she was doing, if she missed him. Watching her ride away in the school bus loaded with Termers had been harder than he had expected. He felt like half of him was missing, like his thoughts were muted and even the colors of the snow-bathed forest floor below were faded and washed out.

"You look like you're not feeling well."

Alex glanced up to find Kalia watching him.

"I think I just..." He hesitated, and went with, "I'm not feeling like myself right now."

"Maybe you should stay at the Academy?" The concern in her voice was unmistakable.

Alex shook his head. "I'd rather help free werewolves. I'll be fine."

She gave him an unconvinced look before turning away.

They landed at the private airfield and boarded Jaze's jet. Alex was grateful they didn't have to use the regular airport. He couldn't imagine trying to get all of the weapons past security.

"This is sweet," Torin exclaimed. He fell into one of the plush chairs. "I could travel like this every day. Hey, Dean, any chance we can take a trip to the Caribbean? I'm dying to get away from this snow."

"Let's focus on the warehouse first," Jaze replied. "Your vacation plans will have to wait."

Torin chuckled and reclined his chair. "It was worth a try."

"You remember we're trying to save lives, right?" Kalia asked, taking a seat across from Torin and buckling her seatbelt. Her face was a bit pale. Alex knew she hated flying. Going from the helicopter to the jet no doubt pushed her comfort limits.

"I'm sure they'll be grateful," Torin replied. "But not as grateful as I'd be digging my toes into the sand of a perfect white beach." He met her gaze. "I could teach you how to snorkel." He moved his eyebrows up and down invitingly.

"Where did you learn how to snorkel?" Kalia asked dryly.

Torin shrugged. "Nowhere. I'm just naturally good at everything. You could learn a lot from me if you wanted to."

Kalia gave a snort of disgust and turned to stare out the window.

Alex had taken the seat behind Torin. He watched Kalia's hands tighten on the armrests as the jet picked up speed.

"Uh, Kalia?"

She looked back at him. Her fear of flying was bright in her eyes.

"Maybe snorkeling wouldn't be so bad," Alex said.

Torin nodded. "See?" He gave Alex a grateful smile. "I think you'd like fish."

"To chase or eat?" Kalia asked. Alex didn't know if it was to avoid looking out the window that made her humor them, but he figured the fact that she was actually speaking to Torin without the note of disgust in her voice was a good sign.

"I'm guessing a fresh-caught halibut would make a fine meal. It wouldn't be that hard to make. I could fry it up over an open fire; tell you stories as we listen to the waves. It would be a very romantic evening," Torin said.

Kalia actually gave a small laugh. "And you would do all of that for me?"

"I was planning to eat the halibut," Torin replied. "But you'd be welcome to a bite or two."

Kalia rolled her eyes and sat back in her seat. "You are a gentleman."

"I know," Torin told her. "That's why the ladies love me."

"What ladies?" Tennison asked from the next seat up as though he couldn't stop himself.

Cassie nudged him with her elbow.

"Your lady, for one," Torin said.

Cassie's smile erased completely. "I have no interest in you, Torin," she replied tersely.

"You keep telling yourself that," Torin told her with a wink.

"Idiot," Kalia muttered. She crossed her arms and looked out the window. When she saw that they were already well on their way, she looked back at Alex. He could tell by her expression that she knew he had used Torin to distract her.

"Thank you," she mouthed.

He shrugged in reply and sat back with a smile.

Jaze came back from the cockpit. "The GPA reports that the warehouse has a few signs of life, but they haven't seen any Extremists. If we're careful, we can get in and out without any problems." He nodded at Tennison. "Tennison, you'll take Terith, Cassie, and Trent on a northwest sweep. Alex, take Torin and Kalia to the southeast. Chet and

Kaynan's teams are already there. They'll take the roof and basement. We'll meet in the middle. I want everyone to stick to their groups." He speared Alex with a look that said he expected strict obedience. "No heroics. Safety and getting our teams out along with the surviving werewolves is our priority."

"Got it," Alex replied. He couldn't shake the tightness in his chest. He didn't know if it was the thought of walking through another warehouse after rescuing Siale, but he had gone with Jaze's pack to other rescues without any problems. Something wasn't right. He kept telling himself that it would go away, but doubt pressed against the back of his mind.

They landed at nightfall on a little strip of pavement near a farm. The GPA's customary black SUVs were there to pick them up.

Agent Sullivan shook Jaze's hand and led the way to the first vehicle.

"Are you okay?" Cassie asked quietly, touching Alex's arm when they were settled inside.

Alex nodded. "I'm fine," he replied. "Just anxious, I guess."

"Nobody would blame you if you don't want to do this one," Tennison told him.

Alex met Jaze's gaze in the rearview mirror. He shook his head. "I want to help."

The dean turned around to face them. "Don't take any risks," he instructed. "We have enough help to sweep the warehouse and get anyone out we can save within fifteen minutes. The General might have it wired to blow, so we'll be quick, efficient, and survive without reckless heroics." Jaze winked.

The words brought a small smile to Alex's face.

"Wired to blow?" Torin repeated. "Are you serious?"

"The General doesn't appreciate us freeing his captives," Trent told the Alpha. "Mouse can usually block the signal, but there may be secondary triggers. We like to play it safe."

"Sounds like a good idea," Torin said, sitting back in his seat. "I don't know what I'm getting myself into."

"Why are you here?" Kalia asked curiously.

Torin glanced behind him at Alex. "Uh, to help my fellow werewolves. I'm always on the lookout for a good cause."

"You are?" Kalia's tone was doubtful.

"Of course," Torin replied.

"This is it," Agent Sullivan said from the driver's seat. He drove slowly into the parking lot of the warehouse. "Blueprints show that this used to be a holding center for produce. It was climate controlled, so there are air ducts and cooling rooms along with eight separate storage areas with adjoining loading docks. Keep your eyes open for anywhere the General might hide his experiments."

"What kind of experiments are we talking about?" Torin asked quietly as they unloaded from the vehicle.

"The worst kind," Trent replied, his tone bitter. "The kind that makes you wish he was locked up like his son."

Alex nodded in agreement. The alarm that was growing in his chest was constricting and causing his heart to skip.

"Kaynan and Chet are in position with their teams," Brock said into their earpieces. "Move in."

"I'm not sure how I feel about taking orders from a human," Torin muttered as he followed Alex around the side of the warehouse behind Jaze and Agent Sullivan's team.

"I'm not sure I like giving them to you," Brock replied sarcastically.

Torin gave Alex a wide-eyed look. "He can hear me?"

"Just like you can hear him," Alex explained. "He's our eye in the sky. He has a lock on the cameras and watches the drone for heat signatures. Without him, there's no way we could have taken as many places as we have."

He motioned for Torin not to ask any more questions. Kalia's arm brushed Alex's. Her eyebrows were pulled together in worry. Alex wondered if she was thinking of the same warehouse where he had gotten trapped rescuing Siale. "It's going to be okay," he whispered.

Torin looked her way. "Oh, yeah. I'll make sure you're just fine," he said. He put an arm around her shoulder and she ducked out from under his grasp. "Just stick with me and nobody will hurt you," he continued as if he didn't notice.

"Quick and silent," Jaze said as he pulled open the door. "Let's get in and out."

Dusky moonlight filtered through the high windows.

Alex led Torin and Kalia southeast down the first corridor. Racks and pallets covered in dust lined the aisles. Alex's nose wrinkled at the smell of death and decay.

"Disgusting," Torin muttered.

They turned a corner and saw the tables.

"Found it," Alex said.

"Check them, but I don't think you'll find anything," Brock said over his earpiece. "No heat signatures on that level."

Alex motioned for Torin and Kalia to take the other side of the tables. He didn't need to check the tables to know that the werewolves on them were dead. No sounds of heartbeats reached his ears, and the green, fresh scent that blanketed the living was nowhere to be found. It was obvious by their condition that they had been dead for weeks.

"These poor werewolves," Kalia said with a hand over her mouth.

"Let's get to the next aisle," Alex told them shortly.

He rounded the corner and stopped short.

"I'm picking up some strange heat signatures," Brock said into their earpieces. "I'm not exactly sure what I'm looking at."

"I think I know," Alex replied.

A scent touched his nose. He turned to see Kaynan standing a few feet away, motionless as though his feet were frozen to the floor.

"What is it?" Jaze asked into his earpiece.

"Bodies, uh, creatures attached to life support, although I'm not sure if they're really alive." Alex took a step forward. The sluggish mass of whatever was on the table twitched.

A glance sideways showed Kalia and Torin close to the wall as if they didn't dare to move. "I don't know what we're looking at," Kalia said, fear and horror making her voice tight.

"Clones."

Everyone looked at Kaynan. The professor's red eyes reflected in the faint moonlight. Dismay showed on his face along with something Alex was surprised to recognize as familiarity. Kaynan had seen such things before.

"These are clones?" Alex repeated quietly.

Kaynan set his hand on a distorted shoulder. The creature beneath his touch let out a little moan through a misshapen mouth. Crooked fangs showed through holes in its cheeks. One limb with two fingers and a claw tried to move, but it was obvious the creature didn't have the muscle structure to do so.

"They're trying to make werewolves." Kaynan swallowed and looked down the long row of tables, each of which contained another deformed creature. "Or something."

"You've seen this before," Alex said.

Kaynan nodded. He put a finger to his earpiece. "We need to clear this warehouse so we can blow it."

"With them in here?" Kalia asked in shock.

Kaynan met her gaze. "It's the nicest thing we can do for them."

He led the way back. "I've cleared the rest of this level."

"Finish with the basement," Jaze told them in their headsets. "We'll meet back at the doors."

Chapter Twenty-two

Alex followed Kaynan numbly down the stairs. He couldn't stop picturing the tables filled with the General's experiments. Nausea made his stomach roll.

"It's horrible," Kalia whispered, grabbing his arm. "How do things like that happen?"

"Bad people who don't care who they hurt to get the power they crave," Alex told her.

A check over her shoulder showed Torin glowering at him. He remembered his promise to help the werewolf gain her trust.

"I'd better catch up to Kaynan," Alex said. "I don't think he's taking it well." He shrugged out of her grasp and hurried down the rest of the cement steps. The professor had already vanished into the darkness.

Alex followed him for a few paces, then froze. In front of him was a round hole sunk into the warehouse floor. Memories flooded over him, images of falling into a hole so similar he couldn't stop the shudders that ran over his skin. He heard Siale's whispered pain, and felt the pile of bodies beneath him. He was overwhelmed with stench, the smell of death and decay so thick it felt like it was choking him.

"Alex, I don't know what you're doing trying to stick me with Torin, but it's not going to..." Kalia's voice faded away when she realized he wasn't listening to her. Kalia followed his gaze to the pit. "What is that?" she asked. She took a step forward.

Alex couldn't move. He couldn't tell her to back away. His voice caught in a throat choked tight with remembered fear. Death had been so close. The bodies overwhelmed him, pulling his thoughts down the cement hole Kalia stood over.

"Alex, what's wrong with you?" Kalia asked. She turned

to face him.

Images warred in Alex's head. He was pinned, trapped beneath cement and wooden beams. He held Siale, trying to slow her bleeding wounds while shielding her from the pile of tortured, lifeless bodies.

He watched in horror as forms rose out of the pit behind Kalia. He tried to call to her and tell her to run. He tried to pull his gun from his holster, but could only succeed in clenching his hands into fists as his heart thundered and skipped, making it hard to breathe.

"I don't understand what's going on," Kalia said, putting her hands on her hips.

The bodies reached up and grabbed her. Kalia let out a scream as she was pulled backwards into the hole. Alex collapsed to his knees on the floor, lost in the clash of memories and reality that threatened to tear his consciousness apart with madness.

"Alex, was that Kalia?" Torin demanded, rushing past him. Torin stared into the cement hole. "Did she fall down there?"

Alex couldn't speak. He kept seeing the bodies reach up and grab her. It couldn't be true.

"Kaynan!" Torin shouted.

The red-eyed werewolf ran into view.

"Something happened to Kalia," Torin said, staring from Alex to the hole. "I heard her scream and she's gone. I can smell other people here."

Kaynan jumped into the hole. The sight of the professor disappearing from view jolted Alex out of the grasp of his fear. He ran to Torin's side.

"You let them take her!" the Alpha shouted. He hit Alex with a haymaker that sent him staggering. "You let her go!" He hit Alex again.

"What is going on?" Jaze demanded in their earpieces.

As Torin quickly explained, Alex heard the drum of footsteps on the stairs. Someone touched his arm. He could tell by the scent that it was Cassie without turning to see. He couldn't tear his eyes away from the hole in the ground.

"Alex, are you okay? Where's Kalia?" Cassie asked.

"The bodies..." Alex's words choked off. He rubbed his eyes. "I don't know."

"You look like you're going to fall over," Tennison said, grabbing his elbow to steady him.

Jaze and Chet ran past them to the cement hole. Before they could climb down, Kaynan called up, "The General's men were here, but they're gone, and they took Kalia. The tunnel leads to a sewage out near the river; it's some sort of drainage tube. There are imprints from a helicopter's skids."

Alex blinked and the sides of the cement hole changed from the decay-covered lining of the body hole to a mesh-sided tube with a grate on top that had been removed. The unemotional side of him spotted the grate leaning near the wall. The other side couldn't process what he had seen; the image of the cement pit and the mesh tunnel clashed in his vision.

"He let her go," Torin was saying. "Alex let them take her."

"Alex, is that true?" Trent asked from beside him.

Alex could feel them all looking at him. He couldn't reply because he didn't know what he had seen. The tube interchanged with the image of the body pit. He saw Kalia grabbed over and over again. The memory of the bodies climbing out shifted. He saw men dressed in black with paint on their faces. He could smell the General faintly. Alex's jaw tightened.

"Alex, no!" Cassie shouted.

Alex jumped into the hole before they could grab him. He half-expected to sink into the pile of bodies. Instead, the impact of the mesh tube along a cement floor jolted through his limbs. He rushed past Kaynan down the tunnel. He couldn't tell if he was running to find Kalia or trying to escape the image of bodies crawling after him.

Alex burst through the end of the tunnel. The grate that had been on the end was lying in the mud. He could smell Kalia's honey and clover scent. Toe marks showed where they had dragged her to the helicopter. Alex studied the tracks, running from the tube to the helicopter skid marks over and over again, desperate for any lead.

"She's not here," Kaynan said.

"There's got to be a way to find her," Alex replied. He shouldered past the professor, his eyes on the ground. "There has to be something."

"Alex, we'll find her," Kaynan told him.

Alex barely heard the professor's voice. He looked for anything, a hair, a piece of cloth, some sort of indication that she didn't vanish into thin air, but there was nothing. He couldn't give up. The mud was churned with his tracks. He couldn't see the marks from her feet through his tears, but he wouldn't stop trying.

"You guys need to get out of there," Brock said into Alex's earpiece.

Alex ripped it out of his ear and threw it on the ground.

"Alex, we'll get her back," Kaynan told him. "We need to leave. We've got to let the place blow."

"There has to be something," Alex said. He stared at the ground without seeing it, but he couldn't stop pacing back and forth from the tube to the marks.

Kaynan grabbed him in a bear hug. Alex's training kicked in. He bent his knees and tried to elbow Kaynan in the chest, then the groin, but the werewolf was ready. Kaynan hooked an arm around his elbow and then the back of his neck, pinning him. Alex tried to struggle, but he couldn't move. His heart thundered in his chest, skipping beats and pounding harder to compensate.

"Breathe," Kaynan said into his ear. "Come on, Alex. Calm down. Take a breath."

"It's my fault she's gone," Alex forced out. His will to fight fled with the words. He sagged in the professor's hold. "I let them take her. I let the General take her."

"We'll get her back, I promise," Kaynan replied. He let go of Alex slowly, ready to grab him again if he showed any sign of fighting back. "We need to go," he said urgently.

Alex gave a numb nod.

Kaynan led him back to the tube. Alex stumbled through the opening. He fell to his knees, then pushed back up to his feet. Kaynan waited for him to collect himself. Alex followed the professor through the darkness.

They were almost to the opening when Alex saw something wedged into a seam of the tube. Alex pulled it free, revealing a small folded piece of paper. He quickly opened it.

"Meet at the park in Greyton. Come alone or your girl will die."

The General's scent was unmistakable.

"Alex?" Jaze called from the top of the tube.

Alex shoved the paper in his pocket and followed Kaynan to the entrance. He jumped and his hands were grabbed by Jaze and Chet.

Cassie caught him in a hug as soon as his feet were on the ground.

"It's okay. We'll find her," she said.

Alex nodded, unable to speak. When she let him go, Jaze

led him up the stairs. The dean's hand on his shoulder grounded him. He heard the footsteps of the other werewolves as they followed the pair up.

When they were clear of the warehouse, Jaze said quietly, "I don't know what happened down there, but I won't give up until Kalia's back at the Academy."

"Me, neither," Alex replied, thinking of the note in his pocket.

He climbed into one of the waiting SUVs and stared out the window. The image of the bodies pulling Kalia into the tunnel played over and over in his head. He leaned against the window and stared unseeing at the passing forest. The view turned bright and the trees around them tipped slightly forward from the repercussion of the warehouse explosion. He was vaguely aware of Cassie rubbing his back, but he couldn't respond. The note burned in his pocket. He had to get to her. He had to make sure she was safe.

***

As soon as Alex was left alone in his quarters, he climbed out the window into the night. Alex jumped to the roof of the green houses, then to the ground. He ran to Trent's workroom and threw the tarp off the motorcycle. Knowing the gates would be closed, Alex pushed the motorcycle through the tunnel that led from the workroom to the Wolf Den cavern beneath the Academy. He shoved his helmet on and sped up the hidden passage to the snow-covered path that led from the forest and met up with the winding road from the school.

"Alex?" Trent's sleepy voice crackled in his ear. "Where are you going?"

"I've got to save Kalia," Alex answered. He pulled over to the side of the road and turned off the motorcycle.

"You need a team." Trent sounded more alert now.

"I've got to do this on my own," Alex replied. He used the key to open the gas cap. "I'm leaving the microchip."

"Don't do it, Alex," Trent replied in alarm. "How am I going to help if you need me?"

"I can't have help," Alex said. He removed the microchip. Knowing the device was expensive, he pulled a knife from the motorcycle's saddlebag and walked a few steps to the closest tree.

"What are you doing?" Trepidation colored Trent's voice.

"I'm hiding the chip so you can find it." Alex cut a deep grove into an aspen that bent at a strange angle about halfway up the trunk. He slipped the chip inside. "Is that the only one?"

Trent was silent for a moment before he replied, "I can track you through the headset's signal."

Alex closed his eyes. "Thank you for your honesty."

"You can't take on the General by yourself," Trent

protested.

"I might not be able to take on the General, but I can save Kalia," Alex said. He took his helmet off.

"Don't do it, Alex." Trent's voice rose. "You can't do this by yourself. They'll kill you!"

"Thank you for all you've done," Alex said. "You've been a true friend."

He pulled the headset from the helmet and hung it in the tree. He could still hear Trent protesting, but chose not to listen. He shoved his helmet back on and crossed back to the motorcycle. Alone with only the note in his pocket, Alex drove down the midnight road.

Chapter Twenty-three

Alex pulled alongside the park just before sunrise. The city was quiet. He remembered Cherish's warnings about gangs. He hoped for their sake that they had the brains to avoid the park that morning.

Alex climbed off the motorcycle. His instincts thrummed; the General's men were near. He walked slowly to the middle of the park, his gaze on the surrounding buildings.

"Put your hands up," a voice called.

The irony that the man hid in the same alley that Alex had fought in the previous winter made a grim smile touch his lips. He raised his hands above his head. His breath fogged in the crisp air. A faint hiss reached his ears before a dart hit his back. Alex chose not to fight the silver as it snaked through his veins. His only chance of finding Kalia was to comply with the General's wishes.

Alex's knees gave out and he collapsed to the ground. The thunder of footsteps sounded loud in his ears as the General's men surrounded him. Hands picked him up roughly and carried him through the snow. Doors to a vehicle were opened and he was thrown inside. The doors slammed shut and tires squealed down the road.

***

Alex's head ached. He kept his eyes closed as he tried to remember what had happened. Unfamiliar beeping sounds, the squeak of shoes on vinyl, the bite of bands around his chest, and a sharp, sterile scent that burned his nose let him know he was in trouble.

He couldn't move. Even the effort it took to try to open his fingers sapped his strength. The only thing that could have such an effect was silver.

Kalia.

Alex's eyes flew open. He was in a wide, low-ceilinged white room. Four guards stood in front of every door while others lined the walls. The scent of silver in the room was almost overpowering.

Beeping near his right ear made Alex want to turn his head, but his muscles wouldn't respond. He shifted his eyes in an attempt to see what was near him.

Four physicians in white lab coats were preparing items on a long gray table. Alex's heart tightened in fear. Past them near the far end of the room was a girl in a chair. Tears streaked her cheeks and her shoulder-length blonde hair was messy. Bruises covered her face and a trickle of blood stained the side of her mouth. Kalia's icy blue gaze met Alex's.

"I thought you might remain unconscious for the procedure."

Alex's lips pulled back in a snarl at the sound of the General's voice. He shifted his eyes to the left and found General Jared Carso watching him from a few paces away, his arms crossed in front of his chest and his gaze impassive. The General's buzzed black hair showed more gray at the temples than Alex remembered. His dark blue eyes held Alex's. "It'd probably be easier on you, but now you're awake and we can't administer more silver, so we'll test the limits of your pain tolerance." A slight smile lifted his lips at the thought.

"What do you want with me?" Alex demanded.

"I want my son," the General replied.

Alex grasped at the chance. "I'll help you find Drogan if you'll let Kalia go."

The General's mouth curved in a humorless smile. "Not Drogan. My other son. " His eyes narrowed. "My men have already located Drogan. I'll have him back at my side shortly. I need my other son."

Alex's heart twisted in his chest at the General's implications. "Why?" he made himself ask.

A hungry light flickered in the General's eyes. "Think of a werewolf with your abilities under my control. The beast you hold inside is more powerful than a dozen of my hounds. I'll make you mine, and use you to tear down your little Academy. Without Jaze's defenses, I'll have your sister in no time."

Ice flooded Alex's veins. He didn't know how the General had figured out about Cassie and the Academy. No one knew, except... His eyes flickered to Kalia.

"I'm so sorry," Kalia said. Tears glittered in her eyes. "They made me tell them everything."

"It's okay," Alex told her despite the fear in his heart for his sister. Jaze and Tennison would protect Cassie. Kalia had no one but him. "I'm going to get you out of here," he told her. "You're going to be alright, I promise."

Kalia nodded, her gaze holding him as if he was her only hope. He tried to move, to break free, to do anything, but the silver held him paralyzed. He could barely swallow.

"As touching as this is, I have a reunion with my son to get to," the General said. He motioned to his physicians.

The table Alex was on rotated with a mechanical hum. The bands held him tight as he was turned over completely.

He stared at the black-flecked white tiles, unsure what was going to happen. Fear made his heartbeat ragged. He tried to force his breathing to calm.

"We've never operated on a werewolf that is awake," a man spoke with a thick accent. "He might not survive."

"He's a Carso. He'll be fine," the General replied. "Proceed."

Burning pain tore into the base of Alex's skull. He tried to move, but he was helpless to do anything but feel the slice of a knife and instruments used to peel his skin back. Something scraped against his skull. Tingles ran down his limbs followed by shards of lightning. Alex gritted his teeth in an attempt not to cry out.

"Leave him alone!" Kalia shouted. The sounds of her struggling came muffled to Alex's ears. "What are you doing to him?"

"Implanting a microchip that will allow me to control your boyfriend's brainwaves and muscular activity," the General replied with a tone of satisfaction. "Alex will be the leader of my hound army."

Pain flooded Alex's entire body in waves of heat and cold so fierce he couldn't think. Yells escaped him and his teeth clenched so hard his jaw felt like it would break. Eventually, the pain subsided. Sharp stabs pierced Alex's skin. Something cold was swabbed over the wound. Gauze was pressed against his neck, then medical tape.

A physician pressed a button and the table slowly rotated back over. A light shined in his eyes. Alex wanted to blink, but his eyelids refused to respond. He felt separate from himself, as though he watched the scene from a distance.

"It's done," the physician announced.

"Alex!" Kalia shouted.

"What should we do with the girl?"

Alex wanted to look at the General, but he couldn't do even that.

"He's mine now," the General replied. "Take her outside and kill her. I'm going to meet Drogan."

Alarm filled Alex's thoughts.

The General's footsteps echoed through the room. A door shut. Other footsteps followed.

"No!" Kalia shouted.

Panic pounded through Alex's heart. He had to save her.

"Alex, help me!"

Kalia's cries tore through him. His mind struggled against the microchip, trying to break free. His heart staggered. The silver was too much. He could barely breathe.

"Alex!" Kalia's voice was muffled. The sound of a door shutting made Alex's heart jump. He tried to move his arms, but they wouldn't listen to him.

"Heartbeat irregular," a physician noted. The sound of a pencil writing on paper was as loud as glass being dragged across cement.

"Alex!"

A gunshot sounded.

Blue surged through Alex's thoughts, chasing away everything else.

"What's happening?" one of the physician's asked.

Alex flexed his expanding muscles. The bands across his chest tightened, then snapped. Alex ripped one hand free, then the other.

A physician attempted to stab him with a needle. Alex grabbed him by the throat and slammed his head into the edge of the table. As the man fell to the ground, two more tried to pin Alex down. He grabbed their heads and slammed them together. The feeling of their skulls collapsing beneath his hands registered in the back of his mind. He threw them to the ground and ripped his ankles free of their bonds.

"Shoot him!" the physician with the thick accent shouted.

Alex was at the man's side in a heartbeat. He ducked as gunfire erupted. Bullets peppered the physician's torso. Alex ran forward, using the man's body as a shield. A bullet tore through Alex's arm. He let out a roar and slammed the physician into four guards.

Every guard in the room charged. Alex grabbed two guns and cracked them across three faces. He spun and slammed the heel of his palm into a guard's face hard enough to shove his nose into his skull. He caught the man before he could fall. Holding an arm and a leg, Alex turned, taking down five more guards. He threw the body at four others charging across the room.

Bullets tugged at Alex's clothes. He broke a guard's arm, caught his knife, and slammed it into another guard's leg. He slammed his elbow against the side of a man's head and spun, connecting with two others. The blue rage drove everything else from his mind.

More men poured into the room. Alex cracked skulls, threw guards across the floor, and used their guns as clubs. He fought until the guards were fighting to get away, and then he chased them down. The only thought in his mind was that no human who had been in that room would leave it. The beast side of him made that thought a reality.

Alex stood in the middle of a pile of bodies. His breath tore through his throat, and blood dripped from his hands to the floor. He didn't know how much of it was his, and he didn't care.

The blue faded from his vision. His muscular beast form lessened, leaving him exhausted and drained.

"Kalia," he whispered.

Alex waded through the bodies to the door they had

taken her out of. He shoved it open with his shoulder, stumbled down the short hallway, and opened the next door to reveal a stretch of snowy ground. Two sets of footprints and the dragging impressions of Kalia's feet as she struggled lined the snow. Alex followed them with his eyes. His heart stopped entirely at the sight of a lone form lying in the distance.

"Kalia!" Alex called. He ran through the snow. Two sets of footprints left the form and made their way back to the building. Alex hoped they had been with the guards who had attacked him.

"Kalia."

Her name came out in a whisper at the sight of the red snow around her body.

Alex fell to his knees. Her eyes were closed. A small red circle occupied the center of her forehead. Alex touched it numbly. His finger came back bloody.

"Oh no." His voice cracked. He wanted to touch her, to hold her, to reassure himself that she was alright. His hands started to shake. He ran his fingers down her beautiful blonde hair, slipping his hand behind her head. The warm damp that met his fingers said everything. "No. No. No. No. No." He shook his head, rocking forward and back on his knees. "No, not you. Please not you."

He gathered Kalia in his arms. The fact that her skin was chilled struck him hard. She used to get so cold before she phased for the first time. He pictured her in the white coat with the fur around the hood. She had always hated that white coat because wearing it made her separate from the werewolves who didn't need anything to shield them from the chill. He would keep her warm.

Alex held her on his lap. Any thought that the General's guards would find him were baseless. He had killed every person in the building. He knew over a hundred bodies lay in the room behind him. They had kept rushing through the doors until there was no one left to attack him. Whoever had shot Kalia lay there with them. He wished he knew who it had been. He would have made them pay.

Instead of anger, Alex felt empty, completely empty. He couldn't think, he couldn't feel. He could only rock back and forth with Kalia in his arms, wishing with every breath that she would open her eyes and tell him that she was okay. He could feel the dampness on his arm that cradled her head. He knew she would never wake up again.

One side of him wanted to phase to wolf form and run. He wanted to run and never look back, to become just a wolf, to live day to day without feeling or thinking about what had happened. The other side refused to leave Kalia in the snow. She had hated being cold, and he wouldn't leave her alone.

Chapter Twenty-four

Alex had no idea how long he sat there. The sun rose and set. The cold his werewolf body usually kept at bay seeped through his limbs, and still he kept his vigil over Kalia. A rhythmic pounding sounded in the distance. Snow battered against him at the force of the blades. Alex couldn't bring himself to look up as forms jumped from the helicopter.

"Alex!" Jaze shouted.

A dozen footsteps rushed toward him. Jaze knelt at his side. The dean's warm hand brushed Kalia's hair gently from her face.

"Oh no," Jaze whispered.

"It's Kalia," Kaynan said quietly behind Alex.

The footsteps around them stopped. Alex found it hard to breathe.

Something damp hit Alex's hand where it held Kalia's shoulder. The warmth pierced through the numbness that surrounded him. He looked up to see tears running down the dean's cheeks.

"Oh, Kalia," Jaze said. He blinked, but the tears kept falling from his dark brown eyes.

"Let me take her," Kaynan said softly. The red-eyed werewolf knelt beside Jaze. Neither the dean nor Alex moved as Kaynan slipped his hands gently beneath her body and lifted her into his arms.

Alex heard the professor walk slowly across the snow to the helicopter. He stared at the ground beneath his knees, unable to lift his gaze from the flood of red.

"Alex." Jaze's voice was broken, hollow.

Alex looked at the dean.

"I failed her," Jaze said.

Fresh tears welled from Alex's eyes. He shook his head,

trying to force his voice to work. It took two tries for the words to break free. "You didn't fail her," he said. He took a breath, then concluded, "I did."

Jaze shook his head. He tried to speak, then gave up and wrapped his arms around Alex. They knelt there in the snow crying for the loss of Kalia's life, for being unable to save the werewolves who looked to them for safety, for not being strong enough to protect everyone, for breaking their promises to keep her safe.

Alex didn't know how long he cried on the dean's shoulder. When Dray and Vance put their hands beneath his arms to help him to his feet, his legs refused to remember how to walk. The professors looped their hands beneath him and carried him to the helicopter.

Alex couldn't look at the blanket in the middle of the chopper. Kalia's scent surrounded him, honey and clove mixed with the coppery tang of blood. He rested his head against the window, wishing he was back in the snow as a tree or a bush, part of the landscape instead of filled with the ache of losing someone else he held dear.

Fingers touched his arm. Alex turned his head slowly to see Lyra beside him.

"You've been shot," she said, her voice quiet beneath the sound of the helicopter.

Alex closed his eyes and rested his head back against the cool glass of the window. He felt the pull of cloth as his sleeve was cut. The cold sting of antiseptic let him know that the numbness surrounding him was mostly emotional. He welcomed the pain that rushed up his arm as she cleaned the wound, and clung to the ache from the tug of string as Lyra sewed the wound shut.

"We'll go back to the Academy and make preparations," Vance said, his voice a deep bass that helped to steady Alex.

"I'll call her parents after we arrive," Jaze said, his words soft and with a slightly lost tone.

"Brock's hoping we can follow the same flight trail to wherever the General lands," Mouse said quietly from the pilot seat.

The General's name triggered something in Alex's mind. His muscles flexed. His fists clenched. A red-blue haze filled his mind. It was all he could do not to turn and attack the werewolves around him.

"Alex, what's wrong?" Lyra asked gently.

"Alex?" Jaze said. A hand touched his shoulder.

Alex grabbed the dean's wrist with lighting quick reflexes. His other hand pinned Jaze by the throat to the door of the helicopter. He stared at the dean, his heart pounding and the red-blue haze trying to surge through his mind. It was all he could do to push it back, to keep his thoughts clear enough that he could try to think.

"The General," he said, staring at Jaze. "He put something in my head." He spoke through gritted teeth as the impulses increased. "He's trying to make me kill you."

Kaynan and Chet moved toward him, but Jaze lifted a hand, signaling for them to wait. He met Alex's gaze. "Alex, you've got to fight through this."

"I...can't," Alex said. Pain flooded his limbs as he fought the compulsions. His fist tried to tighten around Jaze's throat. His arm shook with the effort to keep that from happening.

"Don't let the General win," Jaze said, his voice steady. "You are stronger than he is."

"I'm not," Alex said. He closed his eyes and a single tear leaked free. "He's taken everything from me."

"Then take it back."

Something about the General's words clicked in Alex's mind. The General had taken his parents, had tortured Siale, and had killed Kalia. The General knew about Cassie, and now that he knew, he would stop at nothing to kill her, of that Alex had no doubt. He needed to take back the power the General had over him. He wasn't afraid, he wasn't weak. He was stronger than the General.

Alex pushed the surge of red-blue fog away. His hands shook as he let Jaze go. "Take me to where they're holding Drogan."

The command carried the same tone as an Alpha. Everyone in the helicopter stared at him. Alex repeated himself. "Take me to where they're holding Drogan."

"You need more medical care than I can—"

Alex shook his head and Lyra stopped speaking.

"The General knows where they're holding his son. He's on his way there," Alex said, his voice tight and deep.

"He's trying to control you," Chet said. "Are you sure going there is a good idea?"

Alex met the professor's gaze with a directness that made Chet blink. "It's the only place I can go."

"Do it," Jaze said, watching Alex.

Mouse called someone on the radio. A few minutes later, they circled northwest.

"Agent Sullivan says he hasn't heard any alerts from D Block," Brock's voice said over the intercom.

"Tell him to quadruple his security. We're a half hour out," Jaze replied.

Alex kept his head against the window, concentrating on the cool chill that permeated his skin. It kept the red-blue haze to the edges of his mind, but he couldn't stop shivering. The impassive part of his brain noted that it was the first time he truly remembered being cold. Holding Kalia in the snow for a complete day and night had shaken something deep in his core. With every hard shudder, his heart skipped a beat.

A blanket settled over his shoulders. "Take deep breaths," Jaze said quietly, taking the seat next to him. "I can hear your heart. You need to find a center of calm."

"I can't," Alex replied tightly. "He's in here." He pointed to his head. "If I relax for a second, he'll control me and I'll kill everyone in this helicopter." He kept his gaze away from the green blanket in the middle of the floor. Any thoughts of Kalia would destroy the last vestiges of his self-control.

The tense silence that followed was broken by Brock's voice. "D Block is under attack."

Jaze asked, "How many?"

"More than the GPA has to defend it. The cameras show Extremists storming from above and below. The General's helicopter is on the roof."

"Land us right next to it," Alex said. His hands were clenched into fists so tight his veins stood out along his arms. He fought to keep the red-blue haze under control. His head throbbed and his nerves burned with the pain of fighting the General's commands.

Black windows reflected the moonlight as they approached a tall building in the middle of a city Alex didn't recognize. Mouse landed the helicopter next to another, smaller one. Its rotors still beat slowly.

Jaze grabbed Alex's shoulder before he could jump out of the helicopter. "We need to stick together. Who knows what the General has in mind?"

Alex felt his control slipping. He stepped away from the helicopter and looked up at the dean. "I've got to go ahead." Sharp pain sliced through his head. He grabbed his skull. The pain increased as though it was splitting in two.

"Alex?" Jaze's voice sounded like it was coming from a thousand miles away.

The red-blue haze intensified with the pain. Alex felt a

fierce desire to grab Jaze and hold him up to the helicopter blades. His muscles bulged, tearing his shirt.

"Give me five minutes before following me down," Alex said, his voice deep and scratchy.

"Alex, it's too dangerous—" Jaze protested, but Alex cut him off.

"Please," Alex begged. "I can't control it any longer."

Jaze looked back at the others with uncertainty. Alex knew the thought of him going on without the dean covering him tore Jaze up inside.

"Let him," Kaynan said quietly.

Jaze let out a breath and nodded. "Five minutes, then we're coming. Be careful."

Alex turned to the passage that led from the roof. The instant he shut the door behind him, he let go of the control he had kept so carefully bottled up inside. He morphed in an instant. The beast flooded through him, pushing away all thoughts other than the fact that the General and Drogan were below. The blue haze filled his vision. Only the edges were tinged with red. The General's command was nothing compared to the fire of rage that fueled his drive.

He stormed down the steps. Bodies of GPA agents littered the first landing. The scent of Extremists carried him down to the next level. He threw the door open to the sight of a dozen Extremists on a wide floor filled with monitors.

The thought that any of them would have carried out the order to kill Kalia fueled Alex's fury. Bullets were fired, but Alex didn't feel their impact as he snapped necks and broke bodies in two. The Extremists who tried to fight back were killed first. Those who ran quickly followed.

Alex sucked in a ragged breath as he studied the monitors. A screen marked Sixth Floor Southeast Camera One showed a door opening. Drogan's mismatched eyes locked on the camera for a brief second before he followed other Extremists down the hall. Alex slammed a fist through the monitor, then headed back to the stairs.

He had just reached the sixth floor when an elevator beeped. Instinct made Alex pause beside the door. It opened and Extremist guards flooded out.

"Agent Sullivan's going to have quite the cleanup party."

The sound of the General's voice flooded through Alex like fire. He grabbed two Extremists still waiting in the elevator and threw them out. Before anyone could move, he had removed the General's gun from its holster and had it pressed against the side of the Extremist leader's head.

Silence filled the corridor. The Extremists outside the elevator stared in shock while the General's ragged breaths filled the small space with the scent of his fear.

"Now, Alex. Let's not be too hasty," the General said with a slight tremor in his voice.

"A little late for being rational," Alex replied in a low growl that reverberated through the small chamber.

"You work for me," the General spoke as if hoping the words would make Alex listen to the commands that flooded his mind.

"I work for no one." Alex's finger tightened on the trigger.

The Extremists looked at each other, at a loss as to what to do.

Drogan rounded the corner. The General's son stopped short at the sight before him.

"Dad? Alex?" His mouth stayed open as though he couldn't process what he was seeing.

Alex glared at the man who had killed his parents. "Step back," he growled.

"Let him go, Alex," Drogan said taking another step

forward.

Alex pressed the gun harder against the General's head. The General winced. "Step back," he repeated in a tone that left no doubt as to what he would do if Drogan didn't comply.

Drogan took a step back. The elevator door began to close. Alex couldn't let the Extremist get away so easily. At the last second, he pulled the gun from the General's head and aimed it toward the last sliver of Drogan's chest he could see.

The General had anticipated the move. He elbowed Alex's arm and the bullet buried into the wall. The door closed completely. The General tried to tear the gun from Alex's grasp. Alex pinned the man's wrist against the wall with his hand that held the gun, and drove his other hand into the General's chest.

General Jared Carso stared at him, shock coloring his face more than pain. Alex felt the warmth of the General's blood as it flowed down his arm. The man's rib bones had splintered around Alex's hand and the Extremist's heart beat beneath his fingers.

"You...are...my...son," the General gasped.

Alex grabbed the heart in his fist. "Never," he growled. He squeezed and the General's eyes widened. The heart gave one last beat of protest, then collapsed. The General fell to the floor. His blood pooled around Alex's feet.

The red haze faded along with the blue. Alex had to force his legs to hold with the exhaustion that flooded through him. A moment later, the elevator beeped, then the door opened on the top floor.

"He's here," Jaze said to the others. The dean's eyes went from Alex to the General lying on the ground. Jaze's face washed pale. Alex leaned against the door before he fell over.

"Come on," Jaze said gently, ducking under Alex's arm.

Alex felt the blood on the bottom of his shoes sticking to the marble floor with each step. He felt more than saw Kaynan and Dray hurry into the elevator.

"He's dead," Dray said behind them.

Alex let Jaze help him into the helicopter. Mouse nodded from the pilot seat but didn't ask questions. Alex sat by the window for a moment. He was keenly aware of Kalia's body beneath the blanket on the floor. Alex let out a slow breath and fell to his knees beside the blanket.

"I made him pay, Kalia," he said quietly. "He won't hurt anyone ever again." His voice caught in his throat. "I promised you I would save you, but I couldn't." A different kind of pain flooded through him. He set his head against where Kalia's forehead was beneath the blanket and closed his eyes. "I'm going to miss you," he said, his voice breaking. "I'm so sorry for everything." Tears he had thought he had cried out dripped down his cheeks to the blanket, soaking it.

A hand touched his back. "It's okay to cry," Mouse said quietly. The professor knelt beside him. "She knows you cared."

Alex shook his head, unable to do more than look at the small werewolf. "I don't think she did."

Mouse set a hand on his shoulder. "I saw you two together. She knew."

Alex closed his eyes against a fresh flood of tears. "I hope so."

Mouse helped him back to his seat and quietly cleaned the blood from Alex's hands. Alex leaned against the window and let the chill of the glass sweep him away in a cloud of oblivion.

"There's too many of them," he heard Jaze say a few minutes later. "Torch the other chopper. We've got to get out of here."

The sound of an incendiary grenade being thrown touched Alex's ears before their helicopter lifted off and the building disappeared beneath him.

Chapter Twenty-five

"They're still searching," Brock said, running to meet them as soon as the helicopter landed in the Wolf Den.

Jaze helped Alex down. "Let me know as soon as you hear anything. We can't let Drogan escape."

"Will do," Brock promised. The human's gaze flicked behind Alex to rest on the blanket in the helicopter. The sorrow in his gaze said he already knew what had happened. As Jaze walked by with Alex, Brock patted his shoulder. "You did everyone a service tonight."

Alex nodded without a word. He followed Jaze into the tunnel and up the path to the medical wing. It was the same path he had traveled his first time down into the Wolf Den's secret passageways. The panel at the top slid open and Meredith and Cassie enveloped him in their arms.

"It's okay," Meredith said quietly as sobs tore from Alex.

Cassie's tears damped his torn shirt. He held them both tight. It took a few minutes for his sobs to lessen. He finally stepped back feeling drained dry of any emotion.

Lyra appeared from the tunnel with Mouse at her side.

"You said the General put something in your head," Mouse said quietly.

By Cassie and his mother's alarmed expressions, Alex realized they only knew the basics of what had happened. He nodded. "He wanted to turn me into one of his hounds. Can you remove it?"

Mouse held up a small device. He waved it across Alex's skull. It beeped near his spine. Lyra led him to a bed and motioned for him to take a seat. She examined the back of his head. "The incision has healed, but it should take only a few minutes if we open it back up."

"Get it out." The thought of the microchip still in his

head made him feel claustrophobic from inside his own skin. The fact that anyone who had access to the General's controls could attempt to command him again made him anxious to be as far away from the microchip as possible.

"We could give you an anesthetic—" Meredith began, but Alex shook his head before she could finish.

"I need it out before they make me attack anyone else. I don't know if I'm strong enough to fight it again after everything. I could kill everyone in this school." The admission made Alex feel heavy as though his limbs weighed a thousand pounds each. He bent forward with his head in his hands. "Please cut it out," he said more gently.

His mom touched his shoulder. "Are you okay like that?"

Alex nodded without speaking.

After a moment of silence, something sharp pierced the back of his neck. He heard Cassie's intake of breath and felt blood trickle down his skin.

"Follow the locator," Mouse said quietly at Alex's side. "That's it."

The pressure increased. Alex clenched his jaw against the pain. Lyra and Meredith were much gentler than the General's physicians had been, but it was still his neck.

"A little deeper," Meredith said.

The pain intensified. Alex wondered how much more he could take in his fatigued state.

"Got it," Lyra called out.

The pressure disappeared. The wound was flushed, then gauze was pressed to Alex's neck. He let out a sigh of relief at the sound of the tiny chip being dropped into a metal bowl.

"They controlled you with that?" Cassie asked, her voice tight as if she didn't want to say the words.

Alex tipped his head to look at her. "They tried," he replied.

Before anyone could move, Cassie dumped the microchip on the floor and stomped on it. The small device shattered beneath the heel of her shoe.

"Not anymore," she snapped, stomping on it again for good measure. "Never again."

Cassie sat next to Alex as their mother finished bandaging his neck.

"We know about Kalia," Cassie finally said softly. "I'm so sorry."

Alex didn't speak. She slipped her hand into his and held it tight. "I heard about the General."

"He knew about you," Alex said. He didn't tell her that Kalia had been the one to reveal the secret he had worked so hard to keep hidden. "He would have come after you."

"He deserved it after all he's done," Cassie replied firmly. "Kalia and Mom and Dad would be proud of you."

"I'm not so sure anymore," Alex replied.

"They would," Meredith repeated. She hugged Alex. "You did what you had to."

Alex couldn't stand to be within the walls of the Academy any longer than he had to. It felt like they were closing in with memories of Kalia walking down the hallway or smiling at him from across the Great Hall. He swore he could smell her scent within the hundreds that mingled in the carpets. He couldn't handle the thought that she was gone.

Alex pretended like he was going to his room to lie down, but as soon as Cassie left him at the door, he went back down the stairs and outside. He collapsed in the snow at the base of Jet's statue.

"I couldn't do it," he told his brother. "I couldn't save her. I promised I would, and I didn't. I let her die."

He shivered as the chill of the night wrapped around his ankles, biting at his exposed skin in a way it never had before.

He shook so hard his teeth chattered.

"I failed her, Jet," he forced out.

He sat there shivering for so long he almost got used to the way his heart skipped a beat every time the harder chills shook his body. He was tempted to stay there until his heart couldn't stand it any longer. Perhaps it would give out, exhausted from the arrhythmia. He could just give up at the base of Jet's statue. He leaned his head against the cold stone.

He was swept back to being an eight year old boy. Jet knelt in front of him and Cassie. Their parents had just been killed by Drogan, and Jet was about to leave them at Two. It was the last time they would ever see their older brother.

"I've got to go help save some werewolves," he said in the direct way Alex always appreciated. Jet saw them as peers instead of children. He had always been completely honest with Alex. "You've got to be strong."

"Don't go," Alex pleaded.

"Don't leave us alone," Cassie cried.

Jet put a hand on each of their shoulders and met their gazes one at a time. "I've got to do this. But you have to promise me something."

"What?" Cassie asked with tears on her cheeks.

"You will never stop fighting," Jet said.

"I'm scared," Cassie replied.

"I promise you that you'll never be alone," Jet said quietly, his dark blue eyes passionate and voice soft. "Whatever you do, don't stop fighting. Never stop fighting."

"We won't," Alex promised. He threw his arms around Jet's neck and hugged him tight. Jet held them both for a few moments, something he did very rarely.

Alex could still feel his brother's arm around him. He rose unsteadily and put a hand on the wolf statue.

"I'll never stop fighting," he whispered.

He lifted his hand and looked at the silver seven that had been emblazoned on the wolf's shoulder. According to Jaze, Jet had been given the tattoo when he was in the fighting rings as a way for betters to keep track of the werewolves who fought. Jet had never given up, even when he was shot and left to die.

"How dare you come back here?"

In Alex's despair, the werewolf had come up on him without warning. The anguish in Torin's voice was so raw it tore Alex apart.

Torin grabbed him by the throat and pinned him against the statue. "You killed her," the Alpha shouted. "You killed her!"

"The General killed her," Alex replied, trying to pull Torin's hands away.

Torin drew Alex close to his face. "You let them take her into the hole and didn't stop them. You could have gone after her. She wouldn't have died."

The despair in his voice was thick and brutal, sawing at Alex's heartache without mercy.

"I tried," Alex said past the knot that tightened in his throat.

"You failed," Torin spat. He threw Alex against the statue.

Alex hit it hard and fell to the ground gasping. His head ached where the microchip had been removed. After morphing and killing so many Extremists, he felt like he had been run over by a train. It was hard to push up to his feet.

"Stay down if you know what's good for you," Torin growled.

"You tell me what's good for me," Alex replied, advancing on the werewolf. "You're supposed to be my Alpha, remember?"

He tried to swing a haymaker at the werewolf's head, but Torin blocked it easily. The Alpha ducked under his arm and pulled him across his broad back. Torin spun around and let go, sending Alex crashing back into the statue.

Alex felt his arm snap at the impact. A cry of pain escaped him when he landed on top of it on the ground. He pushed back to his feet with his good arm.

"Give up," Torin shouted.

"Never," Alex growled, rushing at the Alpha.

This time, Torin slammed a haymaker into Alex's jaw followed by a punch to his arm where it had broken. When Alex's knees gave out, Torin threw him to the ground and landed two more punches to his face.

Alex tried to throw him off, but his broken arm refused to respond. He rolled to the side, but Torin hit his shoulder and then the back of his head. Alex's senses fled. When the Alpha climbed off, Alex lay there stunned for a second.

"Get back here, Torin," he called, pushing up to his knees. He coughed and blood colored the snowy ground.

"Give it a rest, Alex," Torin replied from near the statue; disbelief showed in his voice at the fact that Alex was trying to rise.

"I didn't kill her," Alex said, trying to convince himself as well.

Torin let out a roar of rage and kicked Alex in the side so hard it flung him onto his back. The Alpha brought his foot back for another kick, but Alex caught it and rolled, forcing Torin to the ground. Alex grabbed Torin's other leg and gave a sharp jerk, throwing Torin onto his stomach. He slipped his good arm around Torin's throat and drove a knee into the Alpha's back.

Torin sputtered and struggled, but Alex didn't let up. If he gave the slightest pull backwards, the Alpha's spine would snap.

"Yield," Alex growled into the Alpha ear.

Torin hesitated a moment. Alex pressed his knee harder into the werewolf's back. Torin slapped the ground with a cry of pain. "Alright, I yield."

Alex let him go and collapsed near the statue. His broken arm throbbed. He rested it over his knee as he struggled to breathe despite his damaged ribs.

"You just beat me," Torin said, confusion on his face.

Alex ignored him.

Torin dropped to one knee in the snow so that he was face to face with Alex.

"You are a Gray, but you beat me," Torin repeated, trying to get the impact of the words through to Alex. "You beat an Alpha."

Alex turned a weary gaze onto Torin. "I just killed the General who also happened to be my father. I don't care if I just beat you."

Torin stumbled backward.

"You killed the General? You mean you killed General Carso?"

Alex nodded without looking at the Alpha. He was having a hard time focusing his thoughts, and his head ached much worse after the fight.

Torin let out a few sounds as though he wanted to ask questions, but his feet shuffled as though he also wanted to get as far away from Alex as possible. He chose the latter. Alex listened to the Alpha's footsteps as he climbed the stairs to the Academy and disappeared inside.

Chapter Twenty-six

Alex snuck into Pack Kalia's quarters. He could hear the sounds of werewolves sleeping as he walked down the girls' hall and stopped at the first door. He hesitated with his hand on the doorknob.

She should have been in there asleep like the rest of her pack. She deserved to be lost in blissful dreams, swept away by the soft brush of moonlight through the window, but Alex knew that when he opened the door, the room would be empty.

He took a steeling breath and turned the doorknob. The door swung inward as Kalia's clover and honey scent surrounded him. Alex closed his eyes, pretending for a moment that his dear friend was alive and well, that she would greet him with her smile and tease him about the fact that his hair was getting longer than he usually let it grow. He would tell her she liked it that way, and she would deny it even though the sparkle in her eyes said otherwise.

His heart thumped irregularly, reminding him that he was just fooling himself. Kalia was gone, and nothing he could do would bring her back.

Alex stepped inside the room and crossed to the dresser where he knew it would be. The small pouch sat between a picture of Kalia with Boris and another of a younger Kalia sitting at the feet of her parents playing with a porcelain doll.

He remembered it clearly, her sitting on the steps behind the Academy, the setting sun casting the mountains and trees in a wash of gold. It was near the end of the previous term, and she had asked him to join her there.

"I wanted you to know that I kept this," she said as he took a seat next to her.

When he saw the bullet sitting in the pouch, he was

surprised. "Why?"

She studied the small object. "It's my reminder of when you saved my life. You almost died for me."

"I'd do it again," Alex said honestly.

She smiled, but her expression contained a whisper of sorrow. "I know you would. You're like that."

Her comment stung, but he couldn't say why. "Like what?"

She looked at him directly, her icy blue gaze soft. "You'd sacrifice yourself to save anyone. You're like Jet. You're selfless." She looked away, her gaze on the distance.

Alex was quiet a moment before he replied, "It makes you sad that you're not the only one I'd do it for."

She nodded without looking at him. "Does that make me selfish?"

Alex shook his head. "I think we all need someone sometime."

"I can be your someone," she offered with a hint of hope.

Alex shook his head. He didn't want to crush her, but he had to be honest.

"Fine," she said. She took the pouch from his hand. "But you were my someone. I'll remember that."

Alex slipped the pouch in his pocket and hurried out, careful to shut the door behind him to preserve what remained of her scent in the room.

Alex crossed to the next hall and used his nose to find Trent's room. He opened the door soundlessly. Trent lay asleep on the bed, his pillow thrown to one side and blankets rustled as though his sleep had been restless. Alex wondered if Trent suffered nightmares from their experiences together.

He touched Trent on the shoulder. The werewolf jolted awake. He stared up at Alex, his eyes wide.

"W-what's going on?"

"I need a ride," Alex told him.

Trent sat up. "Where are you going?"

"I need to get the motorcycle I left at the park."

Trent shook his head quickly. "The Extremists might be watching it. After what you did, Drogan's going to be out for blood."

Alex's hands curled into fists without him realizing it. "I'm out for blood, too." He moved to the left and the early dawn light fell across his face.

"Alex, what happened?" Trent asked, climbing off his bed. He ran a hand across his buzzed hair as he surveyed Alex's condition. "You look like you tangled with a bear."

"I did," Alex replied. He shoved his hands in his pockets. The pressure to his broken arm made him wince. Though he had stayed by the statue for an hour or so hoping to give his body a chance to heal, it appeared he had put it through too much to expect miracles at the moment.

"Is your arm broken?" Trent asked.

"Would I be asking to ride a motorcycle with a broken arm?" Alex replied, hoping a rhetorical question would throw the werewolf off.

Trent's eyes narrowed. "Yes."

Alex let out a breath. "It's healing."

Trent met his gaze squarely. "Alex, if you don't tell me what's going on, I'm not taking you anywhere, and you're in no shape to drive a motorcycle on your own."

Alex knew Trent's stubborn streak. He had no choice. He leaned against the bed and crossed his arms, resting his healing right one on top of his left. The bruises that ran from the middle of his arm in both directions were dark and angry and it was swollen so badly he couldn't turn his wrist. Riding a motorcycle would be impossible until it healed more.

He gave in. "Torin called me out. He said I killed Kalia."

He studied the floor near the window. A white, fuzzy speck on the carpet held his attention. "We got into a fight."

"That Alpha should be demoted to toilet duty for the rest of the term," Trent muttered. "You were injected with silver a few hours ago, and wiped out pretty much the General's entire army as well as the General. He fights on a coward's terms, attacking when you're weak after something like that."

"I beat him."

Trent stared at Alex. His mouth opened, then closed again. After a moment, he said, "You beat an Alpha?"

Alex nodded. "I was angry. I...I was lost about Kalia. I needed an outlet."

"Did you go rage mode on him?"

Alex thought for a moment, then shook his head, a bit surprised himself. "No. I didn't have to."

Trent leaned against the bed next to Alex and folded his arms as well. "You know what that means, don't you?" he said, glancing at his friend.

"I'm not sure," Alex replied. "I haven't really thought about it."

Trent hesitated, then shook his head as well. "Me, neither. If you were an Alpha, you'd have Torin's pack. I'm not sure how that applies to a Gray. We might have to talk to Jaze."

"Leave it."

"But if you won..."

Alex met Trent's green eyes. "I'm not exactly fit to run a pack."

"Your arm will heal..."

Alex raised his eyebrows meaningfully. "It's not the physical part I'm worried about." He gave his friend a small smile. "It's alright, Trent. I have things I need to do, and this is important. Can you give me to a ride to my motorcycle before anyone's up? I don't think I can handle more questions right now." He rubbed his aching arm. "Torin's interrogation was a bit more than I was ready for."

Trent rose without a word and grabbed a shirt. He followed Alex into Pack Kalia's main room. Alex realized that the pack no longer had an Alpha. He ducked into the hidden passage Trent opened and fought back the urge to hit something.

"This whole place is falling apart," he said quietly.

Trent glanced back at him. "We'll put it back together. We always have."

Alex put his good hand on Trent's shoulder. The scrawny werewolf paused.

"How can you stay so positive?" Alex asked. The thought of Kalia gone was like a hole through his heart. Each beat reminded him that hers no longer did. It was eating him up inside, and it was only the first day after her death. He didn't know how he was going to manage any more without going crazy.

Trent's eyebrows pulled together. He was quiet for a moment, then he said, "Because you need me to."

For some reason, the werewolf's answer made Alex feel a bit better. "So you're feeling lost, too?"

Trent nodded. "Kalia's gone. My best friend is being torn apart with guilt, and Drogan's still out there somewhere ready to take revenge for his father. If I don't pretend to be positive, I might just tear down this place myself."

"Brick by brick?" Alex guessed.

"Brick by brick," Trent replied with a half-smile.

Alex followed Trent through the Wolf Den to the secondary vehicle storage room.

"I have a spare bike," Trent admitted. "It's nothing compared to yours, but I figured it wouldn't hurt to have a backup."

He crossed to the corner and pulled the tarp off of a vehicle nestled between a partially built helicopter and what looked like the parts to a riding lawn mower. The motorcycle he revealed was green and black. It was obvious by the quality of the work that Trent had spent a lot of time on it.

"It's beautiful," Alex said.

Trent gave a proud smile as he shifted it to neutral and pushed it to the middle of the room. "Sometimes the hero needs a sidekick."

Alex laughed, then was flooded with guilt at the emotion. "Kalia's dead," he said bitterly. "And I'm laughing."

Trent put a hand on Alex's shoulder. It was hard for Alex to meet the werewolf's eyes. "Laughter is another outlet. Don't beat yourself up. Would Kalia want you to mope away the rest of your days?" He paused, then said, "Short as they may be?"

Alex thought about Kalia, the way she had started to smile when he befriended her. By the end, before Siale, just a look from him would make her laugh, her blue eyes light and pure joy on her face. She had been happy.

Alex admitted the truth. "She used to get on my case whenever I was down."

Trent nodded. "I figured as much. Remember that."

He handed Alex a helmet and climbed onto the motorcycle.

Alex shoved the helmet on his head with his good hand, then swung his leg over the back of the bike. "If anyone sees us, we'll never live it down."

Trent chuckled. "Don't worry. We'll take the back way out."

When they reached the main road, Alex closed his eyes and listened to the hum of the tires. It was one of his favorite sounds. He leaned against the back rest and let the resonance chase away his thoughts, fears, and aches. For the length of the ride, he just existed.

The sun bathed their shoulders when Trent reached the city of Greyton. Alex opened his eyes to see the skyscrapers towering overhead. Trent drove them through traffic and took the side roads to the small park. Alex felt a rush of relief at the sight of the motorcycle still parked where he had left it.

"Thank you," he said, climbing off.

"How's the arm?" Trent asked.

Alex turned his wrist experimentally. The swelling had gone down and the bruises had lessened quite a bit. "Definitely better than it was. I'll be fine to drive."

Trent nodded. "Good. You can lead the way."

Alex took off his borrowed helmet and strapped it to the back seat of Trent's motorcycle. "I'm not heading straight home."

Trent sighed. "I was afraid you'd say that."

Alex smiled. "You know me pretty well."

"Unfortunately," Trent replied. He pulled something out of his pocket. "At least put these back."

The small tracking microchip and the headset Alex had left in the tree sat on the werewolf's palm. Alex held out his hand.

"Really?" Trent said as though surprised Alex had given in.

Alex nodded. "I owe you for all you've done, and I trust you. Just give me the time I need."

"I will," Trent promised. He hesitated, then pulled something else out of his pocket. It was a stack of bills folded together.

"What's this for?" Alex asked.

Trent gave a small smile. "For a rainy day. I figured you could use it."

Alex watched the werewolf pull away. When Trent was out of sight, Alex crossed to the motorcycle and slipped the headset back into the helmet. He studied the microchip in his hand. As much as he hated being tracked, Trent had been there for him. He used the key to open the gas cap and stuck the microchip back beneath it.

A glance at the clock on the motorcycle's dashboard showed that school would be out soon. Alex started the motorcycle and drove down the road.

Chapter Twenty-seven

"What brings you here?" Cherish asked with a warm smile at the sight of Alex leaning against his motorcycle across the street from her apartment complex.

Alex shoved his hands in his pockets self-consciously. The pressure made his arm twinge and he removed his hands again. "I was, uh, wondering if you know where Josh is."

"Sure," Cherish replied. "He works at the gas station a few blocks away. We can walk there."

"I could take you on my bike," Alex offered.

Cherish kicked at a pile of dirty snow. "I like to walk."

Alex fell in beside her as she cut down an alley. He tried to enjoy the crunch of the snow beneath his feet and scent of wet asphalt mixed with the alive smell of hundreds of people, but he couldn't feel anything other than hollow.

A few minutes later, Cherish broke the silence. "Are you going to tell me why you look like someone just killed your puppy?"

Alex glanced at her. The girl's all-to-perceptive gaze searched his grim expression. He turned his face away from her. "I lost someone I care about."

Cherish's smile fell away. She was quiet for a few minutes longer, then glanced at him. "I'm sorry."

Alex nodded. "Me, too."

"Tell me about her," Cherish prompted.

The sound of people talking on the next street filled Alex's ears as he thought. There were too many memories to go through, too much to process. It made his chest ache.

"Alex, I'm sorry. I shouldn't ask—"

Alex shook his head and she fell silent. He cleared his throat. "Kalia, well, she wasn't easy to get along with at first."

Cherish smiled, asking for more.

"She hated everything about the Academy," Alex told her. "She couldn't phase, so she didn't fit in. If anyone even looked at her, well, it's a good thing looks can't kill because I think every student and professor at the Academy would be dead." He blinked back tears and forced himself to keep talking.

"But she trusted me. I don't know why or how I won her trust, but she started to smile more, and it seemed like she didn't mind the Academy so much. After a while, I started to fall for her."

Cherish glanced at him, but kept silent, her green eyes searching his face as he spoke.

"I thought she might be the one," Alex admitted.

"That's a big deal," Cherish said softly.

Alex nodded. "Especially for werewolves. I just couldn't quite get past the feeling that I was missing something. I cared about her a great deal, but it wasn't how they described it to be."

"That's when you met the girl," Cherish guessed.

Alex wanted to smile. He wanted to let her know much Siale meant to him, but even the action felt unfamiliar. He nodded without a word. The sound of the snow beneath his shoes filled his ears. He finally sighed. "She didn't understand." He stopped walking. Something about the words broke the dam inside of him. The tears started again. "She didn't understand why I didn't love her the way she loved me."

"Oh, Alex," Cherish said. She put her arms around him and held him.

"She kept asking why I didn't feel it the way she did," Alex said, his tears falling in Cherish's black hair.

It took him a minute to collect himself. He finally wiped his eyes and stepped back. "I was just so confused. I love

Siale." The words filled him with warmth and calmed his emotions. They continued their walk down the alley. "And I just wanted Kalia to find someone who was right for her. I was just afraid..."

"That she was too hung up on you to give anyone else a chance?" Cherish finished gently.

Alex nodded. He realized they had reached the gas station. "But I think I went about it the wrong way."

Cherish stopped him before he could reach for the door. "Alex, I trust you, and do you know why?"

Alex shook his head, confused by her line of thought.

Cherish gave him a small smile. "Because even before I knew you were a werewolf, I felt like I saw you, who you are, what you stand for, all of you. You don't hide yourself like so many people do. You don't protect your weaknesses behind a wall of false bravado. You are just you."

"Maybe I need to try harder," Alex said quietly.

Cherish shook her head. "Don't change." She put a hand on his arm. "The reason I tell you that is because Kalia knew how you felt. She knew you were her friend. I can't blame her for wanting something more, but I'm guessing deep down she was just happy you were there for her."

She pulled open the door and went inside. Alex stood on the curb for a few minutes letting her words sink in. He hoped Cherish was right. He hoped with all of his heart.

When he went through the glass door, Josh and Cherish were coming back to meet him. Josh was wearing a black shirt with the gas station's logo in red across the front. His curly brown hair looked somewhat combed. He smiled and held out a hand.

"Hey, man. Cherish said you're looking for me."

"Yeah." Alex shook his hand, feeling suddenly self-conscious. "I have a question for you."

"Shoot," Josh offered.

"How's your tattoo healing up?"

Surprised by the random question, Josh pulled up his sleeve to reveal the firefighter shield. The red was gone and the line work had healed well.

"Faster than I thought it would," Josh replied. "Why?"

"Can you get me in touch with whoever did it?"

Josh glanced at Cherish. She lifted her shoulders in a small shrug.

"Uh, sure," Josh said. "I have the short shift today. I get off in ten minutes. Can you hang around?"

Alex nodded. He followed Cherish to the front of the store. He appreciated the fact that she didn't ask any more questions. Instead, she distracted him with telling him about school and how someone pulled the fire alarm. Apparently it was an occurrence that happened at least twice a week. The principal was trying to crack down on who the culprit was.

A half hour later found Alex at the tattoo parlor where Josh had gotten his tattoo done.

The tattoo artist came around the corner, and Alex couldn't help but stare.

"Hi, I'm Anders," the artist said, holding out his hand while giving Alex a hard look.

"Uh, hi," Alex replied, shaking the hand as the scent of werewolf surrounded him. "I'm Alex."

"You're here to get a tattoo?" Anders asked.

Alex shook himself, chasing his surprise away. "Yes, and I have a special request."

A few minutes later, he was sitting in the chair with his sleeve rolled up.

"Are you sure about this?" Anders asked skeptically.

Alex nodded. He watched the artist withdraw the silver bullet from the pouch he had taken from Kalia's dresser. The werewolf wore medical gloves to keep from touching the silver.

"Silver for a werewolf?" Alex heard Josh whisper to Cherish. "That doesn't seem like a good idea."

"He knows what he's doing," Cherish whispered back.

"I hope so," Jen said. A glance showed the girl holding onto Josh's arm, her bright red hair held back by a cream-colored sash.

Josh had told Alex that Jen usually met him after work so they could be together. She hadn't minded joining them at the tattoo parlor. Tanner and Sarah were also on their way over.

Alex watched Anders open the bullet with a pair of pliers. The scent of the liquid silver inside stung his nose. Anders glanced at him. Alex kept his face calm. Anders carefully poured the silver into a small container that held the silver ink. Alex was glad enough silver had stayed in the bullet to do the job. He settled back in the chair. A few minutes later, the prick of a needle laced his skin.

The silver burned. He knew it would hurt, but the feeling was different, dull, steady, as though he stood too close to a fire and his skin was blistering. He closed his eyes, letting thoughts of Kalia and Jet blur together until the pain of losing each of them became one substantial burn like the tattoo being laced into his skin.

When tattoo artist finished the silver seven, Anders moved his chair around and laid a thin sheet of paper across Alex's other shoulder. He pulled it away, and Alex looked down at the ink on his arm.

It was a wolf crafted in a tribal style with swirling dark lines and its head up, staring at whoever looked at it.

"Black lines and light blue eyes, right?" Anders checked.

Alex nodded.

"Whoa, that's awesome," Tanner said as he and Sarah

walked into the parlor.

Alex returned the boy's smile. "Good to see you again."

"You, too," Tanner replied. "How'd you get your parents to approve?"

"I, uh," Alex looked at Cherish.

"His mother signed the permission slip. No big deal," she said with a quick glance at Anders. The artist appeared to not be listening as he prepared his tools.

"Geesh," Josh said. "I had to argue with my mom for a year to let me get this one. She said she'd kill me if I got another."

"My mom's pretty awesome," Alex replied. He fought back a wry smile at the thought of Cherish signing in the place of Meredith. He hadn't really imagined what his mom would say when he got home.

The thought of returning to the Academy made his stomach twist. Going back to the walls that would remind him of Kalia filled him with nausea, but he had promised Trent. After all the werewolf had done, he couldn't go back on his word.

Alex pulled the folded bills Trent had given him out of his pockets.

"I won't accept your money," Anders said.

Alex's chest tightened in alarm. He wondered if the artist was in league with the Extremists, or if he hated his race and would turn Alex in. Jaze had told him of werewolves selling others out to protect their families.

Alex didn't want his human friends caught in the crossfire. He glanced to where they waited in chairs near the front of the parlor. He lowered his voice. "Why not?"

Anders studied Alex. "Because I heard someone took down the General, and the description they gave made that boy sound a lot like you."

Alex's first instinct was to deny it. The memories didn't even feel real to him. He thought of shoving his hand through the General's chest, of the sticky blood that coated his shoes. He swallowed and nodded.

Anders met his gaze. "You come back here any time you want a tattoo. It'll be free of charge along with anything else you need. We all owe you. That man took so many of our loved ones from us." His eyes glittered darkly. "He deserved to pay for the death of my son."

"I'm sorry you lost him," Alex said quietly.

Anders nodded. "At least I can tell my wife that our son's murderer is dead."

Alex didn't know what to say. After a few moments of silence passed, he went with, "It happened yesterday. How did you hear so quickly?"

Anders smiled. "There's a lot more of us out here than you might think. Word travels quickly, especially when it's good news. Tell Jaze he has our gratitude for all he's done."

"I will," Alex promised.

His arms stung, but he could tell that the wolf tattoo was already healing as he walked with his human friends back to Cherish's house.

"Are you sure you don't want to come inside?" Cherish asked. "My mom said it's pizza night."

"Pizza night!" Josh repeated. He high-fived Tanner. "You need to stay for pizza night," Josh told him. "Mrs. Summers makes them from scratch. They're amazing."

As much as he wanted to stay away from the Academy, Alex replied, "I'd better get going. I don't want anyone to start worrying."

Cherish hugged him carefully. "You're going to be okay," she said, stepping back.

The others looked from Alex to Cherish. "Is something

wrong?"

Cherish gave him a questioning look. Alex replied with a small shrug.

Cherish turned to her friends. "Someone Alex cares about very much was killed yesterday by Extremists."

Sarah's hand flew to her mouth. "Oh my gosh. I'm so sorry!"

"That's horrible," Jen said. She gave him a tight hug that pinned both of his arms. "Are you okay?"

"Jen, seriously," Josh said, pulling her back. "He just got tattooed."

"It's okay," Alex said. "I appreciate it."

"Hang in there," Josh told him seriously. "You can get through this. When I lost my dad, I thought my whole world had fallen apart. It takes a while to find your place in things again."

"Yeah, don't give up," Tanner told him. "We're here for you."

"Thank you," Alex said, touched.

They waited outside Cherish's apartment as he climbed onto his motorcycle. It felt good to know that he had friends at his back as his drove through the evening toward the Academy.

Trent's voice came over the headset. "Testing, testing."

"It's working," Alex replied.

"I just wanted to make sure it wasn't malfunctioning," Trent replied wryly. "The tracking chip says you're heading home."

Alex stifled a smile. "Yeah, well, you can't trust everything you see."

Trent chuckled. "I'll remember that."

Alex drove through the open gates to the main entrance of Trent's workshop. He pulled off his helmet just as Jaze walked into the room.

"I was hoping to find you here," the dean said.

There was something in Jaze's gaze that caught Alex's attention. "What's wrong?"

Jaze let out a sigh and leaned against the door frame. "The GPA is requesting to debrief you. I've asked them to put it off, but they're refusing. They need to know how the General died, and they said too many humans were killed that need to be accounted for."

"But they were Extremists!" Trent protested.

Jaze nodded. "They know the situation, but they have to follow procedures." He met Alex's gaze. "We have no choice on this one."

Alex nodded. "When do they want to talk?"

"Tomorrow morning. We'll take the helicopter to C Block."

"They get credit for coming up with creative names for their buildings," Trent muttered after the dean left.

Alex nodded, but couldn't find anything to say. The thought of meeting with the Global Protection Agency filled him with trepidation. He didn't want to remember what had happened. He wanted to push the memories far away where he would never have to think about them again.

Chapter Twenty-eight

Alex studied the generals of the Global Protection Agency. Seven of them sat on one side of the curved table. Two dozen other agents occupied the seats behind Alex. Jaze, the only other werewolf, sat next to Agent Sullivan near the door. The Agent had given Alex a firm handshake and expressed his condolences when they arrived. Now he sat silently watching the proceedings.

"You said you went into a rage when you heard the gunshots?" a General with short gray hair and a southern accent asked.

Alex nodded. "It must have forced the silver through my system. I could move again, so I did."

"Meaning that you killed ninety-six armed human guards with your bare hands," a woman with an Irish accent replied.

Alex nodded.

Whispers erupted through the room. He could hear the agents behind him talking, but kept his attention on the generals.

"How did you know General Carso was on his way to free his son?" the first general asked.

"He said so before he gave the orders for Kalia's death," Alex replied. He held himself rigid, trying to remain apart from the memories that attempted to storm his mind. He felt exhausted even though the questioning had only started.

"When you landed, you told Jaze to wait while you went below," a man with a thick German accent said, reading from the paper in front of him.

"I asked him," Alex replied.

The man looked up at him. "What was that?"

"I asked him to wait. I didn't tell him." Alex gave an attempt at humor. "You don't tell an Alpha what to do."

The man's eyes narrowed slightly. He turned his attention back to the paper as though Alex hadn't spoken.

"You killed several guards," the man continued.

"Thirteen," the Irish woman noted.

"Then you checked the monitors and found the floor Drogan was on." The man speared him with a look. "The elevator just happened to open when you were walking past."

"Lucky timing, I guess," Alex said dryly.

The man pointed his fountain pen at Alex. "I don't appreciate your tone, young man."

"General Schmidt, Alex is a hero," a woman with long gray hair cut in. "He did this world a huge favor when he killed General Carso."

"All the same," General Schmidt replied, "He can have some respect." The General turned to look at Jaze. "What are teaching these kids at your Academy?"

Jaze rose slowly. The steel in his gaze quieted everyone in the room. When he spoke, his tone reverberated through the air.

"Alex single-handedly accomplished what nobody else in this room has been able to do for the last ten years." Jaze looked like he was struggling to stay calm. It was something Alex had never seen from the dean. "I agreed to this debriefing because of my respect for your organization and our relationship; however, I feel that you have failed to take into account the fact that Alex lost his good friend because of the General. He is seventeen. He needs the time to mourn instead of repeating everything in the report I gave you." Jaze took a calming breath. "If you have questions you need answers for that aren't included in the report, please ask. Otherwise, I'm taking Alex home."

The generals were silent for a few minutes.

General Schmidt finally cleared his throat. "My

apologizes, Dean Carso. I might have overstepped without considering the delicacy of this situation. Give us a minute to collaborate. We'll reconvene and let you know if we have any further questions before you depart."

"Thank you," Jaze replied. He tipped his head at Alex. "Let's wait outside."

Alex leaned against the hallway wall as soon as they were out of the room.

"How are you holding up?" the dean asked.

Alex shook his head. "Not as good as I thought I would." He fell quiet, then said, "They're afraid of me."

Jaze nodded. "Hearing that a single werewolf can kill a hundred humans is a little intimidating."

"Is there a reason you didn't mention the whole rage mode thing?"

"Rage mode?" Jaze asked with a hint of a smile.

Alex gave a small smile back. "Yeah. That's what Trent calls it. Dray referred to it as morphing."

Jaze nodded. "I don't want them afraid of something else. We owe the GPA a great deal. If we can come out of this without damaging our relationship with them, I'll consider it a win. Letting them know about a new ability in one of our students might concern them that werewolves are getting too strong for their trust. We'll keep it to ourselves for now."

Alex slid down the wall so he could sit on the floor. He squeezed his closed eyes with one hand. "Why are they acting so strange about the General's death. I thought they'd be happy."

"They are," Jaze replied. "They're just afraid of what's next." At Alex's questioning look, the dean continued, "Whenever someone in such a powerful position is killed, there's a struggle for who will take his place. I feel like Drogan will step into the position, but we can't know for sure."

"Better the devil you know than the devil you don't," Alex said.

Jaze chuckled. "Has Professor Thorson been quoting Irish proverbs again?"

Alex nodded. "I think he was referring to Torin."

"Probably," Jaze agreed. He sat down next to Alex. After a moment, the dean lifted up Alex's sleeve to reveal the tattooed seven. "I knew I smelled silver and fresh ink last night. Where did you get it done?"

"Greyton," Alex replied, uncertain what the dean's reaction would be.

"And the silver?"

Alex lowered his gaze. "From the bullet Kalia and Siale took out of my arm."

He saw Jaze nod out of the corner of his eye. "The artist has a steady hand. It looks just like Jet's."

Relieved that he wasn't getting scolded, Alex turned and lifted his other sleeve. "This one is for Kalia."

Jaze studied it for a moment in silence. When he sat back, the sorrow in his gaze was clear. "You matched her eyes perfectly."

Alex nodded, pulling his sleeve back down. "I made them mix it until it was just right. Luckily, Anders was pretty patient." He glanced at Jaze. "He's a werewolf."

Jaze smiled. "I thought the name was familiar. You might find that you have a few friends out there after defeating the General."

Alex thought of Anders' words when he tried to pay for the tattoo. "He needed to be stopped."

Jaze tipped his head against the wall with his eyes closed. Alex kept silent, giving the dean his space. When Jaze finally spoke, his words were raw. "I never wanted any of you to get hurt."

"You can't protect everyone."

Jaze ran a hand across his forehead, pushing his blond hair out of his eyes. "My mom told me that once." He tipped his head to look at Alex. "She was right, and it broke me inside to realize it. The same goes for you, Alex. Kalia's death wasn't your fault."

"I should have broken free before they took her," Alex replied. His eyes stung, but he refused to let the tears fall.

Jaze shook his head. "You may learn to control morphing later, but for now, it sounds like the gunshot was what triggered you to do so. We might be mourning for you as well if that hadn't happened."

"Better me than her."

Jaze set a hand on Alex's shoulder. The dean's grip was firm and steadying. "There are many times I have asked myself why I lived when others around me were killed." His gaze was steady as he looked at Alex. "There are times like when your brother died that I felt as though the wrong person lay beneath the earth." Steel showed in his brown gaze. "But I'm here, and because of that, I live for those who didn't survive. Do that for her, Alex. Don't let this destroy you, because in living you can pay tribute to the things she died for."

Alex thought of her body lying in the snow. His throat tightened so that he could barely say, "What did she die for?"

Jaze's voice was firm when he replied, "Her death led you to the General and you killed him. You saved so many lives with that one act. Think of the werewolves we've found who were tortured and killed under the General's hand. Think of Siale, think of the hundreds you've helped me free. The General was behind them. Kalia's death enabled you to stop him."

Alex couldn't accept the note of respect in the dean's voice. He felt like he didn't deserve it. "If I could take back his death so that she would live, I would," he admitted, feeling like he was betraying his very race by saying it.

Instead of loathing, Jaze's expression was filled with understanding. "If saving my mother or Jet meant that Commander Rogart, my uncle Mason, or any of the others were alive, too, I would do it in a heartbeat. You can't deny your instincts. We hold those we love close to us because they complete what we are. A wolf without a pack is like the sky without the sun, dark and meaningless. Even the moon doesn't shine without the sun's light. Our loved ones give us meaning and purpose. We fight because we love them. Don't beat yourself up because you would do anything in your power to have them back."

"What do we do?" Alex asked quietly.

Jaze's answer was firm. "Our job now is to make sure someone worse doesn't take the General's place."

"We won't let that happen," Alex vowed.

Jaze squeezed his shoulder before he rose. Alex caught the sound of footsteps and stood as well.

"We are ready for you," the blonde Irish woman said with a warm smile.

Alex followed Jaze back into the room. Instead of sitting in his chair by Agent Sullivan, the dean crossed the room at Alex's side and stood next to him in front of the board of generals.

"I apologize for my questioning," General Schmidt said.

Alex was amazed to hear that the general's words were sincere.

"At times like these, it's hard not to get a bit overly concerned when the nation is at risk."

"We understand," Jaze said, inclining his head with

respect. "Thank you for your apology."

The general nodded in return. "That being said," he continued. "We have one last question for Alex."

Alex waited on pins and needles. He hoped they didn't ask how he had managed to kill so many men. He wasn't sure how to hide the secret of his morphing from the expectant crowd.

The question came from the last general at the table. He was a slender man with thin white hair and blue-rimmed glasses. "Alex, I am General Baird from Great Britain."

"Pleased to meet you, General," Alex replied politely.

The general continued, "Alex, you have done so much for your nation, much more than one boy your age should have to do. Yet our countries are built on the shoulders of courageous men and women very similar to you. We have survived wars the likes of which no one should hope to see again. But if that day comes..." He leaned forward, his spectacled gaze locked on Alex's. "If that day comes, will you answer our call?"

The significance of General Baird's question ran through Alex. He thought of the things he had seen, of the bodies of slain werewolves he had helped to recover, of those who had been tortured and mutilated. "I will do anything in my power to keep our nations safe," he replied.

General Baird stood and held out a hand. Alex crossed the room and shook it. The Irish woman next to him reached out a hand as well. Alex shook each of them in turn until he made it to General Schmidt.

"We're lucky to have you," the general said.

The GPA had been at the werewolves' side through all of the recovery efforts Alex had been a part of. He knew the teamwork it took to manage a pack; he couldn't imagine everything the generals dealt with on a daily basis. "We're lucky to have you, General," he replied quietly. He met the gazes of the other people behind the table. "All of you. Thank you."

The GPA guards that lined the hallways and doors of the building saluted the two werewolves. To Alex, it was a bit overwhelming, but Jaze nodded at each of them in turn, thanking them with his simple gesture. The Black Team fell in around Alex and Jaze as soon as they reached the outside doors. The team protected them as they made their way to the jet waiting on the private tarmac behind C Block.

Alex leaned his forehead against the window as Mouse prepared the jet for takeoff. A shiver ran down his spine at the cold that washed over his skin.

"You okay?" Jaze asked.

Alex nodded. "Just a chill."

He looked up in time to see the concern on the dean's face. "Werewolves don't normally get chills."

"I can't seem to shake the since Kalia..." His voice died away at the thought of holding her in the snow. He turned back to the window.

A moment later, a blanket settled around his shoulders. "You've been strong," Jaze said. "Try to get some sleep. I know this has taken a lot out of you."

Alex closed his eyes.

Chapter Twenty-nine

When the jet touched down, the Academy's SUV was waiting. As soon as Alex appeared, the vehicle door flew open.

The sight of Siale nearly undid him completely. Alex climbed down the steps on legs that felt like they were made of jelly. He took two steps, then she was in his arms, holding him with tears streaming down her cheeks.

"Oh, Alex, I'm so sorry," she said. She hugged him tight. "I'm so, so sorry about Kalia. It's too much."

Alex held her, the smell of her sage and lavender scent surrounding him, clearing his thoughts and chasing away some of the tightness in his chest.

When Jaze walked past them, Alex met the dean's gaze. "Thank you," he mouthed.

Jaze nodded with a smile.

Before, Alex hadn't known how he was going to face the Academy without Kalia. With Siale's fingers linked in his, he was able to cross to the SUV without feeling like every step closer to the school meant accepting the fact that Kalia was gone. At least with Siale at his side, he felt like he didn't have to hold up completely by himself. If he fell apart, she would be there to pick up the pieces, and she would never judge him, because she knew his darkest flaws and loved him anyway.

They climbed inside the SUV and took the back seat. Alex was surprised to find Trent driving.

"I told them I needed my license," Trent explained. "They said I needed the practice, so here I am."

"I'm not sure logging hours chauffeuring people is legal," Alex said, grateful for the werewolf's presence.

"Another minor detail I convinced them to overlook,"

Trent answered.

Kaynan shook his head from the passenger seat. "It's a good thing your friend isn't going into politics, or we'd all be in trouble."

Trent chuckled. "Don't worry, Professor. If politics were like engines and could be tweaked to run better, I'd love it. As it is, though, free will just poses too much interference."

"Who let the kid behind the wheel?" Mouse asked as he climbed into the middle seat with Jaze. "Haven't you seen him fly a helicopter?"

"Another license I'm working on," Trent said, winking at Alex and Siale in the rearview mirror.

Siale smiled and slipped her hand into Alex's. "You have good friends," she whispered.

Alex nodded. "The best." He stared out the window at the setting sun. Red and gold reflected off the snow, filling it with a million diamonds of light.

Jaze's voice broke through the silence. "Mr. Dickson wants to fly you to his estate for the funeral, Alex. He said Siale is welcome to come as well."

Alex let out a slow breath. "Are any of the other students coming?"

"Her brother Boris, of course, and Torin is insisting that he be there. Cassie and Tennison will join you along with the other members of Pack Kalia."

"Me, too," Trent said. "And Terith. She'd be furious if you left her out."

"Anyone who would like to go is welcome," Jaze replied.

"You don't want to mess with an angry Terith," Trent muttered, staring out the window. "Nobody wants to deal with that."

"I'm so glad you're here," Alex said quietly to Siale. "I don't think I could do it without you."

Siale leaned up and kissed him on the cheek. Alex put his arm around her and held her close through the drive home. When they reached the winding road through the forest, Alex's heart began to skip beats. He tried to breath slowly to force it to calm, but it worsened as they neared the gates. Alex could see werewolves waiting for them inside the Academy. Boris' thick shoulders and Torin's hulking forms were hard to miss.

"Alex, are you alright?" Siale asked.

Alex shook his head.

She put a hand on his chest. "Alex, you need to calm down."

"I can't control it," he said, trying to breathe as each stutter stole the breath from his lungs.

Trent stopped the vehicle.

Jaze turned to look at him. "What's going on?"

"His heart keeps stuttering. He can't stop it."

"I can't go in there," Alex said. Panic filled him at the thought of being within the walls. "I can't face them."

"You don't have to," the dean said. "We can go back to Haroldsburg and—"

Alex opened the door and climbed out.

"Alex!" Trent called.

He tore off his clothes behind a tree and phased. A moment later, Siale was at his side in wolf form. She nudged his shoulder, her gray eyes filled with understanding.

"Go ahead," Alex heard Jaze say to Trent. "He needs some time."

The vehicle door was pulled shut and the SUV continued through the gates.

Alex watched the black iron bars close slowly. Something about the way they locked him out calmed his ragged heartbeat.

He took off across the snow, grateful for the way his wide wolven feet allowed him to run on top of the drifts without sinking in. Siale loped at his side, her lithe, graceful form a gray shadow that leaped logs and bushes with ease.

They took a long loop around the Academy, reaching the forest that Alex knew better than the house he had been raised in. He pushed himself harder and harder, willing his heartbeat to return to normal as he stretched out his legs and covered the ground in a mile-eating run.

When Alex reached the top of the cliff that overlooked the lake, he was half-tempted to jump off. The water below was covered in a layer of ice. The fall would be painful at the very least. He longed for pain, physical pain, that would chase away the ache in his chest.

Siale touched her nose to his shoulder. When he looked at her, the softness of her gaze stole through his chaotic thoughts. Her touch calmed him as no words ever could. He rested his chin on her back and closed his eyes, finding the peace in the center of the whirlwind inside him.

Siale was the first to lift her muzzle to the moon. The notes of her mournful howl filled the hole in Alex's heart, giving him the strength to release his pain.

Alex lifted his muzzle. His howl mingled with hers, the notes interweaving and blanketing the night in a soulful, heartbreaking song of sorrow for Kalia's death. After a few moments, other voices lifted. First, Rafe and Colleen's howls rose from the forest near their cave, and with them, the calls of the pack Alex had fought to save from the General's hounds. Shortly after, voices began to rise from the school as werewolves phased into their wolf forms. Alex could see them massing behind the school, the clouds their breath formed in the cold night billowing over the growing crowd.

Deeper voices joined them as the professors phased as

well. Alex could hear Jaze and Nikki along with Kaynan, Grace, and Vance. Mouse and Lyra lifted their voices, mingling with Gem and Dray.

The howls filled the air, echoing across the mountains and returning to complete the song of sadness for the loss of one of their own.

Alex let his howl die away. He listened to the voices that expressed their love and heartache for Kalia. The sound surrounded him, helping him build walls around his heart to keep his pain at bay, if only for a little while. It reminded him that even though there were struggles between werewolves at the school, they were all one. Mourning Kalia brought them together, and they would be there for each other in whatever way they could.

He led Siale back down the cliff as the last of the howls faded. The forest was silent during their walk back to the Academy. It felt as though even the animals gave tribute to Kalia's passing by maintaining the reverence of the night that still carried the ghost of the wolves' song.

***

Alex and Siale sat in Pack Kalia's common room. Everyone else had gone to bed, but Alex couldn't sleep. Siale sat on the couch with his head pillowed in her lap. She ran her fingers softly through his hair as she quietly sang songs she said her mother used to sing to her when she was little.

Alex closed his eyes and allowed himself to just be. The flames that danced in the fireplace more for comfort than heat played against his eyelids, throwing shadows and light in forms that flickered and twisted in reaching shapes.

Familiar footsteps caught Alex's ears. He turned his head slightly. A door opened, then closed. Another opened, and closed again. The door to Pack Kalia's quarters burst open.

Alex looked up to see Trent standing wide-eyed in the doorway.

"Alex, I've been looking everywhere for you!" Trent exclaimed breathlessly as he hurried across the room.

Alex sat up. "Why? What's wrong?"

Trent waved his arm toward the front of the school. "I, well, uh..." He bent over with his hands on his knees, gasping for air. It took a moment for him to stand up again.

By that time, Alex was on his feet, alarmed at his friend's disheveled state.

Trent waved his hand. "There's someone at the gate asking for you." Trent sucked in a breath. "And he's human."

About the Author

Cheree Alsop has published over 25 books, including two series through Stonehouse Ink. She is the mother of a beautiful, talented daughter and amazing twin sons who fill every day with joy and laughter. She is married to her best friend, Michael, the light of her life and her soulmate who shares her dreams and inspires her by reading the first drafts and giving much appreciated critiques. Cheree is currently working as an independent author and mother. She enjoys reading, riding her motorcycle on warm nights, playing with her twin boys while planning her next book, and rocking out as the bass player of her husband's band.

Cheree and Michael live in Utah where they rock out, enjoy the outdoors, plan great adventures, and never stop dreaming.

You can find Cheree's other books at
www.chereealsop.com

If you like this book, check out
Werewolf Academy Book 5: Lost

TAKEN

Printed in Great Britain
by Amazon